WITHDRAWN

Praise for VICTOR CASS and
Love, Death, and Other War Stories

"It's not your grandma's Pasadena. In his debut novel, *Love, Death, and Other War Stories*...Pasadena police officer Victor Cass shines a harsh light on a town overrun by vicious gangs—a grim landscape only partially redeemed by the love affair between its police detective hero and a fetching L.A. sheriff's deputy."

—*Los Angeles Magazine*

"Cass' book is a thriller."

—*Pasadena Star-News*

"The book is emotionally honest and unflinching in its portrayal of the world of crime as seen through a real police officer's eyes. Its gritty nature is not for the squeamish or conservative."

—*Pasadena Weekly*

"I very much liked [this] book and found it entertaining."

—Chief Bernard K. Melekian, Pasadena Police Department

Love, Death, and Other War Stories

Detective Roy Gildard returns to patrol after an unnerving encounter with the gangster Johnny "One Shot" King, the bloodthirsty leader of the P-9s. Johnny has a knack for beating murder raps and a plan to rule Pasadena's Northwest neighborhood. Johnny's only obstacles are the police and the rival Squiggly Lane Gangsters, whose leader "Satan" just got out of prison.

Roy's efforts to catch Johnny and stay alive almost come to an end at the hands of Karl and Noemi Bernau. The German-Mexican siblings rival Johnny in their murderous endeavors, leaving a bloody wake in Pasadena's immigrant community.

Hot on the trail of Johnny and the Bernaus is Corporal George Denney, a veteran training officer and suspected racist, who is teamed up with the beautiful mixed African-American rookie Officer Ingrid Neilson.

After a crime spree of rape and murder, Johnny finally confronts Roy in a climax that will forever change his life.

Order it today at www.victorcass.com, or at any b seller, including Amazon.com

Telenovela

VICTOR CASS

Outskirts Press, Inc.
Denver, Colorado

Telenovela
All Rights Reserved.
Copyright © 2009 Victor Cass
V5.0

Outskirts Press, Inc.
http://www.outskirtspress.com

ISBN: 978-1-4327-3690-3 paperback
ISBN: 978-1-4327-3710-8 hardback

Library of Congress Control Number: 2008939213

Outskirts Press and the "OP" logo are trademarks belonging to Outskirts Press, Inc.

PRINTED IN THE UNITED STATES OF AMERICA

Also by Victor Cass

(Fiction)

Love, Death, and Other War Stories

(Non-Fiction)

Pasadena Police Department: A Photohistory, 1877-2000

To L.M. and M.R.

Acknowledgements

I would like to thank several people for this book. First, my long time editor, critic, and biggest fan, educator and writer, Dr. Thelma T. Reyna, who also happens to be my mom; my loving and supportive family: father, Victor A. Reyna, Jr., sister, Dr. Christine E. Reyna and her husband, Charles Demes, of Chicago, all of whom read this book in its various stages and gave me useful feedback; Laura Martinez, who assisted me with Spanish translation and the colorful details of Mexican culture while showing me around Tecate and Puerto Nuevo, Mexico; Grace Munakash, with whom I traveled to Argentina, and who helped me with Argentinean cultural references; Dom Gilormini, a talented artist, who helped me produce a great cover; Special Investigator Daleen Ohlinger, of the US Air Force, my best friend and confidant, always there for me throughout the adventures that helped make this book; and finally, my wonderful daughter, Elizabeth Cass, thank you so much for your patience and love.

Prologue

Miriya Fronzini finally got what she wanted. Although her beloved father was dead, and her friend Nathalie was as good as dead, Arturo had delivered the goods. It didn't matter to her that she was soaking wet, her once-lovely locks plastered to her neck like snakes trying to suck out the last bit of her joy. It didn't matter that four years of dreams now felt like a nightmare upon waking. What mattered, all that mattered, was how the fabric of her life was unraveling, thread-by-thread, minute-by-minute, even as Arturo went on bent knee before her.

"Miriya, will you marry me?"

This is how it would happen to me, she said to herself as she sat in stunned silence. Out of breath, dripping from head to toe, and surrounded by people all expecting me to do the right thing. Miriya repeated Arturo's words over and over in her head savoring the bittersweet question she thought she would never hear from him.

Will you marry me?

She scanned the faces ranged all round her: loved

faces, familiar faces, hated faces, their eyes awaiting her verdict. The music in the background was meant to stir souls, and how many times had it done that to Arturo and her, hands and lips locked, eyes flickering with promise? Arturo knew the music, the place, the people—each would work their magic on her.

He knew he needed leverage.

Miriya's cell phone rang briefly before voicemail picked up. Lorena Sandoval, several miles away at the other end of town, needed to get through to Miriya, but she wasn't answering her cell. This wasn't like her. Had Miriya turned it off? Was it too late? Lorena tried calling the restaurant, got a busy signal, and tried again.

She tapped her left foot on the living room floor, rubbed her temple, and murmured, "Come on. Pick up the phone. Pick up the phone." She looked toward the TV, where *Sofia de Amor*, which had been such a part of her confused life lately, taunted her with harrowing familiarity. As the phone beeped in her ear, Lorena swiveled to catch the climactic scenes of the final episode. How had she gotten hooked on this soap opera anyway? Alone in the room, lights low, Lorena marveled at how the *telenovela* had come to mirror the drama in her and Miriya's lives…

"Sofia, Sofia, my love!" Arturo called out to his rain-soaked wife. She stumbled toward him and into his arms.

He stood dangerously close to the edge of the hotel's roof,
as the guns remained leveled at him.

"I'm sorry for everything I've done. Please forgive me.
Can you forgive me? Take me back! We can start over!"

"Arturo, how could you?" Sofia started. She looked
warily at the edge near her feet. She looked up at him, her
wet brown eyes taking in his chiseled features and sensual
lips, as if they could still hold her heart captive. The music
cascaded to ominous heights.

Lorena swallowed and blinked as she stared at the fictional Arturo. Bastard. Lying, scheming bastard who'd tried, in previous episodes, to kill his wife. How could Lorena ignore the similarities to Miriya's Arturo? Where were Miriya and her Arturo now? If only she had said more to Miriya, really tried to warn her.

If I had only screamed out how I felt, Lorena lamented to herself. Why had I been so quiet?

The flickering television screen, with its bellowing soap opera music a familiar, weekly accompaniment in Lorena's house, formed an eerie backdrop now as Lorena dialed Miriya's cell phone number again; still no response.

She felt it was too late. She wasn't going to get through to her friend.

Miriya's soaked black dress clung to her like a dying skin from a past life struggling not to slip off. She shivered as Arturo pressed the diamond and platinum ring into her palm. He held it up first for all at the large, round table to see. He needed leverage. Show the rock, he thought. Show and dazzle. Blind them with the bling. His smile matched the brilliance of the rock. He remained on the floor like a would-be knight, awaiting the crowning sword, his hand now pressing Miriya's thigh.

Miriya looked longingly toward her mother and sisters as if on a game show.

"Say 'yes' and take the rock! The ROCK!" Eva would say. Her older sister never liked the ring her husband had given her.

If only her father, Fabio, were here. He would know what to do.

"Say *ciao* to that *boludo*, *mono*! What's behind curtain number two?"

Arturo frowned.

"Will you marry me, my love?" He knew the answer. This was what Miriya had always wanted. It wasn't so much a question as a command. He knew it. She knew it.

Everyone at the table knew it.

A sudden rising well of warm emotion filled Miriya as if poured from a magical chalice. It surprised her and seemed to drown this four-year-long-dream-moment. She smiled slowly as she thought of a dear friend whom she didn't even know two months ago. Miriya remained silent as the eyes awaited her, and she marveled at how a thirty-year-old woman with an Adonis kneeling before her could only think of Lorena waiting at home and the beach at San Felipe.

Miriya wept.

PART ONE: JUNIOR

"Junior," Fabio Fronzini mumbled in Spanish, from his hospital bed. His gray eyes opened suddenly and he struggled to find his daughter.

"Daddy, I'm here," Miriya said, squeezing his hand. She thought he had fallen asleep.

"Who, who is that with you?"

Miriya glanced at her boyfriend, who stood next to her with his hands tucked hard into the pockets of his leather jacket.

"It's Arturo, Dad. You were just talking to him."

Arturo looked at Fabio as if he were an anthropological artifact in a museum.

"It's me, Mr. Fronzini," he said, also in Spanish, while leaning over slightly. He glanced at Miriya. "Can he hear me?"

"Of course he can hear you," she whispered. "Daddy, what is it? Are you okay?"

Miriya stroked her father's head and face with her free hand, feeling his hot rattled breath struggling to move. Miriya checked the monitors surrounding his bed while Arturo stared blankly at the ceiling. Fabio turned slowly and strained to focus on Miriya's boyfriend.

"Arturo," Fabio began, mustering his strength, "is a good Argentinean man from Buenos Aires. He reminds me of my brother."

Miriya wondered why her father spoke of Arturo as if he weren't there.

Arturo, for his part, observed their interchange with detached curiosity. Fabio cleared the phlegm in his throat, coughed a few times then reached for Miriya's hand.

"Arturo is the son I never had. The son-in-law." Fabio seemed to be drifting.

Miriya shifted uncomfortably in her seat.

Not this again, she thought.

"Fronzinis never have sons," Fabio mumbled.

"Dad, you were adopted," Miriya said, slipping into English.

"I was still cursed!"

This sudden outburst was followed by another round of startling coughs.

"Give me a son, Miriya." Fabio gazed at Arturo until the younger man looked away uneasily.

"Daddy," Miriya said, shooting a quick glance in Arturo's direction, "my baby would be your grandson."

"Grandson," Fabio said. He smiled at Miriya, then Arturo. "Yes, a grandson."

Fabio's voice faded off as his eyes closed.

"Is he?" Arturo hesitated.

"He's asleep!" Miriya snapped at Arturo. She placed her father's hand gently by his side and made sure his monitor's tubes and wires all looked good, nothing tangled. Miriya leaned and kissed her father's lips. She whispered in his ear:

"Te amo, Papi."

As Arturo drove her home from the hospital, Miriya thought about her father and what he'd said. She remembered the stories Fabio told her. She was a stringy little girl then, staring up into a starry night sky. Miriya's favorites were stories about her childhood, especially how she came into the world with her name. Fabio was young and handsome then.

On the night Jimmy Carter locked up the Democratic nomination for President in New York City, Fabio Fronzini paced a smoke-filled waiting room in a Southern California hospital, terrified that the "Fronzini Curse" was still in effect. It didn't matter that he'd been adopted by the son-less Fronzini family at the age of six-months, thirty years prior, in Buenos Aires. He had the name and, in his mind, was beholden to any and all liabilities associated with it. Fabio shook his head when he remembered how he and his new bride had moved to her hometown of Rosario, Argentina's second-largest city, thinking that the change of scenery would impact his namely burden for the better.

"Perhaps now a son may be born to this family," Miriya, his hopeful young wife, had told him.

In the end, it had made no difference, he recalled, while chain-smoking nervously, as his firstborn was a girl, Eva. And now, as he stole glances at the old television set, watching the peanut farmer from Georgia speak to the applause of thousands of delegates while five-year-old Eva sat quietly playing with a doll, Fabio resigned himself to the inevitable.

Eva Fronzini held her clothes-less Barbie by its knotted hair and spun the emaciated doll around like a naked ballerina. Every once in a while she looked at the other unshaven, tired men in the room, all of whom stuffed cigarette butts into orange plastic ashtrays as if stamping out guilty demons of fear and regret. Her father walked back and forth in the cramped room like one of those big cats she had seen at the Los Angeles Zoo. Eva frowned at Fabio as he wrung his hands and combed them through his wavy blonde hair. He hardly glanced at her while muttering under his breath in Spanish. Eva wondered if any of the other men in the room could understand her father's foreign tongue. At one point, Fabio pointed at the TV and spoke in heavily accented English.

"Who is this Carter?" he blurted, stopping in the middle

of the room. "Is he gonna be President or what?"

Eva watched the Americans to see what their reactions to her father would be. No one seemed to pay him any attention, as most of their heavy gazes fell to the tiled floor like those of condemned men. Just then, somebody who looked like a doctor, a benevolent, bespectacled man with mousy brown hair and mutton-chop sideburns, strolled into the room.

"Mr. Fronzini?"

"Yes?" Fabio took one last drag of his cigarette.

"Congratulations, Mr. Fronzini. You're the father of a healthy baby girl."

Eva clutched Barbie to her chest and sighed. The weight of disappointment she felt wasn't for her own eager heart, as she secretly desired a baby sister, but for her poor father. Fabio tried unsuccessfully to mask his feelings and shook the doctor's hand with a tight-lipped smile. Turning to Eva, Fabio called out to her in Spanish as she dutifully slid off the hard plastic chair and reached for her father's hand.

"Let's go see your new sister, little Eva," Fabio said.

"*English*, dad," Eva whispered, rolling her eyes.

"C'mon, c'mon!"

Eva took Fabio's hand and squeezed it.

"Don't worry, Papa," she said. "Girls are better."

Fabio smiled at Eva, with the dark wavy hair and hazel eyes, button nose and thin little lips. Eva had been a blessing, a little angel sent by God from heaven.

But a son….

"What? What did you name her?" Miriya Fronzini asked her husband, in Spanish, from the hospital bed. They had decided not to learn the baby's sex until the delivery, as Fabio had been unable to bear the foreknowledge that he was a marked man. They therefore hadn't discussed names, especially girl names.

Fabio stuck a cigarette in his down-turned mouth as if poking it with a wooden stake, and brought up a plain, silver colored Zippo lighter. He decided that a little flair of *machismo* would best get him out of this current jam.

"Miriya!" he blurted in self-confident defiance. "I named her after you, and why not? Miriya Fronzini— *Junior!*"

He half-laughed at his own humor, which he'd painfully attempted with the nurse when she asked what the child's name would be. He really wanted to cry, not having a son to name after himself.

"*Dios!*" Miriya covered her face with her hands. She had wanted to name a future daughter Luisa, after her beloved grandmother. But it was too late. An unknown staff member of Glendale Adventist Hospital had already typed up the birth certificate. Mrs. Fronzini would be further horrified when she learned that her daughter's name on the certificate actually read: "Miriya Fronzini, Jr."

"What is this?" she demanded later, slapping the birth certificate with her hand when they received it in the mail.

Telenovela

"I was only kidding!" Fabio pleaded with his wife. He didn't think that the nurse was actually listening, or believed that they would truly record "Junior"—on a girl, no less! Miriya, "Senior" would never let her husband live down this error, which she felt would haunt their daughter till her dying days.

Before Miriya, Jr. was old enough to feel different in their adopted homeland, as Eva had, Argentina won the World Cup. Fabio, in a sudden fit of patriotism and homesickness, moved the family back to Rosario where "Junior," as Miriya was affectionately called in English, spent the next four years of her life. Much to her parents' approval, Junior, more so than Eva, was being raised an Argentinean, despite her American citizenship (Eva was born in Rosario). Already enrolled, at the age of five, in the General Belgrano and Beloved Flag School for Girls, Miriya spoke only Spanish, loved *futbol*, singing, ballet, and attended church regularly with her family.

At night, while under the covers, their faces illuminated by a small flashlight, Eva dazzled her younger sister with stories about the United States, few of which Miriya ever believed. Junior couldn't imagine a place better than her beloved Rosario.

"*Vos sos Yanqui!*" Eva said, almost tauntingly to her confused younger sister. "I would be, too, if we were still in America."

Miriya never understood Eva's nostalgia for that distant

land. Eva's memories grew fuzzier as each year passed, much to her distress, and she felt that as long as she talked about America to Miriya, she could cling to her former life and prevent it from slipping away, like a dream lost upon waking.

When Miriya was six years old, during the fourth year of their stay in Argentina, Fabio had had no choice but to move the family back to the United States. Economic opportunities there were too great to resist.

Miriya sobbed quietly when they left their residence on Mitre Street, suffering the loss of friends and a familiar home. She refused to speak to her family, almost pressing her tear-streaked face to the car window as they passed the *Monumento Nacional a la Bandera*, with its towering, sky-blue and white, flag-bedecked tomb of national hero General Belgrano. A glimpse of the mud-brown, choppy water of the Paraña River brought back memories of speed boating with her father, and reminded her of the *Cataratas* of the *Parque Nacional Iguazú*. She longingly thought of these Argentinean wonders of beauty and feared that she would never set eyes on them again.

"But I don't want to be an American!" Miriya cried as the Aerolineas Argentinas flight took off from Buenos Aires.

"You're more American than all of us," Fabio said absentmindedly, as he tried to look brave for his family, gripping the arms of his seat. He had a deathly fear of flying.

"You're returning to your homeland."

"Argentina is my home! I don't even speak English! What will become of me?"

Miriya buried her face in her mother's bosom, as Fabio shrugged his shoulders.

Miriya, Sr. held her daughter tightly, while turning her brown eyes away from her husband's gaze.

"She'll be fine," Fabio said softly.

"Will we ever have a home?" Miriya, Sr. asked.

What else could he do but try to get them back into the mindset of living in America? He harbored a premonition that he would never see Argentina again but said nothing of it. Instead, he held Eva's hand, as the eleven-year-old stared stoically out the window.

Eva was turning into a little woman, Fabio thought, as he gazed lovingly upon her long, black hair. He knew that she would have an easier time of it back in the States, at least at first. Eva still retained some of her knowledge of English and would pick it up quickly. Miriya was the beauty, though. Fabio felt a pang of guilt thinking this about his daughters, but feared that Eva would have trouble with her weight. Miriya would always skate along on her good looks. However they turned out, Fabio was determined to develop their personalities. He wanted happy, lively children. Fabio also swore to himself to keep both of his daughters grounded with good moral values, good eating habits, and, Miriya especially, with humility.

The Fronzinis settled in Pasadena, not far from where Miriya was born. Fabio returned to his old job at the Jet Propulsion Laboratory while Miriya, Sr., raised their children at home. Junior found herself the only non-English speaking pupil in a classroom full of Americans on her first day at her new school, Daniel Webster Elementary School, in East Washington Village, a primarily Armenian neighborhood a few blocks from where the Fronzinis bought a house on Galbreth Street.

"Class, settle down!" Mrs. Talin Avetyan called out, attempting to quiet the vocal first day jitters. Miriya thought that this twenty-something teacher with blonde-streaked brunette hair pulled back in a bun was one of the most beautiful women she had ever seen. Talin had alabaster skin and a fine, pointed nose like a mannequin in a faraway department store.

"I want you all to welcome our newest student, *Miriya*—did I say that right?" Talin raised her eyebrows at the girl amidst the children's snickers. Miriya glanced over her shoulder nervously. "Miriya Fronzini. She comes to us all the way from Argentina, in South America."

"Is she from the Amazon?" someone asked.

"But," Talin continued, her right hand out, arm raised toward the girl, "I understand that Miriya's an American, actually born right here in nearby Glendale."

Miriya's face burned as she stared at her desk. She understood nothing her teacher said, but could almost feel her classmates' comments burning into her neck.

Miriya felt someone tap her. She turned to a small girl with shoulders that slumped forward, pale skin and blonde hair pulled back in a ponytail. She had blue eyes that blinked often behind a pair of thick-rimmed glasses.

"Welcome to America," she said in a froggy voice, holding out her hand. Miriya shook the girl's hand as if it was made of wet rubber. "My name is Veronica Bonkowski. It's okay. My ancestors came from Poland a long time ago, wherever that is. My dad said the Nazis killed most our family because we're Jewish. Are there Jews in South America?"

Miriya forced a smile and politely removed her hand from Veronica's slight grasp.

Could she be a friend? Miriya asked herself. She would have to learn English first. And learn she did.

By the end of the semester, Miriya spoke sufficient English, though with a heavy accent, thanks to Talin's rigorous after-school instruction. Talin felt a soft spot for the Argentinean girl, as the teacher remembered her first day in an English-speaking classroom after having only spoken Armenian the first four years of her life.

"Speak *English*, you foreigner!" Ashley Fleming sneered at Miriya. "What's wrong with you?"

"Noting *es* ron wit me!" Miriya struggled as she sat at her desk, back straight. She tried to ignore her tormenter, a pretty, but mean-faced girl with wavy, brown hair and icy eyes, who sat at the desk to Miriya's left.

"Go back to Mexico!" Ashley spat.

"I'ne not from Mexico! I was born here! I'ne American like zhoo!" Miriya finally turned to her taunting classmate. Miriya felt her face flushing and told herself she wouldn't cry.

"Why don't you shut up, Ashley," Veronica said.

"*You* shut-up, *Polack*!" Ashley tried whispering this epithet as she caught a glimpse of Talin coming back from an errand down the hall. Their teacher was wise enough to know when trouble was brewing.

"All right, you guys," Talin glared at them. "What's going on?"

"Nothing, Miss Avetyan," Ashley said in a singsong voice.

"Ashley's being mean, Miss Avetyan! She told Miriya to go back to Argentina!" Veronica tattled.

At least Veronica got it right, Miriya thought. *Mexico*? How did the other kids think she was from Mexico? Couldn't the *Yanquis* tell the difference between her and the Mexican kids? Their Spanish was so vulgar!

Miriya buried her face in her hands. This was all she needed as she heard the whispers and wisecracks from the other students. Miriya didn't want Veronica to have to stick up for her. She didn't want to have to be protected. She didn't want to stand out, to be different from her American peers. Why couldn't she just be like everyone else, be thought of as the others thought of themselves? She was American, after all!

As Talin reprimanded Ashley, Miriya sat quietly at her desk, wanting just to fade away and disappear. She questioned, in her churning mind, why she did not speak better English. Why did her parents have to speak Spanish at home all the time? They were in America now. They should be helping her practice English so she could talk like her classmates.

She at least didn't want to be mistaken for a Mexican.

Several years later, in fifth grade, Veronica spent the night at Miriya's house so she could see Miriya's new baby sister. Anna Fronzini wasn't actually all that "new," having been born six months prior, but she was new to Veronica, as Miriya's best friend had yet to see the girl.

Veronica, being an only child, was always amazed at how lively dinner at the Fronzini home was. Food was passed around and wooden spoons held high in threatening gestures between political tirades and emotional outbursts. Fabio always had a little more wine than his wife liked and reminisced about Argentina to the point that Miriya, Sr. would scold him for moving the family back to the United States. Eva would jump in and declare how her father's decision to return had been the best thing that had ever happened to her. This would send her mother ranting in a litany of Spanish expletives and insults, aimed mostly at Eva's teen angst, selfishness, and eroding looks.

Miriya got quiet and sat stiffly at the dinner table when-ever her friends were present. Her parents mostly ignored Miriya's sensitivity about their speaking Spanish in front of her non-Spanish-speaking friends. Miriya had admonished them on more than one occasion with the excuse that to do so was rude, as her American friends might think they were talking about them. Adding to Miriya's piling embarrass-ments when they ate was her father's eating habits. Fabio had a habit of chewing with his mouth open and rarely used a napkin. Miriya cringed and sighed in exaggerated tones whenever she saw bits and pieces of food stuck on her fa-ther's mouth or greasing up his fingers. If something could be spilled, Fabio invariably dribbled it down the front of his shirt and onto an ever-increasing girth. Only once in a while would Miriya's mother pick up on the source of her daughter's distress, and subtly gesture to her husband to find a napkin and wipe something—*anything*!

Fabio, for his part, remained clueless to the source of his middle daughter's irritation. He compounded Miriya's frustration by expressing too much parental interest in the family backgrounds and home lives of his daughters' friends. Eva, in eighth grade and already starting to look like her "Goth" friend, Sarah Wilson, with powdered make-up and heavy black eyeliner, sat glumly whenever she wasn't in contact, either physically or by phone, with one of her friends, most of whom Fabio considered riff-raff.

Veronica Bonkowski, on the other hand, had become a welcome and accepted part of Miriya's life.

"Veronica," Fabio began, after sipping from his third full glass of wine. His blonde hair was starting to recede near the top, and he had taken to wearing a goatee lately. "You come from a big family, *no*?"

Veronica shot a sideways glance at Miriya, who said nothing while moving her food around on her plate.

"I'm an only child, Mr. Fronzini," Veronica mumbled. Her glasses were more stylish than they'd been in first grade, and her blonde hair had darkened somewhat. She still dressed like a boy, Fabio noticed.

"Your family, it's like this?" he waved his hand around the table as Eva frowned at him. "You know. Loud. How you say? Boisterous!"

Veronica shrugged as Miriya, Sr. rolled her eyes and mumbled, "Boisterous, he says."

"Not really," Veronica answered him, not knowing what else to do. "My parents don't say a lot."

Fabio raised an eyebrow.

"Really? That's different. I always thought Jewish families were, uh—full of life—like the Argentineans."

Miriya held her breath.

"You know, a lot of people from Latin America—El Salvadorans, Argentineans, Columbians, and even people from the Mediterranean, like the Italians, and those from Eastern Europe—the Russians and the Jews—we full of life

15

and celebration! Always the big family gatherings."

Miriya, Sr., took a long sip of wine and squinted at her husband, while Junior cringed.

"Lots o' laughing, fighting, loving—to the fullest! You know why?" Fabio pointed at Veronica, who shook her head, mesmerized by what she believed to be the longest, politically substantial conversation her friend's father had ever had with her.

"We all come from places where we could be dragged out of our homes, in the middle of the night, and taken out in the street and killed for no reason 'cept the gover'ment want us dead! Before my family come to Argentina, my grandfather was murdered by Mussolini's Blackshirts— shot down in the street like a dog, in Roma."

Veronica gave Miriya a horrified look. Miriya had never heard her father say anything like this before and was equally shocked. She looked into Fabio's glassy eyes as he waved his hands around.

"And we celebrate life—live each day, as if it could be our last, because we never knew when it was going to be our last day. America's a great country. Americans never have to worry 'bout stuff like that. They are not a cold, distant people, as foreigners think. Americans earned their peace, calm, and self-assuredness through strength and freedom. Be thankful, Veronica, for when and where you were born. Be thankful to be American."

He turned to his daughter.

"You, too, Junior."

Miriya, Sr. blew out a gust of air through loose lips while throwing back her hand.

"Well, I don't know where *you* grew up," she said to Fabio in Spanish, while collecting her dirty dishes. "But no one in my family was ever dragged out of their house and shot in a ditch!"

"What do you expect from you provincials in Rosario!" Fabio retorted. "Fascists your family was!"

And that was how it usually started between the two. Junior sighed and motioned with her head for Veronica to join them in Anna's room. The child was fast asleep in her crib, unaware of the Spanish insults being hurled between her parents in the dining room.

"She's so little," Veronica mumbled, taking the infant's hand in her own.

Miriya said nothing as she leaned against the crib, her face cradled in her bent elbow.

"You like being a 'junior'?" Veronica finally asked.

Miriya managed a shrug.

"Sometimes I wish I had my own name," she replied, reaching for her baby sister's cheek. "I guess it would be better if they could at least say 'joon-ior' instead of 'hoon-ior'."

Veronica laughed, which seemed to ease the nervous energy between them. Eva appeared at the door, backlit and officious, like a midget sentry.

"Mom said for you guys to leave Anna alone and let her sleep," Eva said this as if reading aloud a shopping list at a hardware store. She then turned and stomped off to the privacy of her bedroom and punk rock music.

Later, Miriya and Veronica played with Barbies on the floor behind the living room couch. The girls were unusually quiet, and Miriya, Sr. hardly noticed them as she sat on the couch, captivated by the TV's nightly fare. Veronica leaned over every so often to get a look at what her friend's mother was watching. It reminded her of the soap opera that her own mother watched, *Guiding Light*, but it was in Spanish.

"What's your mom watching?" Veronica asked.

"Huh?" Miriya looked up from a half-clothed Skipper doll.

"On TV. What is that she's watching?"

Miriya stood up on her knees and cocked her head back to get a look at the screen from over the top of the couch. She quickly ducked down as if being shot at from outside a trench.

"*Telenovela*," Miriya said with a rare Spanish accent.

"What?" Veronica was confused at this alien word.

"She's watching some *telenovela*. It's one of those Mexican TV shows like *As the World Turns*. You know those weird shows that look funny? My dad calls them soap operas, or something like that."

Veronica made a curious face.

"Are they good?"

"I dunno. I don't really watch them. They're in Spanish."

"The women in them are pretty."

As the girls prepared for bed, Miriya heard the sound of her mother laughing quietly in the kitchen. Miriya, Sr. always spent her final hour before bed meticulously scrubbing, polishing, wiping, and sweeping every tile, crevice, appliance, and protruding piece of plumbing in the capital of her domestic empire, much to her husband's displeasure. Fabio, always eager to get his wife to bed so that she could see to her more uxorial duties, spent an equal amount of time trying to coax his maid into abandoning her nightly ritual.

Junior couldn't help but try and steal glimpses of her parents' private interplay, as on this night, peering out from behind the protective cover of their refrigerator. She held her breath at the spectacle of her mother's smile and squinting brown eyes. Miriya, Sr. looked young, like some of the teenage girls Junior saw in the neighborhood. Honey brown skin of bare, tired arms and achy shoulders glowed with each twist and turn as Miriya, Sr. lazily tried to avoid Fabio's groping hands. The nails on her hands and feet, alive with taut pleasure, flashed brilliant red with each playful whack or kick at her husband's legs as he tucked them close behind her.

Miriya, Sr. took hold of her husband's left arm, as he squeezed her tightly around her waist from behind. She used her right hand to reach behind her head and move aside her long train of dark hair, exposing the left side of her face and neck to Fabio's hungry breath.

This must be what love looks like, young Miriya thought to herself.

The thought stayed with her as she slunk back to her room and crawled into her sleeping bag on the floor next to Veronica's. Miriya snickered to herself in mild embarrassment as she remembered wanting to "marry" her daddy when she was a small child. The silly notions of a beloved daughter aside, Miriya wondered if she would ever find a boy who would look after her and protect her the way Fabio did.

Miriya awoke later, in the still darkness of her bedroom, as she always did, ignorant of the exact time, but confident in the belief that everyone in the world must have been fast asleep. She knew what was coming, as her heart beat faster and the butterflies fluttered in the pit of her stomach. She always feigned sleep when Fabio crept past her open door, letting a sliver of hallway light guide him to his sleeping daughter.

Fabio stared at his child for a brief moment before nudging her and whispering her name. It was a personal challenge to the little girl to see how authentic she could make each "waking" appear to her father, when the reality was that she could hardly contain her excitement as if it were Christmas morning.

"Wake up, Junior. C'mon, little *mono*." He called her monkey.

Miriya yawned and pushed herself up on her elbow. She glanced toward Veronica to make sure her friend was asleep, and then raised her skinny arms toward her father. Fabio gently gathered his baby around his waist, her tired head resting on his shoulder.

"Hi, daddy," she whispered.

"C'mon, baby. You wanna see the stars?"

"Yeah."

Every morning for the last six months, after his family had gone to sleep, Fabio would stealthily slink out of bed, taking with him the faint smell of sweaty lovemaking, and seek out his middle daughter. He had promised his wife to quit smoking, but could not resist the relaxing pull of one or two illicit cigarettes, lit and sucked on in the cool night air, his daughter warming him by his side.

Miriya cherished these nightly meetings like no other thing in her life, just her and her daddy, up late, staring at heaven in the dark. Here, his eating habits were all but forgotten and he could speak all the Spanish he wanted.

"Daddy, *there*! Up there!"

Fabio blew a cloud of blue smoke toward the patch of starry blackness.

"Where?"

"Right *there*, next to those three little stars. You can barely see it," Miriya said in her own rusty Spanish.

Miriya squinted and aimed her pointed finger, keeping it straight and stiff. Fabio leaned over, his stubble scratching against her brown arms, as he tried to align his own vision with her little finger, as if he aimed a small rifle. Sure enough, there was the faint star, its twinkle almost invisible to the naked eye—apparently the farthest and most remote star they had yet to discover.

"Man, there it is," he said in exaggerated awe. He leaned back in the worn cushion of the wooden deck bench that cradled the two of them. Fabio hugged Miriya closer to him, gently squeezing her frail torso. He took another drag of his cigarette and let the smoke leak slowly from his contented lips like cloudy bubbles.

"How far away do you think it is, daddy?"

Fabio shook his head.

"That little star? Could be thousands—*millions* of light years away. We might even be looking at its ghost."

"Wow!"

Fabio had explained to Miriya once that many of the stars they gazed at didn't even exist anymore, as the light from their glow had traveled so far, and for so many millions of years, just to be seen by them on Earth, that the original stars beaming the light no longer existed—burned out long ago—and only their "ghosts" were visible now.

"What happens when the light finishes coming to us?" Miriya had asked at the time, about the ghost stars.

"*Blip*," Fabio made a flash with his outstretched fingers. "It'll just disappear from the sky."

Now, Miriya sat content that she had located a ghost star, or at least a suspected one. She turned her head.

"Daddy, you think that little girl out there is sitting with *her* daddy now, looking up at us?"

Fabio dutifully checked his watch.

"Yeah, maybe. I don't know what time it could be on her planet, but I'm sure on one of those faraway worlds it's nighttime."

Miriya sighed.

"I wonder if I'll ever get to meet her."

Fabio glanced at the straight, dark brown messy hair on his girl's head, and saw her light brown eyes sweeping the night sky under her bangs. He chuckled while sucking in some more smoke.

"You will, baby."

"I will? When?"

"In heaven." He tried unsuccessfully to blow smoke rings. He never could.

"For real?"

"In heaven you get to meet anybody you ever wanted, no matter where they from. You get the answers to all your questions. All secrets are revealed."

Miriya considered this.

"I hope she's nice."

Fabio smiled.

Life is good, he thought.

"Miriya! *MIRIYA!*" screamed her mother, storming into the echoing high school auditorium. Miriya, Sr. wore her salt and pepper hair up in a bun. Her hips, now wider than her shoulders and stuffed tightly into a pair of tan Capri pants, swished side to side with each step down the aisle. Her thick toes burst from wood-soled sandals that made a *clunk-clunk-clunk* sound as she made her way across the sloping, polished concrete floor.

"*Donde esta Miriya?* Where is she? Come, Miriya!" Her mother practically clapped her hands, as the drama teacher, Ms. Tafoya, looked on with mild shock.

Seventeen-year-old Miriya Fronzini cringed at the sound of her mother's voice as it echoed through the cavernous auditorium. The lithe high school junior stood, her wispy, straight hair now streaked with blonde highlights, in torn blue jeans and flip-flops, her small breasts jutting braless through a black tank top.

"Oh, no," Veronica mumbled, making a face and glancing sideways toward Miriya.

"Who's that?" Karen Velez whispered at Veronica. Karen was the sixteen-year-old stage crew director who'd been spending a lot of time with Veronica. Karen wore black, plastic-rimmed glasses, short, dyed-black spiky hair, and a nose piercing. Karen was skinny and preferred baggy clothes that concealed her slimness.

"Miriya's mom."

"What now?" Miriya mumbled under her breath.

Miriya walked toward the edge of the stage as if there were a hundred foot drop awaiting her. Veronica watched her friend's breasts jiggle with each annoyed step then quickly averted her gaze, as she knew Karen was next to her and might be watching. Veronica glanced down at her own cleavage, more pronounced due to her arms being folded under her large chest.

"Mom! *What?*" Miriya stood arms akimbo.

"Don't you 'what' me! You need to come home now, and study for your AP test."

Miriya rolled her eyes.

"Mom, the play's in a week."

"And the test is in two days!"

"Fine!" Miriya preferred leaving quickly and with as little scene as possible, as opposed to having to endure her mother's thick accent in front of all of her friends and peers.

"I'm sorry, ma'am," Miriya, Sr. turned to her daughter's teacher. "But she must study."

Ms. Tafoya, her bleached blonde hair pulled back in a very short ponytail, thought better of saying anything as she adjusted the black-framed glasses on her nose.

Veronica pretended not to see Miriya wave at her. Miriya climbed down from the stage, gathered her backpack and baggy hooded sweatshirt, and shuffled sullenly out of the auditorium with her mother.

Veronica, wearing a V-neck white T-shirt, un-tucked from a pair of worn, Vietnam-era jungle fatigues, and Doc Marten low quarter boots, sighed while running her hands through her short, blue-dyed hair. She wore contacts most of the time now, instead of the hip, cat-eye glasses she wore when studying.

"Hey," Karen said, touching Veronica's arm. "I'm over here."

After watching Miriya leave, one of the stagehands, a chunky football player who had known the girls since first grade, turned to Veronica and said:

"You gonna be okay without your girlfriend?" He added under his breath:

"Carpet muncher."

"Fuck off," Veronica mumbled.

He high-five'd a snickering buddy who had overheard the brief interchange.

Later that night, Junior was alone in her bedroom studying. She heard a familiar knock at the door.

"Come in," she called out. Miriya sat up, closed her book, and tucked a bare foot under her other leg. Fabio opened her door slowly and poked his head in as if entering a forbidding tomb. He was surprised that she wasn't playing her music or talking on the phone.

"Hi, daddy."

"Hey, Junior. What are you doing?"

She sighed.

"Studying for my stupid AP test." She motioned to her books.

Fabio approached the teen's bed as if was possibly booby-trapped and sat carefully on its edge. He hadn't worn a goatee in a couple of years and his hair, receding further near the top, was longer and slightly disheveled.

"It's almost midnight," he mumbled. "What is this?"

He picked up her book.

"U.S. history? You gonna run for president or some'ting?"

She shook her head.

"Then why you gotta take this test?"

"'Cause mom will flip if I don't, and she'll really flip if I don't pass it."

Fabio smirked but said nothing.

"I need a cigarette." He motioned with his head. "You wanna see the stars?"

Miriya beamed.

"Let's go," he said.

Fabio took a long drag of his cigarette while looking up at the night sky. Miriya sat slouched over, her skinny legs extended out. She wiggled her toes in her flip-flop sandals.

"Any thoughts about where you want to go to college?" Fabio asked.

"No, not yet. I'm not sure I want to go. I just want to be done with school."

"You know you could at least go to a junior college. You got the grades for it. You've really improved."

Miriya shrugged her shoulders.

"I'm just not sure what I want to do," she said.

"What do you like?"

"I like fashion and beauty stuff," Miriya mumbled. "Maybe I can work for a magazine."

Fabio tried blowing smoke rings; still couldn't do it.

"You could be a fashion designer," he mused. "Either way, you probably still gotta go to school for that kind of stuff."

"Maybe I'll just marry a rich guy." Miriya laughed.

Fabio shook his head.

"I don't see how that's gonna happen. You break up with your boyfriends after only a month or two. What happened to the last guy who was calling here all the time? What was his name?"

"Eric." Miriya said, shaking her head. "He was lame."

"He seemed nice enough."

"He was immature, just like the rest. They all just want to hang out with their stupid guy friends. Even when we went out, he wanted his friends to tag along. Why can't boys just be wise, mature, and romantic like you? Mom's lucky she found a good man."

"Oh, c'mon, *mono*," Fabio chuckled. "I'm old. I made all the same mistakes these boys are making. Just ask your mother."

"You're a hard act to follow, daddy. I'm afraid I'm gonna be really picky."

"They say a girl looks for a man who was like her father."

"Well, I just hope he doesn't smoke."

Fabio coughed.

"And that he's a little thinner," Miriya said, poking him in the stomach.

"Hey!"

"And has more hair up top!" Miriya laughed, reaching up to rub his head.

"Watch the hair! Watch the hair!" Fabio said, trying to dodge her hand.

As they laughed, Fabio started coughing some more.

Miriya frowned.

Late in the fifth year of the War on Terrorism, which their friend Karen had gone off to fight in, Junior, now thirty-years-old, made one of her daily trips to the critical care unit of Huntington Memorial Hospital, where Fabio was laid up in the twilight stages of terminal lung cancer. Although saddened by her beloved father's impending death, Miriya was determined to make his last days as memorable and happy for him as she could.

The charge nurse on duty, a middle-aged Caucasian woman with graying blonde hair, sharp eyes to match, and a thin mouth that resembled a slit in her face, thought she could set her watch to the younger Fronzini's visits.

"Hi, Louise," Miriya said, smiling as she breezed by her station with flowers in her hand. The senior nurse acknowledged the girl with a quick smile as a Filipino medical assistant approached.

"There goes Fronzini Junior," she said to Louise, "with flowers and good cheer for her daddy."

"I think it's sweet. Poor thing," the charge Nurse replied, shaking her head.

Miriya squeezed past a couple of orderlies removing dinner trays and changing IV bags. Fabio sat up in bed and watched his daughter throw out the old flowers from last week and replace them with her new bouquet. The beeping monitors and Darth Vader-like sound of Fabio's respirator were only partially drowned out by the Spanish-language TV station he watched with passing interest now that Junior was there.

Miriya checked the work of the now-departed orderlies to make sure that everything looked right and that her father was comfortable. She hugged and kissed Fabio then pulled up a chair so she could hold his hand and talk to him. They liked to sit in silence at first, collecting their thoughts and considering each other in their collective memories.

Miriya glanced up at the TV as a graphic announced that they were watching a show called *Sofia de Amor…*

A pretty, fair-skinned woman with almond-shaped brown eyes and a flowing mane of streaked blonde hair,

Sofia de Amor, who looked about 35, put on her earrings and admired her form in front of a long mirror. There was an alluring and obviously much younger woman in the muted uniform of a housekeeper, in a well-to-do Latin household, standing behind her. Carmen Santiago, maybe 25 or so, had straight, dark hair in a ponytail, wide, inno-cent-looking eyes and an overeager countenance.

"You look beautiful, Mrs. de Amor," Carmen said, glancing at her own reflection.

"Thank you, dear Carmen." Sofia turned and took hold of the younger girl's arms. "I'm so happy! Arturo has been so busy lately. Secretive. He's asked me to meet him tonight for a surprise dinner. I think he's going to announce that he's booked our cruise for that second honeymoon I've been talking about. I've looked forward to this for so long."

"I'm glad for you, Mrs. de Amor." Carmen frowned slightly as Sofia turned back to the mirror.

"What's this?" Miriya asked her father, in Spanish. He was glued to the Mexican soap opera.

"*Sofia de Amor*," Fabio replied with a raspy voice. "A *telenovela*. It's pretty good."

Miriya watched with growing concern as he tried to clear his throat. Fabio's faded eyes fluttered in her direction like sick moths. He blinked several times while squeezing her hand.

"How was work, *mono*?" Fabio finally said. He still

called her "monkey," among other things.

Miriya worked at a local beauty spa, Burke Williams, and often regaled her family with stories about the elite clientele who frequented it.

"Oh, it was fine. You remember Suzy, my Armenian boss? She's been really good about flexing my hours so that I can see you as much as I can."

"It makes me happy to see you."

A gurgling sound bubbled up from the depths of his throat as Fabio shifted uncomfortably in his bed. He looked distressed, which worried Miriya, but he cleared his airway for more tired breathing and seemed relieved. Junior took a deep breath to calm down as Fabio turned to her.

"You were always my favorite, Junior," he mumbled.

"Oh, daddy, you probably say that to Eva and Anna, too," Miriya said, finding a smile somewhere.

"It's true," he said, turning back to the TV. Without looking at her, he asked: "How are things with that boyfriend of yours? Is he going to make you an honest woman anytime soon?"

"Well, I think he's going to ask me to marry him next week. He's got this big night planned for everyone. He even invited Mama. Anna's going with her boyfriend. He invited you, too, but I told him...Well, you know, I told him that you might not be up for it."

"I might be in heaven by then," Fabio said, calmly.

Miriya's face wrinkled.

"So tell him to hurry up," he continued. "I'm not going to be around forever, Junior. I would like to see your children, even if it's looking down upon them from the stars."

You can't die, Daddy, Miriya thought. You've always been in my life. You can't leave me.

She sat quietly knowing that if she tried to speak, she would break down crying. Instead, she carefully sat on Fabio's bed and watched *Sofia de Amor*. She found herself snuggling up next to her father, as if she were sitting by his side, a tiny little girl, eyes full of wonder at a night sky, long ago.

Sofia de Amor sat across from her husband, Arturo, amid the hustle and bustle of a crowded swanky restaurant. Sofia's eyes sparkled with loving anticipation as Arturo took her hand in his. He was a strong, handsome man with deep blue eyes, hair slicked back, and a rugged, unshaven appearance. His dress was impeccable.

"Sofia, my love," Arturo started.

"Yes, Arturo?"

"I have some news."

Sofia's eyes widened.

"I have a business opportunity in Guanajuato. I'll have to leave on Monday."

Sofia frowned. This was obviously not what she expected.

"How long will you be gone?"

"Just a week, but it will be very busy, very high profile. It's a deal we've been working on for months now. That might explain a lot of my late nights. I would have asked you to go along with me, but I know that you have an important week coming up at work."

"Well, yes, but...You couldn't schedule this trip for another time? You know how much I've always wanted to go to Guanajuato with you."

"I'm sorry, my love, but I could not."

"I-I-I don't know what to say. This wasn't what I expected."

"I'm afraid there's more," he said in a somber tone. "I'm going to need someone to assist me with photocopying, errands, transcription, ironing my clothes and preparing the things I need. All of our assistants at work are tied up with other duties related to this project, so I have asked Carmen to come along as my assistant."

"Carmen? Our housekeeper?" Sofia bit her lip, trying hard to conceal the hurt and fear welling up inside her.

"I'm sorry, my love. I had no other alternative. You know that she's helped me before when I've worked at home under deadlines. She's the only other person familiar with the things I need, with the type of work I do. I'll arrange for another housekeeper to come in and take care of our home while I'm gone."

Sofia was speechless, devastated.

PART TWO:
RED

Lorena Sandoval stared blankly at the copy-machine repairman sitting across from her, and wondered how long she could maintain her closed-lipped smile. Joe seemed nice enough to Lorena, although *gabachos*, white guys, weren't her type. She had met Joe in passing, at work, seeing him several times over a month-long period as he completed jobs in other offices throughout her building. Lorena was flattered when Joe nervously asked her out to dinner after engaging in their usual small talk by the elevator. She had not been on a date in three months. Now, Lorena was thankful that her boss used a different repair service than the one Joe worked for.

"So, uh, how old are you again?" Joe asked, talking with his mouth full. He wiped it on a soiled napkin he kept crinkled up like a ball of paper by his plate.

"Twenty-one," Lorena replied. She took a quick sip of her wine.

"Wow. Amazing. I don't think I've ever gone out with someone as young as you. Most of the girls I date are twenty-five, twenty-six—older women, you know? I'm gonna be thirty-eight in February."

"Age is just a number." Lorena took a deep breath and glanced at her nearly empty plate, as if wishing it were a magazine.

"Yeah, that's what this other Hispanic girl I went out with said—I met her on Yahoo Personals. Nice girl. She was from Argentina."

Lorena made a face.

"What's wrong?" Joe asked. "You don't like Argentineans?"

"Eh—I dunno," Lorena said, sighing. "The ones I've met think they're better than us *beaners* because their Spanish sounds like Italian and they say '*ciao*' instead of '*adios*.' It's like they want to be European instead of *Latino*. Get over yourselves."

She chuckled after this and took another sip of wine.

"Whatever," Joe continued. "I guess all you Hispanic women are cool with older guys. You must mature faster, or something. You like older men?"

I'm reconsidering, Lorena thought.

"Show me the older man and I'll tell you if I like him or not." Lorena sought out their waiter and wondered where their bill was.

"Good answer," Joe said, pointing at her with his fork.

"You're sharp. Quick. I like that in a girl. You'd be surprised at some of the chicks I've gone out with lately—one-date wonders! They just sat across from me. Hardly said a word. I don't think there was too much upstairs, if you catch my meaning."

Joe tapped his left temple with his greasy fork when he said "upstairs," leaving a spot of gravy near his eyebrow.

"Imagine that," Lorena replied, her smile broadening in honest amusement. She had to look away while wiping her mouth with her napkin.

Joe drove Lorena home while filling the silence between them with a long-winded autobiography that began when his first pet died in kindergarten, and ended with his decision to drop out of junior college and enroll in a vocational school, which partly explained his current career. His stories were mildly amusing, with some parts even genuinely hilarious, sending Lorena into several fits of laughter. She appreciated Joe's efforts, despite her foreknowledge that she would end up the subject of a "one-date wonder" story on one of his future outings.

"Here it is, on the left," Lorena said, pointing out her parents' house, now dark.

Joe pulled over across the street. Lorena held her breath as he put the gear in park, pulled up the emergency brake, but did not turn off the ignition. She exhaled slowly and looked at Joe, fighting the urge to reach for the door handle.

Joe thanked her for the date. Lorena reciprocated, thinking of the good parts of their date so that her farewell rang honest and warm. She then stepped out of his car in good form, deftly avoiding any issue of a goodnight kiss. Lorena was sure she would not hear from Joe again.

Once inside her house, Lorena was surprised to see her *abuelita*, Julia, sitting alone in the silence of their darkened kitchen. Everyone else was in bed and Lorena smelled hot tea.

Lorena kissed Julia on the cheek and greeted her in Spanish. Julia watched her granddaughter open the refrigerator door and pull out a carton of orange juice.

"Was he a nice man?" Julia inquired as she stirred her tea.

"He was all right," Lorena replied in Spanish. "Not really my type, but it was nice to be taken out."

Julia looked into her teacup as if staring into a magic oracle. She had seen this look on Lorena's face before. Julia had seen it in her mother's eyes, and even in her own, as she looked into a dirty mirror, years ago. Lorena watched her stoic *abuelita* in reverent silence, as if somehow connected spiritually, almost as if she could read Julia's thoughts. Lorena saw the lines etched in her grandmother's face and wondered what she was like as a woman her own age.

What have your eyes seen? Lorena wondered. Have you ever known love, grandmother?

While Julia's mind was lost in the haze of memory, Lorena thought about Joe, and about her own limited love life. Her mother, Isabel, had told her stories about the bad luck the women in their family had had with men, love, and marriage, which correlated somehow to the themes of Lorena's own upbringing. In the quiet of their kitchen, both Lorena and Julia retreated into their thoughts, going back to a faraway place in a faraway time, to the land of the scorpions.

When Isabel Cuevas was a child, she witnessed the birth of a stillborn boy. A woman not originally from her village in Durango, Mexico, had birthed the baby aided by a wizened *partera*, who happened to be Isabel's own *abuelita*, Juana. Juana had tried in vain to save the distressed infant, but the baby had been badly tangled in his own umbilical cord and in breech position. Juana had not seen the pregnant woman prior to this tragic birth. She would have been able to detect the complication and maybe save the baby, though there were no doctors, let alone a hospital, in the tiny village of Maria de Jesus del Real, in the mountainous, remote state of Durango. No police, no doctors, not even an *alcalde*, or mayor. The town was "governed," in any stretched sense of the word, by an *ad hoc* gathering, when appropriate, of the men of the village, a motley smattering of quiet, pious types, but also *rancheros*, *bandidos*, and *borrachos*, all of whom made livings by the meager products, whether livestock or plant, cultivated

on sparse farms scattered here and there, by highway rob-
bery and drug smuggling, or by the woven goods and store-
front wares made and sold by their women.

The women of the village relied heavily on Juana, who
also read tarot cards and attended to their pregnancies.
When they couldn't pay in pesos, the grateful *señoras* and
señoritas delivered fruit and vegetables from their own gardens. Juana, her brown, wrinkled face like that of a walnut,
would graciously accept the humble tributes, thanking her
dusty clients in soft-spoken, short sentences. Juana, in
widow's black, with mostly silver-white, wavy hair framing
her round face, would take the food to her kitchen where
she would resourcefully use it for her family's meals.

Her own daughter, twenty-eight-year-old Julia, had
long since stopped listening to her mother. Julia, whose
restless black eyes were always fixed upon the red horizon,
had little use for Juana's "folk" wisdom. The girl always
seemed happiest when a man's rough hands were on her
hips and there was music blaring nearby. Julia's lovers
came and went, each with flowers and broken promises
chipping away at her beauty and vitality. Soon, the lines
around her eyes and mouth were etched deeper with tears
of pain rather than those of joy, as she settled for a man—
Jose Cuevas—who was the nicest, beat her the least, and
gave her a child—Isabel—someone that she could love un-
conditionally and who would love her back.

Once proud and confident, Julia spent her days desperately trying to keep tabs on Isabel's father, who came and went when he pleased, often staying gone for several days on end, with no word as to when he would return. Whenever Jose Cuevas suddenly reappeared, tinkering inside the raised hood of a beat-up car standing like an old monument to Mexican progress on their barren patch of land, Julia would forget her seething anger of the past few days, wait on him hand and foot, and pray that he would take her to their one church and marry her before God and the *Virgen*.

Juana glanced at Isabel as the six-year-old stood on a rickety stool to watch her *abuelita* prepare a meal. Isabel had a quiet, soft mouth and heaven-turned, mahogany eyes as deep as a well, with a soul as open and clean as a baptismal dress. Juana called Isabel her little "brown nut" and liked to comb her long, black hair at least a hundred times each night while telling stories about Julia, at her age. Now, as the two of them stood over boiling pots and flame, like scientist and apprentice, Juana carefully considered the roundabout ways the child inquired about her mother and father.

Juana had never approved of Isabel's dad, whose own father had killed a man in cold blood for getting one of his daughters pregnant and refusing to marry her. Juana had known men like Jose, lazy dreamers who drifted through town and life like a leaf in the wind, stopping only to pick up the dirt on a momentary layover until the next gust carried it away.

"Your heart lets you know who you love. Your eyes let you know who loves you." Juana's *dichos* never came with explanations, as if Isabel's young mind was hard-wired at birth to wrap itself around such traditional family wisdom.

Years later, Julia watched as her daughter, Isabel, her fine, dark features made-up in pious dignity, married twenty-three-year-old Gerardo Sandoval in a modest ceremony held before the rustically decorative altar of the *Iglesia de la Enunciación de Santa Maria*, their town's only church. As the middle-aged, bespectacled priest with the matted comb-over hairdo administered the vows in Spanish, Julia found her eyes roaming around the small, stuffy interior, taking in the colorful iconic statues of the Virgin Mary and the crucified Christ, blood painted ghoulishly dripping from the hands, feet, and chest. The powerful reach of the Roman Catholic Church moved Julia. God had found His way to Durango, even to her flyspeck of a village, tucked away in a mountain range hidden from the world.

Returning her gaze to her daughter, as Isabel leaned to kiss Gerardo, Julia envied the girl. This was supposed to be Julia's dream, here, in this church marrying Jose Cuevas. Now, Jose was long gone to who-knows-what new life. He had run off with a green-eyed, seventeen-year-old girl he had met on one of his forays into the state capital. The day he had told her that he was leaving was the only day that

Julia had ever cursed in her life. She had stood, immobile at their doorway as Jose turned his back to her and walked along the gravel path toward a waiting pick-up truck. Julia had spat in his direction and yelled:

"*Pinche perro cabrón!*"

That was five years ago, and she had not heard from the man since.

Julia took a deep breath of the stale church air, forcing herself to be happy for her daughter's sake. The new Señora Sandoval turned to her mother and hugged her warmly. Gerardo was congratulated by his family members while Julia stood alone, her mother, Juana, having died seven years prior. Now it was just Isabel and Gerardo, and their children, if they had any. Julia was looking at the future. It was her daughter's time now, for happiness, for a new life.

And a new life Isabel and Gerardo would have, in America! Gerardo Sandoval, although raised most of his life in an even more remote village in Durango than Isabel's—in fact, the only access there when he was a child was by donkey—had actually been born in the United States. His father, a migrant farm worker, had been living with Gerardo's mother at the time of his birth, in an immigrant community in Atwater, California. They had returned to Durango when Gerardo was two years old, and they had never been back since. However, as Gerardo was always reminded, as if it were an ace up his sleeve, he had American citizenship, and he could return to that country anytime he wanted, his birth certificate coveted like a brick of gold.

Gerardo Sandoval was raised on the old family story that the men in their family were descended from a *conquistador* with hair as fiery red as Cortes'. This apocryphal tale explained the rust-colored hair, freckles, creamy skin, and eyes ranging in color from green to hazel that Gerardo and his brothers were born with. Gerardo, himself a provincially handsome man who kept his collar-length hair pulled back in a short ponytail, liked to wear a neatly-trimmed beard and a wide, flat-brimmed straw hat with a short, pillbox crown surrounded by a black silk band.

Before settling down with the alluring Isabel, Gerardo had nurtured a reputation in his hometown and elsewhere as "comfortable in the company of pretty ladies," as his own mother had once commented with mild disapproval. Isabel, not having known a man she was attracted to until Gerardo entered her world, was ignorant of the classic womanizer's wily ways. All Isabel understood was that her life, while she was in the state capital on vacation, had been turned upside down the day she met the green-eyed, red-haired, well-dressed man who smelled pretty. Isabel noticed that other women cast approving glances at Gerardo, as he and Isabel walked hand-in-hand, but in her naïve mind she could not blame them. Gerardo was like a beautiful peacock, his virile colors spread out behind him like a magical aura.

Isabel was even more enamored with her choice of husband when she learned that he was an American. He was her ticket out of the harsh land of scorpions from whence she came and would deliver her to a world only dreamed of before. In this new world, Isabel would raise a family with opportunities that she never had, because her children would be living in the United States, with access to education and plentiful work. This would all be possible because of Gerardo Sandoval, her guardian angel.

The Sandovals eventually settled in Pasadena, California, where Gerardo had a young cousin—a *chilanga*, originally from Mexico City—named Ruby Vasquez. Ruby, who would introduce them to other distant relatives in the area, was a wise 23-year-old, desperately cheerful, with skin the color of old piano keys, Indian eyes heavy with thick mascara and false lashes like inverted Venus Fly-Traps. She had a large, bleached-blonde coif with a lower flip that stuck out like a flying nun's habit. Ruby was recently separated from a good-for-nothing American husband, had no children, and was more than happy to help get Gerardo and Isabel acquainted with their new country. The young newcomers bought a modest house in Northwest Pasadena—an economically depressed section of town— and found themselves among mostly African-American families of various incomes and lifestyles. There were few

Hispanic families on Montana Street, where their house was situated.

Ruby was equally ecstatic, being childless, when Isabel gave birth to Cecilia. This child, with black hair and eyes to match, was a spitting image of her mother, even down to her olive skin and soft temperament. A son, Francisco, handsome and dark like Isabel's father, followed Cecilia five years later. Ruby helped raise the children like a dear aunt, providing countless hours of babysitting entertainment through her colorful stories of growing up in Mexico City, all embellished in her singsong voice and regional vernacular. Isabel was grateful, being exhausted all the time, but soon Ruby met a new man whom she would soon marry, leaving little time for Isabel's children.

Isabel, alarmed at her weight gain and increasingly frustrated because she felt like a single mom, was slightly relieved when her aging mother, Julia, moved into a house Gerardo had bought as a retirement investment in Tecate, Mexico, near the U.S. border.

This meant that the children could spend summers with their *abuelita*, Julia, now ironically enough full of folk wisdom and traditional values that Isabel felt would do her children some good, while she tended to her marriage.

As Gerardo aged, he abandoned his beard and wore his hair shorter, slicked back.

He was still lean and fit but had taken to drinking increasingly greater quantities of beer and had withdrawn from Isabel since she had embraced the role of mother and homemaker. He was not very happy working as an auto mechanic for a large, balding Armenian with gold chains, bad breath, and a large Cuban cigar sticking out of his mouth, lit or unlit, at any given moment. Gerardo dreamed of starting his own auto repair shop and saw in Ruby's new husband, Pedro Morales, a potential business partner in such a venture. Pedro was originally from Guadalajara, Mexico, where he had owned his own auto mechanic business.

Gerardo and Pedro spent many a night drinking beer and working under the hood of one car or another in the Sandovals' backyard, where they schemed, planned, and plotted on the where's, when's, and how's of getting their own shop underway. Isabel was already pregnant with their third child, due to be born right around the time of Francisco's fifth year.

On October 31, 1985, the same day that Anna Fronzini was born, in the same hospital and down the hall from her delivery room, Lorena Sandoval entered the world with barely a peep. Gerardo was amazed as her little softball-sized head, gripped gently in the bloody latex-gloved hands of the obstetrician, was pulled from Isabel's open abdomen. Lorena let out a faint cry, which was gone as soon as her 6 lb. 0 oz. little body was placed in a warm blanket. Gerardo was wide-eyed as a pair of scissors was placed in his hands.

Forgetting his fear of only moments before, when they learned that a prolapsed umbilical cord would necessitate an immediate emergency C-section, Gerardo now fumbled with the scissors as he cut her rubbery, ivory-yellowish cord, which appeared to magically seal itself off upon its being severed, a single drop of blood squirting out.

"*Mi 'jita linda*," he mumbled to himself, staring into baby Lorena's wide-open blue-gray eyes. The girl appeared to seek out her father among the operating room staff, locking onto his watery green eyes. Gerardo thought she smiled at him.

"I want to see her!" Isabel cried out in Spanish. She was in a drugged stupor, her eyes half-closed.

Gerardo went to Isabel and rubbed her forehead.

"I saw her," he soothed his wife. "She's beautiful with a perfect, round little head. Everything's okay."

Lorena was born to be daddy's little girl. In between running his new auto shop—P & G Auto Repair—and taking care of his family, Gerardo doted on his baby girl, whom he was pleased to see had his creamy skin, faint freckles, and red hair, which grew out in beautiful, dark auburn waves and curls. Lorena's round face beamed like a full moon with tiny dimples whenever her wide mouth parted in a smile. Her now big, brown eyes were shaped like a cat's and grew wide with excitement whenever Gerardo came through the back door at night, after a long day at the shop. She never cared that her father's hands were dirty, as she ran into his arms screaming, "*Papi! Papi!*"

Cecilia and Francisco treated their baby sister like a doll, dressing her up and starring her in various play-acting scenarios. Of course, Lorena worshiped her older brother and had to do whatever he was doing, much to his occasional annoyance. She would cry and tattle when he would not share a toy or include her in whatever he and the neighborhood boys were doing. Then she would smile in glee when Isabel scolded Francisco, telling him to let Lorena play.

Dutifully, the elder Sandoval siblings spoke only English to their sister as she grew up, while their parents spoke only Spanish to Lorena, that being the main language spoken in their home. Gerardo and Isabel had never gained a mastery of English to the point that they were comfortable speaking it. They knew enough to do business and enroll their children in school.

"Get the camera, get the camera!" Gerardo said, putting down his third Budweiser. Ruby frowned as she grabbed her Kodak instamatic.

"What are you doing?" Isabel asked, as Pedro looked on with mild curiosity.

Lorena, small at three-years-old, with hair down to just below her shoulders, was dressed in a white satin and lace Sunday school special, with matching lace socks and shiny patent-leather baby doll shoes.

"*Ven aqui, muñeca,*" Gerardo commanded.

Gerardo lifted his daughter and positioned her so that she stood on the arm of a worn green sofa in their back patio area. He placed his open right palm near her feet and asked her to stand in his hand.

"*No manches, guey!*" Ruby laughed, shaking her head.

"*Que 'tas haciendo, Gerardo?*" Isabel asked, wide-eyed.

Lorena smiled to herself, as she and her father had per-fected this stunt unbeknownst to the others.

"*Watch,* mami!" Lorena yelled.

Once her feet were touching in the center of Gerardo's large, calloused hand, he let out a faint grunt and lifted the petite girl up into the air. She held the folds of her dress out like a crowned baby Jesus idol, grinning from ear to ear, as Ruby snapped what would become one of Lorena's most cherished photos of her and her father.

"*Ai, Gerardo!*" Isabel gasped, instinctively standing up to position herself close to her daughter in case she fell over. This was not necessary, as Gerardo then quickly grabbed Lorena with his left arm, and flung her over to him.

Lorena was raised to feel proud of her roots in a tradi-tional Mexican household, while attending American schools and reciting the Pledge of Allegiance like all of the other children. During her summers in Tecate, Lorena was

enthralled by the poor, cinderblock homes, many unfin-
ished with rusted re-bar protruding from graffiti-
emblazoned foundations like eerie Aztec ruins, while
neighborhood boys played soccer in the dirt roads they
called streets. Lorena roamed these rocky, uneven byways
around Julia's house, playing with Cecilia and Francisco, as
well as with their Mexican neighbor girl, Lourdes Gon-
zalez, who wore sky blue eye shadow and pink lipstick on
her brown face. Lourdes had a pronounced over bite and
covered her mouth when she laughed. She always wore her
long black hair separated into two braided pigtails that
hung over her pre-pubescent chest.

Lorena grew to love Mexican candy bought at the corner store, especially the salty *tamarindos*, washed down
with orange Fanta. She paid no mind when the kids in her
Tecate neighborhood teased them as being *Americanos*,
since she, as she spoke fluent Spanish and had family in
Tecate, was naturally accepted as one of them. Lorena was
particularly struck by one of the boys that lived near Julia,
Carlos Perez, on whom Lourdes had a young girl's crush.
Lourdes, who was two-years older than Lorena, confessed
that Carlos had kissed her on the cheek by the side of her
mother's house. Carlos, although awkward and lanky in
colored-striped tube socks and soccer shorts, with a per-
petually sweaty clump of hair hanging down his forehead,
had an innocent boy's good looks, with large doe-eyes and
full lips.

Several years later, as a pre-teen, Lorena would be sitting with Carlos in Tecate, watching a sunset by a grassless soccer field, as he put his arm around her and whispered in her ear: "*Chiquita*." She felt a tingle in the pit of her stomach that she recognized in the future as nascent sexual arousal. Lorena always thought that Mexican children, boys and girls, were born with a natural, instinctive knowledge of all things sexual. Julia, sensing her American granddaughter's interest in the boys in the neighborhood, cautioned her to cherish her virtue like a secret gift that she should only relinquish upon finding a worthy man who truly loved her.

"Why buy the cow when the milk is free?" Julia asked the girl in Spanish, one summer while teaching her to make *ceviche*. "Don't make the same mistakes as I did, *mi 'ija*. Many men will promise you the moon, but once you give yourself to them, they lose interest and are gone. A man good enough to marry you will not lose interest so soon. It's only fair, your love for their hand in marriage. Never settle for less."

Isabel was always pleased when she greeted her children at the end of the summer. Pleased and proud of how her mother had raised them, making them attend a summer school in Tecate, taught entirely in Spanish, complete with uniforms and strict discipline. Julia taught the girls how to cook traditional dishes, knowledge Isabel tried to build upon in her own kitchen, often getting assistance from Lorena, who had learned a technique or two from her grandmother. Isabel's children possessed a raw, natural affinity for all things culturally Mexican that was evident in the cherished traditions and artifacts they brought back to America. Scorpion-encrusted souvenirs, colorful ceramic piggy banks, handmade dolls and toys, Mexican coins, and the firecrackers Francisco liked to blow things up with, were held in the same esteem as her children's taste for rice and beans, *carne asada*, *mole*, *tamales* at Christmastime, and various other delicacies prepared by Isabel and her mother, Julia, who started spending more time with the family as she got older.

Lorena especially cherished family gatherings, Sunday *carne asada* barbeques being her favorite. She would play with her siblings and cousins, while the adults cooked, laughed, drank beer, and told ribald jokes in Spanish, which the children would eavesdrop on, laughing at the humorous stories and expressions, untranslatable in English.

On Sundays, Lorena sat as reverently as she could in the large wooden pews of St. Andrew's Church, resisting the urge to make faces or secretly whisper things to Francisco or Cecilia. Whenever Isabel caught Lorena, she would reach down and pinch her thigh:

"*Cállese!*" Isabel whispered loudly.

"*Ai!*" Lorena rubbed her thigh, half-laughing and half-wanting to cry.

There was a large replica of the original Virgin of Guadalupe icon hanging in the living room of the Sandoval home, along with various other Catholic artifacts, crucifixes of every shape, size, and style in almost every room of the house, as well as *santitos*, candles, and cards with prayers, in both Spanish and English, visible on every shelf, table, nook or cranny. One of the few books in the house, aside from a set of the Encyclopedia Britannica that Gerardo had proudly bought upon Cecilia's entry into kindergarten, was a Holy Bible. Lorena said her prayers almost nightly, could not walk past a statue of the Virgin or a crucified Jesus without making the sign of the cross, and, when she was in fourth grade, per tradition, received her first Holy Communion at St. Andrew's.

Unlike most of their peers, the Sandoval children were not allowed to go to their school friends' houses to play, do homework, or socialize. They were not allowed to linger on campus past the time that school let out. Girlfriends came over to spend the night in Lorena's bedroom. Lorena never saw the inside of one of her friends' homes. When Cecilia was dating Victor Olivas—her future husband—in high school and in her first year in college, Francisco or Lorena would accompany their sister as chaperones. Even nine-year-old Lorena, awkward and lanky with long, curly red hair, was irritated by this, as she often had to sit, bored to tears, and entertain herself in the living room, while Cecilia and Victor were on the couch across from her, chastely holding hands and talking in lovers' code.

Ruby did her best to advocate for the children, arguing that Francisco and Lorena had to have some fun once in a while. Otherwise they would rebel later.

"They can have as much fun as they want right here at home," Isabel replied, wiping her hands on her apron. "There's nothing but trouble for them out there in the streets. I see all the little *negritos* and *peloncitos* running around out there, and where are their parents, huh? Little *cholitas* getting pregnant, dropping out of school. Not my kids, *cabrona!*"

"*Ándele, guey*," Ruby said with a flick of her hand. "We'll see."

Isabel Sandoval stuck to her rules, and, backed by Gerardo's quiet, neglectful support and Julia's homespun wisdom (she had moved into their house when Francisco was in high school), created a loving and supportive family environment, built upon a foundation of traditional Mexican and Christian values. It wasn't long before Cecilia Sandoval became Cecilia Olivas, in a beautiful ceremony at St. Andrew's Church. She graduated from college and took a decent-paying job at a local engineering firm. She would bear Victor two sons and a daughter, and would raise her children in the same manner as Isabel had raised her. Francisco graduated from high school with a 3.5 GPA, lettered in varsity football and track, and worked as a cadet at the Pasadena Police Department, while majoring in criminal justice at Cal State L.A.

Lorena Sandoval was no less successful. She attended John Muir High School like her brother and sister before her, dutifully walking the four blocks to and from school everyday without getting distracted by the African-American and Hispanic youths, who were dressed in full hip-hop gear, hanging out at the bus stops and street corners.

"Yo, what up, *Red*!" they called out to her.

"Hello, boys," she replied politely, always with her full, mischievous smile.

"When yo' mama gonna let you go out on dates?" asked Artemis Jones, a tall inside linebacker with dark skin and a natural afro.

Lorena clucked her tongue while wagging a delicate index finger side to side.

"C'mon, Red!"

"No-no-no, mister," she said for added effect. "Not allowed."

But the boys respected her for this and left her alone. She was from their 'hood, after all.

Lorena served in student government as vice-president in her junior year, and as president in her senior year. She was voted junior year homecoming queen and "best eyes" and "best smile" in her senior yearbook. Like every good Pasadena girl, she tried out for the Tournament of Roses Royal Court, making it to the second round of judging. Lorena proudly kept her numbered entry card and affiliated accoutrements as souvenirs, along with a photograph of herself holding a bouquet of red roses.

Lorena dated one boy in high school, beginning in her junior year. He was a senior at the time, James Estevez, and came from a good family in Pasadena. He played football and planned on going to UCLA after graduating. Even though his buddies called him "Jim" or "Jimmy," Lorena never called him anything other than "James" or "Babe." She thought that he was nice, with boyish good looks, short, spiky hair and a crooked grin. Although Hispanic, James was not *Latino*, as she explained meant growing up "in the culture." His grandfather on his father's side was the most recent immigrant, and James' parents didn't speak Spanish at home—James couldn't speak a lick. Lorena told him that she would overlook this but would try to teach him herself, because she had to marry a Mexican, not a *pocho*.

On the day that James had asked Lorena to be his official "girlfriend," meaning that they would be committed and would see no others (James felt that this would speed up the process of Lorena relinquishing her virginity), she asked him to do something that took him completely by surprise.

"James, before I accept," she began, taking a deep breath. "I would like you to meet with my parents and talk to them about this."

James frowned, shifting uncomfortably in his letterman's jacket.

"What do you mean?"

"I want you to tell them that you would like us to become official."

Lorena made quotation marks with the first two fingers on each hand as she said "official."

"You know, tell them what your intentions are with me."

She gave him a closed-lip smile while raising her eyebrows. He stymied a rude chuckle.

"Babe! I'm not asking your hand in marriage."

Lorena didn't laugh.

"Babe, c'mon," James realized that he was on the verge of striking out.

"James, if you love me like you say you do, you'll do this little thing for me."

"Babe, that's *weird*! I've never had to do something like this before."

Lorena looked away. She placed her hands on her knees and tapped her feet, unsure of where they were headed.

"Babe, that's how I was raised," Lorena said, matter-of-factly. "You know my family means a lot to me, and I respect them. I want them to know what's going on with me—*I* want to know what your intentions are, too; that you'll be around for the long haul. By doing this little thing for me—it won't hurt—I'll know that your love is true."

"You *know* I love you!" James protested.

"You say you do," Lorena said, unconvinced. "And I

love you. But your *heart* lets you know who you love, and your *eyes* let you know who loves you."

James chuckled.

"Oh, Mexican folk wisdom! How can I compete against that?"

Lorena laughed, and her boyfriend agreed to let her eyes see his love for her.

"You'll see," Lorena said, putting her arm around him and kissing him on the cheek. "It won't be so bad."

James accomplished this task, and Lorena's parents found him acceptable and were impressed with the fact that their daughter always made James come to her door and wait in the living room, where he had to at least speak with Isabel. Lorena's mother always took this opportunity to talk to James about his family, what he wanted to do with his life, and to ask him to please not keep her daughter "out too late," which he understood meant between 11:00 PM and midnight.

Lorena was never ready on time, opting to "present" herself to James with dramatic effect, usually with a red flower in her hair, bright, Latin-colored frilly tops with scooped or V-necks, padded push-up bras, festive, knee-length skirts, her long, thin bare legs always ending in high heeled, strapped sandals, toes painted by her but made to look professionally done.

Lorena truly thought that she loved James, being that he was her first boyfriend.

She kept him waiting for her virginity all through her senior year, past prom night, and well into her first semester at a vocational school where she had registered for training as a legal secretary. After some discomfort upon their first making love, Lorena was surprised to find that she enjoyed being physical with her man, and it seemed to deepen their bond. Was marriage far off? Lorena told herself that she would at least finish school first.

Lorena had the grades and background for a four-year college, but knew that her parents probably couldn't afford two children at a university. Lorena also made no secret of the fact that she craved a simple life of marriage and family, and after a few years of being a legal secretary somewhere, she would probably settle down and be a housewife; if not with James, then with some other Prince Charming, if he was out there.

James kept pressuring Lorena to move in with him, but she would never budge, reminding him that she would never leave home until she had a ring on her finger.

"An *engagement* ring?" James asked, hopeful.

"Nice try, mister," Lorena said, coyly. "A *wedding* ring, thank you."

In an oddly calculated move that Lorena figured was James' attempt at softening up her parents' position on her living arrangements, he sat down with Isabel and Gerardo, bravely advising them that their daughter was no longer a virgin, and that their relationship had been taken to "the next level." Lorena sat on the couch with James, in stunned silence, resisting the urge to bury her face in her hands. Gerardo, stone-faced and without saying a word, stood up and left the room while Isabel looked heartbroken. Lorena did the only thing she could think of as a dutiful daughter and asked a worried and confused James to leave.

Once James had gone, Lorena tried consoling her mother, explaining that she had no idea her boyfriend was going to do this. Isabel believed her daughter but was still distraught at the news that Lorena had not saved herself for marriage. Isabel was realistic enough to know that Lorena had been intimate with James to some degree, possibly even sleeping with him, but as it was not confirmed, she could live with the illusion that Lorena had retained her chastity. Now that the truth was thrown in her face—in Gerardo's face—the damage had been done. Lorena's father could not be consoled. He was furious at her, but in reality was taking his anger at James out on his teary-eyed daughter.

Gerardo told Lorena that he never wanted to see James again, especially anywhere near his house. Lorena was crushed, not because of the thought of losing James (actually, she was furious, hurt, and turned off by his latest "talk" with her parents), but because she feared that she had wounded her father deeply. The possibility that her father would look at her differently from now on, somehow love her less, was almost too much to bear for the poor girl.

Out of respect for her family, but especially for her father, Lorena ended the relationship with James, who took it stoically. Lorena was hurt that James didn't say much, that there were no tears or expressions of undying love. She went home and cried later, convinced that what they had was not really love. Lorena told herself that she would tread carefully with the next man she got involved with. She knew that she was a good woman who deserved a good, traditional man with family values, who would respect her *and* the relationship she had with her family. Only marriage-minded suitors need apply, she told herself.

Lorena immersed herself in school, looked forward to entering the workforce, and as for love, she would worry about that when the time came.

Several years later, two nights after Miriya brought Fabio new flowers in his hospital bed, Lorena Sandoval, now an office manager and legal secretary at the Fayed Law Corporation, got off late from work and stopped at a local bookstore before going home. It was a Friday night, and like every other Friday night before, Lorena had no plans except going home to be with her family and to go to bed. One of the few friends that she had from work, Lupe, had called her earlier to see if she wanted to meet her and her boyfriend for drinks later. Lorena briefly considered this but was tired and had a common aversion to feeling like a third wheel, so she had declined.

After greeting her parents and *abuelita*, Julia, she chit-chatted with Francisco before shutting herself in her bedroom to change out of her work clothes. She donned a pair of jeans and a tight T-shirt that read *Everyone Loves a Latin Girl*, threw on a pair of flip-flops, and soon emerged to get some orange juice from the refrigerator.

Julia sat at their kitchen table, still as a mummy wrapped in a black knit shawl, and watched her granddaughter shuffle from one corner of the kitchen to the other, mindlessly reheating what was made for dinner earlier.

"No one sees the diamond's brilliance if its kept in a box," Julia said, in Spanish.

Lorena frowned at this, too tired to decipher the *dicho*.

"I'll get my diamond one of these days; I'm in no hurry," was all she thought to say. Lorena sat next to her grandmother and ate her food in silence, staring wide-eyed at what Julia thought must have been the salt-and-pepper shakers.

Julia turned her attention back to the TV. *Sofia de Amor* was on. Lorena rarely watched *telenovelas* unless she had seen them from the start and been hooked, so she ignored what Julia was engrossed by.

Arturo de Amor had booked separate hotel rooms for him and Carmen. However, not long after unpacking and settling in, Arturo knocked on Carmen's door. She let him in and they embraced with wild abandon, kissing and grasping at each other feverishly.

"*Ai, dios mio*," muttered Julia at the TV, shaking her head at Carmen and Arturo's shenanigans.

Lorena finished her food and excused herself from the table. Curiously, she felt a sudden pang of loneliness and found herself at the doorway of her brother's bedroom. Francisco was hunched over in front of his computer, checking his latest lineup from Match.com. Smiling, he scratched his goatee and finally turned to her.

"What's up, Red? Whatchoo doin'?"

Lorena shrugged and plopped down on his bed behind him, only mildly interested in what he was up to. She stared at a small shrine that Francisco had made for his best friend, Ricky, whom she had also been close to. Ricardo and her brother had been inseparable, and had spent many days and nights jamming out in Francisco's room—Ricky on his bass guitar and Francisco on his drum set. Ricky made no secret of his crush on Lorena, but never pursued her out of respect for Francisco, and perhaps, because he knew that he was not Lorena's type. He was too wild, had too much *machismo* for Lorena.

She smiled to herself, thinking of the three of them laughing and joking around. Lorena remembered how she would pretend to be Gwen Stefani, belting out No Doubt lyrics while they backed her instrumentally.

Lorena had prayed for Ricky when he joined the Marines shortly after 9/11. She had gone with Francisco to San Diego when Ricky had graduated from boot camp, and thought he looked sharp in his uniform. Ricky had been part of the initial ground force in 2003, when Saddam Hussein had been deposed. Sadly, on his second tour of duty, Ricky was killed in Fallouja. Lorena had grieved with Francisco, and the two of them placed flowers and a small American flag at his grave each Memorial Day. And now, as she looked at the photo of Ricky in his Marine Corps "blues," with his cocky grin, she missed him.

"I got one of those dog tags," Fernando said, breaking the silence.

"Huh?" Lorena blinked, composing herself.

"Those remembrance tags that you can get with the engraved photo of your friend or family member that was killed. I can get you one if you like."

Lorena took a deep breath and nodded.

"Cool," she mumbled. She glanced at his computer screen, eagerly seeking a distraction.

"Oooh! *Match.com*? Don't you have a girlfriend?" she asked, turning her attention to a tattered poster of Jim Morrison on his wall.

"So?" Francisco mumbled calmly. "I can shop around for new parts, can't I? Get an upgrade."

"Maybe you can find a *sancha* on eBay," Lorena said, smiling. She looked at his drum set. "Hey, can I bang on your drums?"

"Go ahead."

Lorena got up and maneuvered around the drum set cramped into the corner of his room. She picked up the drumsticks and tried to twirl them.

"Okay, Ringo," Francisco said. "Why don't you try online dating?"

Lorena banged on the drums as if she knew what she was doing.

"Does this sound like that one Pink Floyd song?" she yelled over the cacophony of her *doom-doom-da-da-da-dum-da-dum-doom-doom*!

"No." He clicked onto a male's profile. "Check this guy out, Red."

"Huh?"

"C'mere! Look at these guys on-line."

Lorena hung up the drumsticks and returned to Francisco's computer.

"What am I looking at?"

"Look at the kinda guys that go on these sites. You might find Mr. Right online."

"Are you trying to play match-maker?"

"No, I'm just tired of seeing my sister home on Friday nights."

"You're here, ain'tchoo?"

"Yeah, but I'm going out in an hour."

"With *sanchita* number one or *sanchita* number two?" Lorena laughed.

"*Cállate, cabrona!*" Francisco blurted. "*Con mi novia!*"

"Big balla, shot-calla," Lorena added in her best ghetto accent. "Oh, he's *hot*! Go back to that guy! They got *Latinos* on this?"

Francisco laughed.

PART THREE: MIRIYA AND LORENA

Miriya Fronzini, Jr., stood before a full-length mirror and envied the confident smile of the woman looking back at her. *This is all you. This is your night,* she told herself, hoping eventually, that she would believe it. Miriya had almost forgotten that Veronica Bonkowski was by her side, there to help her feel every bit herself. Veronica's hands flittered and fussed over Miriya's form-fitting, black bead-and-sequined evening gown, picking off hairs, smoothing uppity beads, and finally zipping up the open back as if sealing a precious cargo. Miriya, for her part, couldn't keep her fingers off her blonde-streaked auburn hair, which she had curled for tonight as she often did on special occasions, and lamented its fine uselessness. Veronica however, approved, beaming at her best friend.

"You look beautiful," she said. "As always."

"Thanks," Miriya replied, forcing a smile. "You look stunning yourself."

Veronica's hands instinctively went toward the small bulge in her tummy, pressing down on her satiny, emerald green cocktail dress, low cut in the front and topped with a string of pearls. Her short, collar-length hair, currently dyed platinum blonde and combed back, gave her an air of elegance she usually eschewed. She had powder-puffed her alabaster skin as a final touch, which gave her a sparkly glow. To complement her attire, she wore bright red lipstick, although probably more for shock value, Miriya thought.

"I'm just glad I can still fit into this dress." Veronica turned sideways and sucked in her stomach. Although not overweight, Veronica had grown softer over the years, which accentuated her natural curves.

"You look like you're toning up." Miriya examined her friend's reflection.

"I'm trying," Veronica moaned. "24-Hour Fitness five days a week."

Miriya nodded while evaluating her friend's figure.

"You look good. You're lucky. You have big natural boobs. I had to buy mine," Miriya said, with a mischievous smile.

Veronica still referred to Miriya as her "Argentinean friend" when talking about her to other people. The girls remained best friends through high school and junior college, Veronica opting to continue her education at UCLA, graduating with a degree in English. Miriya had received an

A.A. degree and had considered transferring to a university. She quickly realized, however, that continuing her education would not help subsidize her shopping habit, so she entered the workforce. Miriya got a job at Burke Williams Spa in Old Pasadena, through a college buddy, Suzy Hovsepian. It was not long before Miriya was a manager there.

"So, uh," Veronica began, "what do you think's gonna happen tonight?"

Miriya shrugged coyly.

"Who knows? When Arturo said he wanted to gather everyone for a special announcement, I thought, this could be it!"

Veronica squealed with excitement.

"Oh, my God! Can you imagine?" she added.

"Trust me, I've been waiting for this for a while," Miriya said with fleeting gloominess. "I'm thirty years old. Most every girl I know is already married and having kids. *I* want kids, and I don't have a lot of time if I'm going to give my parents grandchildren. I don't know how long…"

Miriya paused for a moment, her face wrinkling as her eyes welled with tears.

"…how long my daddy has."

Miriya wiped her face and quickly composed herself. Veronica reached out for Miriya's slumping shoulder.

"I know how much you wish he could be there tonight." Veronica felt that she too, was going to cry.

"He's the best man I've ever known."

"I know," Veronica agreed.

"Hey," Miriya said, turning to Veronica, "thanks for everything. You've been my best friend for so long. I know we've gone through spells when we weren't close, like in college, but you've been supportive. Thanks for never giving up on us."

"I'd never give up on you, silly," Veronica said, still with a froggy edge to her voice.

Later that evening, Miriya and Veronica arrived at Café Santorini, where their friends and family eagerly awaited them like pop idol fans at a red carpet event. Suzy Hovsepian, Nathalie Faresi, and Taylor Jorgensen fleshed out Miriya's inner circle and formed the first wave of greeters. Behind them, Miriya saw her younger sister, Anna, and her boyfriend, Chris, as well as Miriya, Sr., and two of Arturo's Argentinean buddies, Carlo and Jorge, milling around some tables that had been pushed together for the large party. Miriya's older sister, Eva, and her husband, Jim, had opted to remain at the hospital to take care of Fabio.

Suzy hugged Miriya first and whispered in her ear:

"Best of wishes, sweetie."

"Thanks." Miriya replied, feeling better at the sight of Suzy's smiling face.

When they met in college, Suzy had taken an immediate liking to Miriya. She was one of the few non-Armenian women whom Suzy had ever made an effort to get to know. Miriya seemed friendly and honest to Suzy, who felt that most women were fake, catty bitches either secretly judging or competing with her, or out trying to steal whatever man was momentarily in her life. Suzy also happened to be a twenty-eight-year-old virgin, holding out for a good, wealthy Lebanese-Armenian man who would treat her lovingly and give her a large family. She detested men who paid her attention just to get into her pants.

Suzy stood aside so Miriya could hug and greet Nathalie and Taylor. Taylor had originally grown on Miriya slowly. They, too, met in college, having only one class together. Taylor, tall and thin, with a self-conscious slouch, began her acquaintance with Miriya as just that, an acquaintance. Miriya would see Taylor eating lunch or reading by herself and would sit with her, engaging the girl in friendly small talk. Miriya thought that Taylor had a pretty face with classic Nordic features, blue eyes, a fine nose, and long blonde hair—just the type of look that most guys noticed fast. Taylor was quiet and somewhat shy when she first met Miriya. Soon, through Miriya's quiet influence, Taylor discovered her own femininity, using make-up, getting her hair done and taking better care of herself. Once boys started noticing her more, Taylor tried to depend less on Miriya, opting instead to find her own social attitude.

"You look great, Taylor!" Miriya nodded her head in approval. Taylor wore a red tube top and tight black Capri pants. Her long, thin feet were displayed prominently in black sandals.

"Thanks. You, too." Taylor turned to Miriya's boyfriend, who stood impatiently to the side. "Here's Arturo."

Thirty-five-year-old Arturo Suarez stood at the head of the table, pointing and waving guests to their seats like a well-dressed CEO of a modeling agency. He wore a charcoal-gray pinstriped suit complete with orange and blue diagonally striped tie. At 6' 3," 220 pounds, Arturo fit the image of the imposing, fit hero who would sweep Miriya off her feet to a blissful, happily-ever-after. Argentinean by birth, he had lived in Los Angeles long enough to have a barely perceptible accent and a Hollywood *über*sexual's polished looks. He had long, slicked-back, blonde-streaked hair that came to just below his ears, and sharp, wandering gray eyes that hid under thick, neatly groomed brows. A classic square jaw, complete with slightly dimpled chin, framed his tanned face, shiny from organic aftershave balms and anti-wrinkle lotions.

Miriya gave him a quick, passionate kiss on the lips.

"Hi, *mono*," she said. Miriya turned, waved and smiled at everyone she couldn't reach.

"Hi, love. I'm trying to get everyone settled. I saved you a place by me," Arturo motioned with his arm. Miriya saw that he looked stressed.

"Sit down, *boludo*!" Jorge said, elbowing Carlo. They chuckled as Arturo made a face at them. Jorge Müller had short, spiky blonde hair and a goatee to match. Arturo often teased him about his German heritage, claiming that Jorge was one of the "Berlin Müllers" who escaped to South America after the war. Arturo liked to think that Jorge's family was probably still wanted by some anti-Nazi tribunal somewhere.

Carlo Seccia sat with arms folded across his chest. More of the strong, silent type, Carlo kept his dark hair slicked back and always had a day-old beard. He was self-conscious about looking at Arturo's girlfriend, Miriya, on whom he had a secret, if innocent, crush.

"Does everyone have a menu?" Arturo asked the group. He glanced at a passing waiter and tried to get his attention.

"Baby!" Miriya, seated to his right, reached for his hand. "We're fine. Sit down and relax."

Arturo sat sheepishly and smiled at Miriya. She squeezed his hand and leaned over to kiss him.

"You look so handsome," she whispered in his ear.

"You look beautiful," he countered.

Twenty-seven-year-old Nathalie Faresi took a slow sip of her strong Cosmopolitan and cautiously watched the couple. Persian and unmarried, Nathalie would be considered a spinster in her culture, which she eschewed to the disdain of her family. Her friends, Miriya included, shared the artist's disbelief that she did not have a man of her own. Nathalie, always well dressed, coifed, and made-up, had the type of svelte figure and alluring exotic looks that many men craved. She was also a sophisticated, successful woman of independent means. Still, she was single. While happy for Miriya, whom she truly liked, Nathalie couldn't fight off faint pangs of envy as she admired the handsome couple.

After ordering drinks and food, the group settled into a dull buzz of anticipation, eager to learn why Arturo had convened this formal gathering. Miriya, too, could hardly contain her excitement and turned to her boyfriend. She watched Arturo absentmindedly butter some bread and tear into it like a savage, nervously chewing with his mouth open. Miriya cringed slightly at the sight of breadcrumbs stuck to the corner of his mouth. She delicately cleared her throat to get his attention and made a quick wiping motion with her hand. Arturo got the hint and reached for a napkin.

Arturo, sensing that his friends, girlfriend, and her family could wait no longer, smiled and cleared his throat loudly, as if to get everyone's attention. Miriya sat up straighter, beaming regally from ear to ear as Veronica, seated to her right, reached over and squeezed her thigh.

"I would like to first thank all of you for coming tonight," Arturo said with dramatic reverence, as a waiter filled their wine glasses and delivered beers. "Especially you, Mrs. Fronzini! Thank you, ma'am."

Miriya, Sr., nodded at Arturo with a tight-lipped smile. To her, he was the son that Fabio never had.

"I only wish that Mr. Fronzini could be here with us,"

Arturo added, giving his girlfriend a warm smile.

Don't cry, Miriya told herself.

"He wanted to be here, trust me," Miriya, Sr., said with a distant look in her eyes. She turned to her youngest and placed a wrinkled hand on her thigh. Dyed-blonde, green-eyed Anna Fronzini took her mother's hand in hers. Anna glanced at her older sister and winked at her. Anna wore a cream-colored camisole with spaghetti straps and tight black slacks with gray pinstripes. She was the "mama's girl" of Miriya, Sr.'s daughters and was never far from her favorite shopping partner.

"The reason that I called for this dinner tonight is to celebrate the official announcement…"

Miriya frowned slightly.

"…of the forming of our real estate investment company, Patagonia Investment Corporation, along with my partners, Carlo Seccia and Jorge Müller."

Miriya took a deep breath as the three men patted each other on their backs and shook hands proudly. Miriya, Sr. looked impressed. She always knew that Arturo was the right man to take care of her daughter. He was going places! Veronica tried hard to widen her tight-lipped smile while Miriya, visibly disappointed, put on her best face and started clapping for her man.

"Congratulations, babe!" she said, as others joined in the applause. "I'm happy for you."

Arturo leaned over and kissed her.

"It's for us, baby. For our future."

Miriya's feelings toward the news improved the more she considered the possibilities of Arturo's growing maturity and drive toward achieving his career goals. The once part-time doorman/bouncer and wireless customer service representative appeared on the right track to a stable future, especially if he and Miriya were going to get married and start a family.

Nathalie glanced sideways at Suzy and Taylor. They offered their congratulations as if in a daze. The three of them had expected Miriya to walk away from this night with a big rock on her finger. While Nathalie truly felt bad for Miriya, she was overcome by a strong sense of relief, which helped to calm her pounding heart. She caught Arturo's happy eyes in hers and gave him a look. He seemed puzzled by this and frowned slightly, as if silently seeking clarification.

Nathalie quickly looked at Miriya, then mouthed to Arturo: "Miss you." Arturo nodded slightly and turned back toward Miriya. Nathalie sat up straighter and glanced around the table to make sure nobody was paying attention to her. Taylor Jorgensen rolled her eyes.

None of Miriya's friends mentioned anything about dashed expectations or false hope. They all offered warm praise and congratulations to whom they all figured was the group's next successful couple, soon to be engaged, married, and set up in a big house, with matching BMWs in the driveway, and all the trimmings of the good life, *if* Arturo's big dreams paid off. Miriya, too, tried to see the silver lining to the gray clouds of Arturo's lofty plans. She was happy for him. Miriya was wise enough to know that no man was ready for marriage if he wasn't secure in his career and ability to provide for a future wife and family. Arturo was a good man. He had spent many an evening awake in bed, as they had held each other and stared at the ceiling, talking openly about his dreams of being able to give her the finer things in life. She was worth it, he always told her, squeezing her tightly.

On the drive to Arturo's place later that evening, Miriya was pleased to see her man wired, excitedly gesturing while discussing the company and its potential for growth. She watched him with a warm smile on her face.

"I'm telling you, babe, Jorge and Carlo are solid team players, totally dedicated to this venture. They're real go-getters!"

"As are you, baby," she said.

Arturo was too modest to talk about himself and drove in silence for a bit. Miriya used the quiet time to remember previous Arturo Suarez get-rich-quick schemes. Arturo was known to dream big and live above his means.

"We're finding investment properties and setting up meetings with potential investors. Soon we'll be getting the capital to really get things going for us. Things will start taking off. You watch, babe! A year from now, *watch,* you'll see! We'll be set up, you and I. We're on our way, baby."

Miriya decided to give him the benefit of the doubt and be supportive.

"I'm so proud of you."

"My big, strong man," Miriya purred, rubbing the inside of Arturo's muscled thighs. He sat, proud and naked on his leather desk chair, as if the king of a new corporate empire yet to be born. Miriya, too, was nude, on her knees before him, looking sensuously up from under her dark eyelashes.

Arturo reached out and gently took hold of an amber wave of Miriya's fine hair, holding it away from her face to afford him a better view. Miriya smiled at him crookedly while slowly stroking him. Miriya loved the feel of his alert manhood in her hands. Arturo had opened her eyes several years prior when he told her that if a woman truly loved a man, she would *love his cock*.

"Never look at my cock as something separate from me," he had told her. "It is not something disgusting you have to put your mouth on. It is an extension of me—the man you love. Therefore, love my cock as you would love me. Kiss it the way you would kiss me. When you kneel before me, worship my cock as you would worship me. That is love."

Miriya was blown away. Before Arturo, she had been

ambivalent if not slightly repulsed at the thought of fellatio. Maybe men sensed this, she had wondered. What had she been doing wrong? Arturo had presented this aspect of lovemaking in a whole new light. Miriya felt empowered now, not only over Arturo, whom she realized loved a woman going down on him almost as much, if not more, than being inside her, but also over her friends, whom she believed still didn't get the secret to adoring a man completely.

Love the cock.

"Oh, baby, baby, baby," Arturo moaned. Miriya licked her hand, using her saliva to lubricate the process. She put her hair behind her ears while Arturo helped to hold the rest behind her head.

"You like that, baby?" she asked, looking up at him with eyes half-closed.

"Oh, yeah, yeah! Spit on it."

She did as she was told while gently caressing his quivering source with her wet fingers.

Arturo threw his head back and groaned loudly.

"Oh, shit, man! That feels *sooo* intense!"

Miriya pulled one of Arturo's large testicles into her mouth, sucking on it gently as his body shook. She buried her face further beneath his sack, letting her tongue dance and tickle the sensitive spot below. Arturo pulled away, as it tickled him down there. Miriya chuckled mischievously and sat up straight. She then took him into her mouth again.

"Oh, God!"

Miriya looked up at him and smiled.

"God's not doing this," she teased.

"You got that right! Oh, fuck yeah, babe! Suck it." His breathing grew heavy as his stomach rose and sank with each bob of Miriya's head. She followed her lips with her hands, spitting on him again every once in a while. Miriya used her free hand to massage his testicles between her thumb and fingers.

"Oh, baby! Yeah! Work those balls! Massage 'em! Oh, fuck yeah! You're getting me all worked up...Oh, yeah!...*Yeah!*"

Miriya increased the tempo of her strokes, bobbing and weaving her head up and down and around his glistening shaft, using her tongue to caress his swollen head. She tasted his sticky pre-seminal fluid, already starting to leak out and mix with her saliva. He was close, real close. Miriya ignored the pain in her neck and her burning jaw muscles, keeping her ear tuned to the change in Arturo's breathing and the pitch of his moaning. She prepared herself mentally to relax her throat muscles. She anticipated the warm squirts into the back of her mouth and prepared to start swallowing.

Arturo's eyes widened as he felt himself stiffen up. His toes curled and his balls tightened as if they were going to retract up into his stomach.

"Oh, *fuuuuck*! I'm *gonna come!*"

Miriya squinted and let out a faint moan as his first salty shot hit the back of her throat. She paused for a second up near the top of his shaft, keeping her lips wrapped tightly around her head as she quickly jerked him off, each upstroke sending another warm squirt into her mouth. She dutifully swallowed Arturo's sticky nectar, squeezing his cock as if to get every last drop out, while gently sucking what was left into her mouth. She pulled away, catching her breath and thinking that semen smelled like bleach. Arturo trembled in a total ecstatic collapse. Miriya then licked and kissed his slowly softening penis.

"Oh…my…God," Arturo moaned, bringing his hands to his face. "That was the *fuckin'* best blowjob I ever had."

"That's what you always say," Miriya said, smiling proudly.

"It's the truth, babe."

Arturo slowly stood up from his desk chair.

"Lookit," Miriya said, pointing. "The chair's all wet and gooey."

"I'll wipe that off," Arturo said, struggling to maintain his balance. Miriya stood up in all her golden brown naked glory, her body glistening with a fine layer of sweat. Arturo couldn't resist the urge to cup her large breasts in his still hungry hands, and felt the give of the bulbous saline sacks underneath their smooth, soft skin. He leaned over and kissed each erect brown nipple. Arturo then kissed her on the mouth, tasting him on her lips.

"Thank you, baby."

"I love you, baby," Miriya replied, wiping her mouth. She pulled him closer, wanting to kiss and play some more.

"*Whew*! That was just what I needed," Arturo said, gently extricating his body from her loving grasp. He walked into the bathroom and proceeded to brush his teeth.

Miriya frowned and sat on the edge of the bed.

"Uh, hello? What about me?" she mumbled under her breath.

Miriya sighed and threw herself backward.

Not again, she thought. She stared at the ceiling and listened to Arturo gargle. Oh, well, this was for him. He deserves it.

Ramin Fayed stuck what was left of a half-eaten glazed twist from Pronto Donuts in his mouth to free up his right hand, as his left arm precariously balanced a thin, black leather briefcase, a dark green umbrella, and a café mocha from Starbucks. The thirty-eight-year-old Persian attorney, originally from Tehran, was late for the third day in a row, thanks to an ovulating and impatient wife. He didn't mind so much since he was the boss of the Fayed Law Corporation, a one-lawyer, upscale ambulance-chasing outfit hidden away in a neat series of offices on the third floor of the historic Braley Building in Old Pasadena. Besides, Ramin knew that his twenty-one-year-old office manager and administrative assistant, Lorena Sandoval, who always arrived before he did, would have his caseload and court appearance calendar up and running, his phone messages neatly arranged in order of importance, and his personal appointments—Dr. Moritz, lunch with law school buddy, etc.—scheduled to his approval.

Thank God for Lorena, Ramin thought to himself as he fumbled with his keys.

At that moment, the door to the community lavatory opened down the hall. Ramin froze, inadvertently clamping down on the donut in his mouth. A tall Caucasian man with little gray eyes and a blonde, wind-swept coif that whitened at the temple, glided snakelike toward the swarthy Iranian. Ramin tried to compose himself, standing taller to meet his smirking floor mate just as the glazed twist broke off and plopped to the floor.

"Lost your donut there, eh, Fayed?" Chet Rasmussen said through a half-chortle. He smoothed the wide lapels of his dark Men's Wearhouse suit.

Ramin swallowed the remains of his donut and glanced down at the rest. He wiped some crumbs off his chin and forced a smile.

"Good morning, Chet." They never shook hands.

Chet had a rusty, leathery complexion cracked full of hard lines that made his forty-five-year-old face look fifty. Ramin found himself casually searching for signs of melanoma.

"Read the paper today?" he asked, holding up a folded

copy. Ramin flinched every time Chet dropped his pro-
nouns.

"Not yet," Ramin mumbled, looking toward the restroom. "I see you did, though."

"Yeah, do most of my reading on the crapper," Chet
said shamelessly, holding up a fist and belching. "See them
Eye-rain-ee-unz are up to their old tricks again."

Chet held his folded newspaper up in the air, shaking it
like a tambourine.

"Oh?" Ramin could hardly keep from rolling his eyes.

"Just can't wait to get their hands on a nuke and attack
the West."

"Well, they are one of the Axis of Evil, right?" Ramin
humored Chet.

Chet hated the fact that he couldn't tell whether Ramin
had an accent or not.

"That's right." Chet nodded, squinting at Ramin.
"You're one of them Muslims from Iran, aren't you? How
do you feel about all this?"

"I'm a Christian, Chet, remember? We go through this
at least once a week. I was a minority in Tehran. My family
had to flee the country in the middle of the night."

Ramin checked his watch as Chet nodded and licked his
lips.

"Fair enough, Fayed. Just don't forget about the war.
Figure out whose side you're on," Chet said, pointing a
bony finger at him. He turned to walk toward his office,

much to Ramin's relief.

"I'm on the side of democracy," Ramin called out.

Chet ignored him and disappeared behind his office door.

"USA number one!" Ramin grinned, holding up a thumb. He walked through the door of the Fayed Law Corporation, shaking his head. He nearly slammed the door shut behind him, leaned against it and sighed.

Lorena sat erect at her desk, prim and proper, with her dark red hair pulled back in a tight bun. Her full lips widened at the corners in her trademark toothy smile at the sight of her flustered boss. Lorena, suddenly realizing that she was chit-chatting socially on the company line, looked guiltily up at Ramin through dark-framed cat eye glasses, nonprescription, which she thought made her look more professional. Lorena held up her phone, which Ramin saw she held with both hands, her right palm covering the mouthpiece.

"Our buddy Chet?" Lorena asked, hoping to distract him.

"How did you know?" Ramin thought maybe she had heard them.

"Because you always have that look on your face after one of your run-ins with him," she said in her naïve, yet all-knowing way.

"He's starting to bug the shit out of me," Ramin said in slightly accented English. "Axis of Evil-this! Al Qaeda-that!

He thinks all Middle Eastern people are terrorists."

"You're not a terrorist, Ramin," Lorena said, smiling. "You're a *lawyer*."

Ramin chuckled.

"Yes. They're worse, aren't they?" he said, stealing her punch line.

"You said it, not me."

"Anything noteworthy?" Ramin asked.

"That doctor—whatever her name is." Lorena checked a Post-It. "Dr. Joanne Pesci called again. She thinks you're purposely avoiding her."

"I am," Ramin said, straight-faced. "I don't want to talk to her."

"I'm running out of creative roadblocks."

"Just tell her that I'm not interested. We already have a doctor that we use on our cases. We don't need a new one."

Lorena smiled and brought the phone back up to her ear, giving Ramin the not-so-subtle hint that she was busy. He motioned toward his office as Lorena winked at him, as if to say, "Bye." She watched her boss shuffle away out of ear-shot.

"So, anyway," Lorena continued, checking her finger-nails, "what happened next? He's in the shower…"

The girl on the other line was Guadalupe "Lupe" Mercado, the twenty-four-year-old receptionist down the hall at Rasmussen Streeter & Brinkley—Chet's law firm, specializing in personal injury and worker's compensation, somewhat of a competitor of Fayed Law Corporation, since Ramin handled similar cases. The difference between the two law firms was that Ramin also dabbled in immigration law.

"Right!" Lupe said in hushed tones. "He gets out. He's drying himself off, and he just gets this, I don't know—*feeling*—that Bridget's up to something."

Lorena frowned.

"*Qué?*"

"You *know*, girl! Sneaking around. *Snooping!*" Lupe explained.

"Oh, right." Lorena saw where this was headed.

"So he opens his bathroom door really quietly, hoping to catch her, and he pops into his bedroom. And would you believe she throws down his cell phone?"

Lorena let out an exaggerated gasp.

"NO!" she blurted.

"*Si, guey,*" Lupe continued. "Bitch was checkin' his cell phone to see who he was callin' an' who was callin' him. Bridget goes off because she sees that Rafa called Teresa twice in the last two days, and Teresa called him last night at *midnight*."

"Oooh, *girl*! That's past 'booty time'," Lorena smiled at their friend Rafael's rascality. Teresa was his ex-girlfriend, twice removed.

"*Pero*, GIRL!" Lupe's Spanglish dripped with drama. "Teresa's not even his *sancha!*"

"*Ándale, guey, no manches*!" Lorena could thank her second cousin Ruby for being able to match Lupe's crude style. Besides, Lorena got a kick out of talking this way with Lupe. "I thought—*who's* he seein'?"

"Karla."

"*Who*?" The name wasn't ringing a bell for Lorena.

"*Karlita, 'mana*! *La Flaquita* from Bodega, with the big *tatas*. The bar girl?"

"Are they fake?" Lorena had to know.

"I don't know, girl! They look fake."

"So what happened with Rafa and Bridget?" Lorena asked, only mildly interested now that she knew he wasn't seeing his ex-girlfriend.

"She dumped him!" Lupe chuckled.

Lorena shook her head.

"Mmm-mmm-mmm. How do you like that? Kicked to the curb over a chick Rafa wasn't even seeing."

"She always got the chicks wrong. Never knew who he was really boning," Lupe agreed.

"Everybody's cheating on everybody," Lorena said woefully.

While on her lunch break at Equator, Lorena thought about her friend Lupe's story and shook her head, relieved that there wasn't a man in her life. Love was too complicated. There were too many ways that a girl's heart could be broken, her hopes dashed. She only had to think of James to know that she had made the right decision to immerse herself in work, family, and her Christian faith. She would decide when, where, and with whom to open her heart again.

Lorena sat alone on one of the coffee house's plush sofas and overheard a woman's voice nearby. The conversation reminded her how silly love sounded, especially over the phone.

"I don't want to hear your excuses, *boludo*!" the woman said in Spanish. "All I know is that I haven't seen you in three days, and it's bullshit!"

Lorena cocked her head to the conversation behind her, recognizing the accent as Argentinean Spanish.

"*Arturo*! Stop it! Stop giving me your lies! I'm getting tired of your shit! I've invested too much time; I've given way too much as your girlfriend to take this from you. You're selfish and inconsiderate...What?"

Lorena smiled to herself after hearing some of the different words used by the South American. Some she recognized, others she had no clue as to their meaning. Lorena glanced up at the woman, and was struck by her stark beauty.

"So?...So what, Arturo! That doesn't mean anything to me."

Lorena turned away and finished her iced coffee, content to listen only. She could almost hear each of the twists and turns of the Argentinean's body, as she sighed and huffed to whatever this Arturo was telling her.

"Yes...Yes....Well, yes...Fine! Fine, okay, I guess you have a point, Arturo...I thought we weren't...Stop it! I was really upset, babe."

Lorena smirked at the softening of the Argentinean's tone.

"Fine...All right, all right...I guess...Yes...Of course I love you...Yes! I love you, *mono! Ciao.*"

Lorena raised her eyebrows.

That was interesting, Lorena thought. I'm sure whoever this Arturo is...

She considered Lupe and chuckled.

...He's probably cheating on her.

"*My* boyfriend's not cheating on me," Miriya said a week later, forcing a nervous laugh. She gripped her cell phone tighter. "Why would you even suggest that? That doesn't sound very supportive."

"Look, I'm sorry. I'm trying to be supportive. I just say, show me a guy who's not cheating and I'll give you a million bucks." Veronica tried to picture the expression on Miriya's face.

"Oh." Miriya was almost relieved. "So you're not talking about Arturo specifically, but just, kind of, men in general, right?"

"Yeah, whatever," Veronica mumbled. "Are you coming or not? We're all here waiting for you."

"Yeah, yeah. I'm almost there."

"Cool. Late."

Veronica hung up before Miriya said goodbye. Miriya shook her head with a puzzled grin. She hated when Veronica said "Late." Only some of Miriya's male friends used that type of phone sign-off.

Equator was nestled in the center of the cramped Mills Place, more of a glorified alley than a side street, which ran north and south through Old Pasadena, connecting the bustling Colorado Boulevard on the north, with Green Street on the south. Just across the alley from Equator was Burke Williams Spa, where Miriya and Suzy worked.

"Is she coming?" Suzy asked Veronica. Suzy had messy waves of jet-black hair that draped the sides of a long, angular face with delicate features, open brown eyes, and a small mouth whose closed lips moved with each thought.

"Yeah, she said she's almost here." Veronica sat between Suzy and Nathalie in one of Equator's heavy wood and metal chairs. Veronica felt out of place among these women, whom she felt only tolerated her because of her lifelong affiliation with Miriya. Miriya, Suzy and the others were what Veronica called the "beautiful people"—pretty "in crowd" types, who always wore make-up, shopped for the latest styles, and dressed as if they could go to a club at any given moment. Veronica, on the other hand, dyed her hair blue, had too many tattoos, and her nail polish was usually chipped.

Veronica watched Suzy and Nathalie closely, constantly evaluating and comparing their looks, wondering what differences, if any, there were between Persians and Armenians. Both had light tan-olive complexions, smooth and clear, although Nathalie tended to wear more make-up. Both women had large manes of hair, which Suzy almost always wore down, while Nathalie preferred intricate, stylish buns and ponytails. Veronica thought that Nathalie's light brown eyes were prettier, but her nose was bigger. Nathalie had the sensuous mouth, but Suzy had the soulful face. Where Nathalie was more fashion-conscious, being an interior designer, and was always dressed to the nines no matter what she was doing, Suzy was more down to Earth, equally comfortable in sweats and flip-flops as a club dress. Suzy worked out in the gym as much as Nathalie, the two of them often going together, but Nathalie's thin, svelte figure was easier to maintain than her friend's soft curves. Even though Suzy sometimes poked gentle fun at her own butt and thighs, the thickness of which fluctuated like the stock market, they all admired her large, natural breasts, which she could, at times, be self-conscious about.

Veronica caught Nathalie glancing down at her own neckline, and remembered how she had openly debated her plans to get a boob job. This had occurred shortly after Miriya had had her breasts done, going from a respectable B cup to a full D. Veronica had thought that Nathalie was unusually interested in the procedure at the time, asking Miriya all kinds of questions—Nathalie had even asked to see them! Miriya, however, never showed off her enhanced chest, always tasteful in her dress and neckline. Whenever Miriya showed up to one of their outings, Nathalie always checked her out to see what she wore and how her breasts looked in the outfit.

Taylor Jorgensen licked her lips while tugging at the ends of her blonde hair. She glanced toward Equator's entrance to make sure Miriya wasn't walking in at that moment.

"Hey, have you guys heard anything more about Miriya's dad?" she asked.

Suzy made a face.

"Just that he's in intensive care."

"How much longer does he have?"

Suzy shook her head while Veronica stared at her feet.

"I dunno." Suzy couldn't imagine losing one of her parents.

"Hey, here she is," Nathalie said, lifting her chin in the direction of the entrance. She smiled warmly and waved at Miriya as she bounded in, grinning from ear to ear with shopping bags in hand.

"Hey, guys. Sorry I'm late."

"Yeah, lunch is almost over. Where were you?" Suzy asked, checking her watch.

"I had to get gifts for Anna and Arturo's dad. Their birthdays are coming up, almost on the same day. Weird, huh?"

It was Miriya's day off. She wore tight jeans, wood-heeled open toe sandals, and a midriff-baring, white, gauzy top, with red and turquoise beads near the scoop neck line, complete with billowy, long sleeves. Veronica noticed that she wore a white stone-studded belly-button ring. She looked Nathalie's way to see if she noticed.

"Hey, did you hear the latest?" Taylor asked, her 5'11" frame hunched over, her chin practically resting on her knee.

Miriya frowned and shook her head.

"No, what?"

"Karen's flying in tomorrow," Veronica said, pushing her glasses up on her nose. "From Walter Reed."

Miriya swallowed.

"Oh. Oh, wow!" She was at a loss for words. "How is she? I mean, you know…"

Veronica shrugged her shoulders.

"Okay, I guess. Her spirits are up. You know how Karen is. She still thinks the Army has a place for her. She's hoping to get re-assigned somewhere."

Suzy frowned, dumbfounded.

"Do they do that? She's missing an arm, right?"

"I dunno, maybe. I'm sure there's plenty of stuff she can do," Veronica said, doubting her own optimism.

"Of course there is!" Miriya said. "C'mon, the military's so short-staffed anyway, they'd be relieved to have her. I'm sure Karen will do just fine."

Miriya was suddenly all smiles.

"I can't wait to see her."

I wonder if she and Veronica are still together, Miriya thought. It's been a long time.

Lorena glanced at her watch and took a last sip of her iced mocha. Equator was not her favorite coffeehouse, but it was close to her office. For that reason, she often popped in for a salad or a post-lunch coffee. Equator had an interesting clientele, attracting a motley assortment of alternative types, artists, beatniks, skater kids with dyed hair and piercings, who sat at the hard tables outside, squinting suspiciously at passersby while smoking on hookahs provided by the swarthy establishment. The few corporate folks who came in to work on laptops and talk on cell phones, mostly all Caucasian, intrigued Lorena, as did the well-dressed "glamour girls," no doubt trendy boutique employees, food service managers, or spa workers.

Lately, Lorena had come to notice a group of young women who seemed to meet there around lunchtime at least thrice weekly. An avid people-watcher, Lorena was struck by the ethnic diversity of the group, two of whom appeared to be Middle Easterners. There were two *gueritas*, one of whom Lorena thought might be gay or bi-sexual, based upon her tattoos, piercings, and "manly" clothes.

One girl stuck out—the prettiest of the clique, in Lorena's opinion—and she recognized her as the Argentinean from a week prior. Now here she was again, among her friends, dressed in a manner that, although not Lorena's personal style, she appreciated as being chic. Lorena watched Miriya as long as she could without being noticed. Lorena was struck by Miriya's persistent smile, which bubbled to the surface of her glowing face as if ready to break out into polite or genuine laughter at any given moment. This gave the Argentinean's sparkly brown eyes a squinty quality, revealing dainty crow's feet at their corners.

Lorena stood and threw her empty cup away. It was time to go back to work. She walked out of Equator without looking at Miriya or her friends. Lorena's elegant stride, back erect and head held high, caught Miriya's attention and she glanced up at the legal secretary for a split second. The girl looked familiar to Miriya, but then she turned her attention back to a story that Suzy was telling.

Lorena pulled into her driveway that evening craving a hot bath. It was a nightly routine for her to wash away her work day upon returning home. She knew that either her mother, Isabel, or *abuelita*, Julia, would be preparing dinner, while her father worked on cars and a six-pack of Bud Light in their backyard.

"*Que onde, mi 'ija?*" Gerardo said to her, wiping his greasy hands on a rag. His aging, rugged features were illuminated by a small, caged light bulb hanging from the open hood of a 1966 Ford Mustang, his latest passion. He loved old Mustangs and had refurbished two of them in the last year.

"Hey, dad," Lorena replied in English. She asked him in Spanish if Francisco was home. He replied that he was at his girlfriend Lizette's house.

As Lorena walked through her back door, which faced their rear driveway, she was hit with the luxurious smell of *chile rellenos* and *arroz con frijoles*. Lorena sauntered into the kitchen and dropped her keys on the green tile counter-top. Isabel and her mother, Julia, sat at the kitchen table while a small TV aired the latest episode of a favorite *telenovela, Sofia de Amor*.

Isabel, at the head of the table, greeted her daughter with a warm smile, arms outstretched to embrace Lorena, who bent down to dutifully kiss her mother on the cheek. Lorena walked over to her *abuelita* and kissed her the same. Julia's silvery hair was kept braided up in a bun, like a woven crown, her wrinkled face a roadmap to her past. She hardly said anything these days, unless she was getting into it with Isabel, or uttering some surprising wisecrack or ribald comment that would send Lorena and Francisco into fits of laughter.

Isabel appreciated having her mother in her household, as was culturally accepted. Julia, however, was still her mother, and admonished Isabel with apropos *dichos,* when-ever she thought her daughter was doing something wrong. Lorena was struck by the realization that daughters and mothers would never cease to butt heads, no matter how old they got.

Isabel, in recent years, had begun wearing her dyed black hair in a short, manageable style befitting a middle-aged woman. She had long since stopped nagging Gerardo about his drinking and had just accepted it with dignified resignation. She longed for the days when he paid her attention, spending most of her nights going to bed alone, while her husband's head remained inside the hood of a car until all hours of the morning. Sometimes Gerardo would go to Tecate by himself, for several days on end. He told Isabel that he was visiting his brothers, who lived nearby, but she could only imagine what else he was up to.

While Lorena often thought about her parents' marriage (she wasn't blind), she never broached the subject with either of them.

"Is that *Sofia de Amor*?" Lorena asked while opening the refrigerator. She found what she was looking for and poured a glass of orange juice.

"Yes, come watch if you'd like," Julia replied.

Lorena stood between the two women and cast a cynical eye toward the program. Mexican *telenovelas* differed from American soap operas in that while "As The World Turns" will have run for 30 odd years, each *novela* aired for only a specified number of weeks, the story playing itself out to a definite conclusion, when a new story—a new *telenovela*—would take its place.

Lorena frowned, only vaguely familiar with the plotline of *Sofia de Amor*—Sofia being the name of the main character in this particular *novela*...

Carmen heard the unmistakable click-clack-clicking of Sofia's high heels on the white marble floor of the foyer. She was home early and sent Carmen into a panic.

"My love, I must go. She's here," Carmen said, quickly hanging up the phone in the kitchen.

"Hello? Carmen?" Sofia called out, frowning to herself.

Sofia put the mail down and stood in front of a large mirror. She quickly checked out her trim and toned thirty-five-year-old figure, which was the envy of many of the women at the office.

"Not bad," Sofia said out loud, "for a veteran. We'll see how long the looks hold up."

Sofia sighed and blew a strand of hair out of her face.

"Yes, Mrs. De Amor? How are you today? Home early, I see."

Carmen wore a simple, muted housekeeper's dress that hugged her figure in a flattering manner. Sofia always noticed and paused to take a breath before speaking to the girl.

"Yes, I'm fine, Carmen, thank you. I had to get a head start with some paperwork here at home. Arturo and I are going to dinner tonight. He has some making up to do after

being gone a week. I'm sure you enjoyed your stay in Gua-najuato."

Carmen frowned. Arturo hadn't mentioned this.

"It was agreeable. I had little time for pleasure; just work, work, work. Where will you two be dining?"

"At the Revolution Café most likely. Arturo loves that restaurant."

"Yes, I know," Carmen said, looking at the floor.

Sofia smiled and cocked her head sideways. She reached up and let her long mane of blond-streaked hair roll down across her shoulder. Her brown plastic hair clip made a hard sound as it landed carelessly on the nearby marble table.

"And you?" Sofia asked. "What will you do with your-self this evening?"

Carmen glanced sideways at Sofia.

"I will be going out with a girlfriend later. Perhaps you know the place?" Carmen said with a demure smile. "Ar-gento's."

Sofia frowned.

"Argento's? How do you know of that place?"

"I go out, Mrs. De Amor."

"What's Argento's?" Lorena asked, as dramatic music blared from the TV.

"That's her husband's, Arturo's, favorite restaurant," Isabel said, without taking her eyes off the screen.

"Drama!" Lorena shook her head in mock horror.

"You're watching it, aren't you?" Julia smirked at her granddaughter.

Lorena turned and entered the peaceful sanctuary of her bedroom. She closed the door behind her and sat on her white, four-poster bed, which she had had since she was in the eighth grade. A white diaphanous canopy hung from the posts, giving her bed a fairy tale quality that she adored. She had strung a rope of little blue lights all around the top of her bedposts to add to the atmosphere she was after. On the circular nightstands that flanked each side of the headboard, she had fragrant candles as well as a used incense holder next to the photo of her standing in the palm of her father's hand.

The books that adorned her childhood bookcase were eclectic if not thematic. There was a heavy, two-volume definitive astrology guide, which she referred to as the "red" and "blue" books. She had a well-worn copy of a book of supernatural occurrences, including "true" ghost stories and the occult, a book of vampires, a history of the *Virgen de Guadalupe*, and a guide to the "Haunted Places of Pasadena."

Not one to get overly gushy regarding movie stars, Lorena did have one single magazine-cut-out photo of Johnny Depp thumb-tacked to a cluttered bulletin board. There was a crucifix on her wall, a small figurine of the Virgin Mary on a nightstand, as well as the blue and gold tassel from her high school graduation mortarboard hanging from the corner of a cracked mirror. "Couples photos" of her and her high school grad night and prom night dance dates were stuck all along the frame of this mirror, as well as those of her girlfriends and their dates.

Lorena's bedroom hadn't changed much since high school, except that now she woke up early every morning during the week to shower, get dressed in business attire, and go to work. On the weekends Lorena tried to catch up with her sleep. Unless, of course, Cecilia and her husband were over, and Lorena's niece and nephew sneaked into her room to wake up their *Nina*.

Lorena slipped off her work shoes and stretched her toes as her cell phone rang.

"Hello?"

"*Qué onde, pinche changa?*" It was Lupe from work.

"What's up, *cabrona?*"

Lorena talked while slipping out of her pants. She plopped down onto her bed, clad only in her blouse and panties, and stretched out her bare legs. Lorena had an unusual habit of sticking one of her legs out at a ninety-degree angle and curling her toes until her foot cramped.

"Ow, ow—my foot!" Lorena kicked her leg out while wiggling her toes.

"Are you doing that weird thing again with your foot?"

"Shut-up! Yes."

"I don't know why you like that."

"I'm obsessed by it."

"*Girl*, if Chet doesn't quit with his bullshit, I swear."

"What now?" Lorena stuck her fingers between her toes.

"All that *pinche pendejo* does is talk shit about Mexicans an' how they all hate Americans, and are all being recruited by *Al Qaeda*, 'cept he calls them *Al Quesadilla*."

"Wuuuuut?" Lorena said in a dull hum. "You need to compare notes with Ramin." Lorena chuckled. "*Al Quesadilla*," she said aloud to herself.

"Hey!" Lupe switched gears. "Have you been to Blick's lately?"

"*Bleek's*?" Lorena imitated Lupe's accent. "What's that?"

"Blick's Art Supplies? It used to be the Art Store."

"Oh, yeah, the, uh, the one across the street from my work?"

"*Sí, estúpida!*"

"*Cállate, cabrona!* No, why?"

"*Girl*, I went in there the other day to look for a journal book and I caught a glimpse of the manager—*oooh*, girl!"

"What?"

"Talk about a *papi chulo!*"

"He was cute?" Lorena considered doing her toes.

"Boy was *foine!*"

"*Ándele, guey*. Why you tellin' me?"

"Because, *cabrona*, you need to go in and see him. He's tall, dark, and handsome—just your type."

"*Latino?*"

"*Sí, guey*…I think. Could be white."

Lorena considered this for a moment. She hadn't met anybody that remotely interested her in months. She had only been on two dates since she was with James, but nothing had come from them.

"I'll check it out," Lorena said in a noncommittal way.

"Girl, how long has it been since you *poon-poon*'d?"

Lorena thought for a moment.

"Not since James," she admitted. "I've only been with one man."

"How long?"

"It's probably been a year."

"You need to get back in the game."

"We'll see," Lorena mumbled. "I've been doing a lot of thinking lately. Reading the Bible an' stuff. I'm considering saving myself for marriage."

"*Cállate, guey!*" Lupe shot back. "You getting' all born again?"

"*Sí, pendeja.* You could use a little religion yourself."

"*Ai, Santa Lorena!*"

"Good morning, Fayed Law Corporation," Lorena said, cradling the phone receiver on her shoulder. She was typing up a motion for Ramin.

"Hi, Ms. Sandoval?"

Uh-oh.

"Yes."

"This is Dr. Pesci again, Ms. Sandoval. I don't mean to be a bother, but I can't shake the feeling that Mr. Fayed's giving me the run-around."

Lorena rolled her eyes and grabbed the receiver.

"Dr. Pesci, uh, I'm sorry but Mr. Fayed already uses the services of another medical group for his clients' evaluations. I don't think he's interested in…"

"Well, you tell Mr. Fayed that I think it's rude of him to not have spoken to me in person."

"Dr. Pesci, I'm sorry but he's been really busy."

"Sure. Whatever!"

She hung up on Lorena.

"Bitch," Lorena muttered under her breath. "Forgive me, Jesus."

She shook her head.

Ramin emerged from his office looking frazzled.

"Lorena, I totally forgot about this default that I need prepared before I go into court at 1:30," he said. "I'm up to my neck in paperwork. I'll need copies of these, too."

He handed her a stack of legal documents.

"So, put this motion I'm typing up on hold?" she looked up at him.

He frowned.

"Which one is that again?" He glanced at her screen while rubbing his five-o-clock shadow. "Shit. No, I need that, too. Can you get all of it done by one?"

"Not a problem."

"You're the best!"

Ramin turned and slipped back into his office.

Lorena was relieved that she finished everything in time for lunch. Ramin would spend most of the afternoon in court, which meant that Lorena could take a longer break than normal. She walked out of the Braley Building, into the crisp October air and glanced across the street toward Blick's.

She checked her watch and thought, Oh, what the heck.

A short while later, Lorena found herself casually checking out the tubes of Windsor & Newton oil paints, wondering why they were more expensive than the Blick's brands at the head of the adjacent aisle. There was a bespectacled, spiky-haired young man with a piercing under his lower lip and tattoos on both arms, helping a lanky Asian girl with red-dyed hair and sunglasses fill an order for an upcoming art class of some sort. Lorena sneaked a peek at the employee's nametag: JORGE. She decided that he was *not* the manager that Lupe had spoken of, since Jorge was rather short and pudgy.

Lorena had straightened her hair this morning, opting to leave it down, and did not wear her glasses. She had on a red beret that she wore at a jaunty tilt, which she hoped matched her lipstick. Her white, woolen-gloved hands were tucked into the pockets of a knee-length, black wool women's top coat, under which she wore a long-sleeved gray cardigan, a black skirt and high, black leather boots with heels that added three inches to her 5' 6" height. These heels made a slow, pronounced "click-clack" sound on the white tile floor as she turned the corner of the aisle, trying hard to focus on the art supplies as if she were shopping.

"Hi, do you need any help with anything?" came a husky male voice from behind her. She turned and stood facing a tall, not so dark, Caucasian or mixed Hispanic-looking man with black hair slicked back so that it brushed against the open collar of his long-sleeved, white shirt. He wore neatly trimmed sideburns down to just below his ear-lobes, but was otherwise clean-shaven. Lorena decided that he had open, honest brown eyes, an engaging smile, and that he was probably wearing Allure cologne, or at least it smelled like it. His manager's nametag read: STEVEN.

"Anything at all?" Steven asked again, raising an eye-brow.

"I'm sorry." Lorena chuckled, free from embarrassment. "I don't really know what I'm looking for."

Steven frowned.

"So…you're not an artist?" Steven was obviously amused.

"Can't say I am." Lorena quickly looked around the store, hoping to notice something—*anything*—to which she could claim an interest in purchasing. "I'm just on my lunch break and found myself drawn to this store. I've never been inside, you see."

"Ever had an urge to take up art?" He stood comfortably, one arm across his chest, the elbow of the other resting against the folded arm while he rubbed his chin thoughtfully.

Lorena started to nod.

"Actually, not really," she blurted. "I don't think I have any talents in that direction, although I used to draw horses and unicorns and stuff when I was a kid."

She thought that sounded lame.

"That's something," he said. "What do you do now?—I'm Steven, by the way."

He stuck out a firm hand, which she shook, and was taken in by her woolen glove and how he could still feel her slender, delicate fingers underneath.

"Hi, Steven. Lorena. I'm an office manager-slash-legal secretary at a law firm not far from here."

"How not far?"

Lorena chuckled.

"Close. Real close."

"Walking distance?"

She knew he was flirting now.

"Something like that," she said, coyly. "Are you wearing Allure?"

He was only mildly taken aback and looked around, blushing.

"Yup. Yeah. You, uh, caught me wearing cologne to work."

He cleared his throat as Lorena nodded slowly.

"Well, it was nice meeting you, Steven."

"Oh, okay. Nice meeting you, too, Lau—"

"Lorena."

"Lorena. Got it!"

"Don't forget, mister," she said, holding up a finger.

"Oh, I won't."

Lorena turned and slowly walked out of the store without glancing back at Steven. Jorge watched the girl leave and approached his manager from behind.

"What's up with that?" Jorge asked.

Steven shook his head.

"Unbelievable," he replied. "That is the hottest girl I've seen walk in here in at least a month! And she's not even an artist."

"What'd she want?"

"Hopefully *me*."

Jorge raised an eyebrow.

"What about Sugar Mama?"

"What about her? She has a man," Steven said, getting tense.

"Okay," Jorge mumbled. "I just thought you were all sprung over her."

"Like I said. She has a man. I'm just *el otro*."

While walking to Equator, Lorena decided to give Lupe a call.

"Hello?" Lupe sounded busy.

"I saw him!"

"*Qué?*"

"*Papi chulo, 'mana!*"

"*No chingas, guey!*" Lupe yelled. "What happened?"

"Mmm-mmm-mmm," Lorena hummed. "That boy is one handsome dude."

"Did you say anything to him?"

"We had a whole conversation."

"Did you give him the digits?"

"Huh?" Lorena frowned. "Aw, *hell* no! You know I'm not like that."

"*Cállate, cabrona! Porqué?* This was your chance!"

"No, no, no. That comes much later, if at all."

"Still holding out for Mr. Right and marriage? I don't get you, girl. I woulda been all over homeboy!"

"Hey, you have a man!"

"I know. I can *look!*—Shit, I gotta go. Here comes Chet!"

Lorena snapped her cell phone shut and slipped it into her purse. She stepped into Equator and noticed the Argentinean girl sitting by herself, finishing a salad. Lorena flashed Miriya a tight-lipped smile of acknowledgement, which was politely returned. Miriya recognized the young, redheaded girl as being a regular there.

Lorena was not prepared for what she saw next.

Veronica, whom Lorena recognized, walked in first

and scanned the interior for her friends. Veronica was slightly disappointed that it was only Miriya, but was relieved that at least her best friend was there. Miriya smiled at Veronica and braced herself for the reunion with Karen.

Specialist Karen L. Velez, United States Army Reserve, trailed Veronica, wearing the standard Army Class "A" enlisted women's uniform, consisting of the short-waist, olive green blouse, matching skirt, tan nylons, and plain, black high-heeled shoes. Karen's dark hair was pulled back in a regulation bun (she left her issue hat in the car). On her chest were two rows of awards, the most notable being the Bronze Star, Purple Heart, Iraq Campaign and Global War on Terrorism Service ribbons. On her upper right sleeve, which Miriya noticed was empty from the mid-bicep down and folded up, was the "theater patch" of the 3rd Infantry Division. Miriya thought that Karen would be wearing a prosthesis but was glad that she wouldn't have to stare at a hook.

"Hey, Miriya," Karen said, smiling.

Miriya stood, beaming, and gave her old high school classmate a warm hug.

"Hi, Karen. I'm so glad to see you!" Miriya stepped back, still holding onto Karen's left arm. "Look at you!"

Lorena, seated not ten feet away, was fixated on the soldier. Lorena noticed the girl's missing arm and, realizing that she was probably an Iraq veteran, made the sign of the cross.

The three women sat down around a low wood table.

"We were so worried about you when we heard," Miriya said, taking on an appropriately somber tone. Karen, eyes averted, nodded her head slowly. "What happened, if you don't mind talking about it? I mean, are you hurt anywhere else? Is everything okay?"

Veronica shifted uncomfortably in her chair as Karen cleared her voice.

"Well, as you all probably heard, it was a roadside bomb—near Baghdad. Lost my arm, and, uh…suffered some shrapnel wounds in my back and right side. I had a couple of operations, but I'm lucky." Karen took a slow deep breath. "Three of my fellow soldiers were killed."

"My God," Miriya mumbled, shaking her head.

"I got a prosthetic arm they taught me to use. I don't like to wear it in uniform."

"Do we know anybody else in the war?" Miriya asked. Karen had been the only one she knew of.

"You remember Dan MacMillan?" Karen asked, turning to Veronica.

"He played football in high school, right?"

"Oh, yeah," Miriya said.

"Yeah, he's a Marine in Iraq. I actually bumped into him while I was there. Cornell Wheatley, tall, black guy in our fourth period English class? He's in the Army. I wanna say he's in Afghanistan, though. Those are the only ones I know of."

"We're real proud of you, Karen," Miriya said. "Serving our country an' all. Look at you—all those ribbons! You're a war hero!"

"Hardly." Karen smirked. "I was just doin' my duty."

"Are we making progress in Iraq?" Veronica said. "We hear so much negative stuff in the news."

"They don't know shit," Karen mumbled. "It's complicated, but...we're making progress. It's gonna take a while, that's all. Rome wasn't built in a day."

As they talked, Karen searched Veronica's face for clues, watched her every time that Miriya spoke. Veronica seemed to notice and sat rigidly, reaching out and squeezing Karen's hand at intervals. It was hard being away from Veronica for so long, but Karen had needed to get away. As a reservist since college, the war in Iraq had given her the perfect opportunity.

Karen couldn't blame either of her old friends for what happened. Miriya was innocent and probably never had a clue that Veronica had romantic feelings toward her. This had prevented Veronica from moving forward with Karen, into a deeper, more meaningful relationship. Veronica couldn't help how she felt and Karen didn't want to force it.

Karen had told everyone that she was volunteering for Iraq duty because she believed in what her country was doing there and in the rest of the world. It had been better than saying: "I gotta get outta here. The one I love loves someone else." Things might be more difficult now that she was missing an arm, but she had no hard feelings or regrets about anything. As Karen told her friends at Equator:

"I was there for the elections. To see the looks on the Iraqis' faces after they voted made it all worth it."

As she arrived home later that evening, Lorena had a hard time clearing her head of the jumble of thoughts, feelings, and emotions relating to the day's events. Seeing the soldier friend of the Argentinean girl had made her think of Ricky. Lorena couldn't help but wonder if she should have cared for him the same way he had cared for her. She tried to remember the last conversation they had ever had, but sadly, could not. She cried a bit on the drive home, but knew she would feel better after reading from her Bible. Lorena was also curious as to why the Argentinean girl lingered in the back of her mind. Lorena didn't know her from Eve. She was a stranger, but there was something about the girl that Lorena found endearing, from what she had seen of her. Lorena could not put her finger on it, but knew enough to trust her instincts about people.

"Dad?" Lorena called out while closing the driveway gate behind her. There was evidence of Gerardo's automotive tinkering, but he was nowhere to be found. Nobody was home. She found a note written in Spanish, in her mother's handwriting, on top of their kitchen counter, indicating that the family had run some errands and gone out to dinner without her.

"Wuuuuuuut?" Lorena hummed out loud. "Fine! Eat without me. It's not my fault I had to stay late at work."

She poured herself a bowl of cereal and sat at the dinner table after kicking off her shoes. Lorena absently turned on the TV, not expecting to find much of anything, and actually thought that she would go to bed early and masturbate. It wasn't something that she did often but it helped her relieve tension and sleep.

"You call this news? Lies! All *lies!*" She laughed at herself as she changed channels. "What the..."

Sofia de Amor was on.

Sofia knocked on the bathroom door before opening it cautiously.

"Arturo?" He was in the shower.

"Yes? Sofia... my love, is that you? You're home late?"

Lorena got only a vague idea of how Arturo looked with water running over his damp hair. She wondered whether he was "all that."

Sofia frowned.

"Why are you showering?" she asked, quickly scanning the bathroom.

Arturo thought for a moment.

"I wanted to smell clean and beautiful for you."

"Where's Carmen?"

"Uh, she had to go home early. She wasn't feeling well."

"What do you want to do for dinner?" Sofia looked un-convinced.

"Whatever you want—we could go out."

"We'll discuss it when you get out."

Sofia closed the door behind her and made a beeline to their bedroom. She stopped in the doorway, striking a defiant pose and quickly took in the scene before her. Bed made, floor vacuumed, no clothes lying around. She got down on her hands and knees and looked under the bed. Sofia stood and leaned over the bed, stretching her arms out to her sides for support as she lowered her face to within inches of the comforter. She took several short sniffs, half-hoping to catch a whiff of her.

"Oh, no she didn't!" Lorena blurted out loud.

Sofia looked for Arturo's cell phone. She found it on top of a desk in their bedroom, plugged into its charger. There was an open laptop computer on the desk.

Sofia checked the call history on the phone. A close-up revealed several calls placed to and from Carmen. Sofia nodded her head with the unmistakable look of sick realization.

"What are you doing calling our housekeeper at one in the morning?" Sofia said out loud.

"'Cause he's *cheating* on you, idiot!" Lorena yelled at the TV. She remembered Lupe's story about their friend getting caught because his girlfriend checked his cell phone.

I gotta remember that, she thought as she stood and retrieved a Corona from the refrigerator. Later:

"I think my husband's having an affair with my housekeeper," Sofia told the burly, mustachioed man with a black leather coat and bolo tie.

"What would you like me to do, Mrs. De Amor?"

"You're supposed to be the best private detective around. I want you to follow Arturo and Carmen. I need hard evidence of his infidelity. He stands to lose a lot in a nasty divorce."

"I think I can find out the truth...if you can handle it."

"Mr. Solorzano, I can handle anything. I am Sofia de Amor."

"Oooh, this shit's getting *good*!" Lorena said.

PART FOUR:
ENTER THE BOYFRIEND

Miriya considered the paperwork on her desk the way one stared at a small puddle of water on a countertop—harmless, but probably needing attending to later. It was going to be one of those days, thanks to him.

Suzy sat nearby on the phone, but Miriya could hardly hear her voice. Gone were the duties and responsibilities of running Burke Williams Spa. Miriya's mind ran free elsewhere.

That was how he made her feel.

He was her special friend who in an alternative universe she would have lived happily ever after with. When Arturo was emotionally unavailable, *he* was there for her. When Arturo was selfish in bed, *he* was a generous and thrilling partner, sweet in his tenderness and passionate eroticism. Whenever she found the time to meet him for a forbidden afternoon tryst, she could not get the experience out of her mind, and played the scene like a racy film, over and over in her head, as she did now. She had been in his arms only the day before, but could still smell him.

Miriya liked to remember how they met. It was such a chance encounter, she felt they were destined to cross paths. She remembered a breezy night just over a year ago, as she left Moose McGillicuddy's bar in Old Pasadena after meeting her friends for happy hour. Her car was parked in a parking structure a couple of blocks away.

She walked by herself and stood, shivering, at the corner of Colorado Boulevard and Raymond Avenue, where an unusual diagonal crosswalk was meant to coordinate the smooth flow of car and pedestrian traffic. As she stepped off the curb, a deep, soft voice called out to her:

"Whoa, watch out. You can't cross yet."

Miriya stopped and turned around.

"I'm sorry?"

She faced a pleasant-looking young man in a coat and tie, who looked as though he had maybe one drink somewhere, but no more. His brown eyes were clear and friendly, and his dark hair was just starting to grow over his ears.

"Yeah, uh, you have to wait for the little white guy..."

The man held out two downward-turned fingers to indicate a person walking, an image that flashed white on the crosswalk control boxes, along with a red hand for "DON'T WALK."

Miriya, although buzzed, found herself pleasantly amused.

"Thanks, I guess."

"I just saved your life," he said, straight-faced.

She found herself slowing her normal fast-paced stride so that she could cross the intersection with the curious stranger. Unlike most men, he did not try to engage her in typical pick-up small talk. He had said his piece and seemed content in quiet contemplation.

"Am I getting an escort, too?" Miriya just had to ask.

"If you'd like," he said, looking at her. "At least you know you can trust me."

"I don't even know you," she chuckled.

He stuck out his hand.

"Hi, I'm..."

Even as she shook his hand and he told her his name, it passed through her consciousness like a fleeting thought, and she immediately cringed that she couldn't remember the name he gave her.

"I'm Miriya," she smiled warmly. "And my car's parked just down here."

"Miriya? That's the prettiest name I've heard in a month-and-a-half."

Miriya laughed.

"Thanks. What was the last pretty name you heard, a month-and-a-half ago?"

"Annelise. She was a cute blonde girl from Norway who popped into my work."

"Oh? Where do you work?"

"Around here."

"You're not going to tell me?" Miriya was surprised.

"And have you coming around—stalking me? I don't even know you."

Miriya shook her head.

"You're cute," she said. "Does your girlfriend know you're talking to me?"

"You're here, aren't you?"

Miriya laughed and turned to him.

"I don't think I'm your girlfriend, yet."

"Yet, huh?"

He considered her.

"Nah, I can tell," he said, continuing their walk.

"You can tell what?"

"I can tell you already have a boyfriend."

"What if I do?"

"Then I'll be sad."

"Why?"

"Because it will confirm what I've always known."

"What's that?"

"That all the good ones are taken."

Miriya got quiet.

"I *am* a good one," she started, thinking of Arturo. She took a deep breath. "But I'm not taken."

She didn't know why she lied to him. He made her feel something she hadn't felt in a long time, causing a stomach churning that made her body almost shake.

"You're just teasing me," he said, waving her off.

"No, I'm not."

He stopped in his tracks and looked around. He thrust his hands into his pockets while taking a deep breath.

"I'll tell you what," he began. "Give me a ride to my car, and I'll consider it."

They met the next day for coffee, and the day after that they were in bed. Miriya remembered the day that she confessed that she had a boyfriend of just over three years. She was at his apartment after agreeing to model for him. She was thrilled at the thought of posing nude in front of him, twisting and turning her golden-brown body for him to admire. He had set up some canvases and oil paints and looked every part the struggling artist, frowning with each brush stroke, asking Miriya to remain still, to hold her pose.

Miriya tossed her hair back over her shoulder and shifted to a more comfortable position.

"Did you move?" He looked up at her.

"No," she said with a mischievous smile. "My arms were getting tired."

"I'll make you tired," he said.

"Oooh, stop it!"

"I'll run you ragged."

"Dirty boy! I bet you get all your girlfriends to model for you. Where'd you get these art supplies anyway?"

"Where do you think?"

"Oh, yeah...*duh!*...What part are you painting now?"

"Your titties."

"Can you paint them bigger?" Miriya laughed.

"They're already big enough."

"Nah, I've thought about getting an upgrade—making them bigger. My boyfriend said he'd pay—"

Miriya's blood froze and she brought her hand to her mouth. He frowned and looked up at Miriya. At first he said nothing, and tried to focus on what he was doing. Then he put his brush down and approached her.

Miriya brought her legs up and wrapped her arms around them, resting her head on her knees. She bit her lip as he sat next to her.

"You got a boyfriend?" he asked.

Miriya took a deep breath.

"Yes. I'm sorry...I'm so sorry I didn't say anything about this sooner."

He stared at the floor and then turned to her.

"How long?"

"Just over three years."

"What's his name?"

"Arturo."

"*Arturo?*"

"He's Argentinean, too."

"Do you love him?"

Miriya considered this and then nodded reluctantly.

"Yes, I do, but I've fallen for you, too."

"Why?"

"You're just...different. I can't explain it. Arturo and I don't have the best relationship."

"This probably isn't going to help," he said.

Miriya just shrugged and looked at him pleadingly. He hated when she gave him her loveable looks. She was irresistible to him. He knew he was falling hard for her, too.

"How do you feel?" Miriya asked.

He shrugged.

"I dunno, a little sad. Like the fantasy has...evaporated."

Miriya got closer to him, unwrapping her naked arms and legs and slipping them around him like a serpentine siren.

"It doesn't have to," she whispered into his ear. She kissed him gently and he closed his eyes as a tingling sensation spread across his back and shoulders. "I adore you, I do. I don't want to lose you."

He turned and kissed her full on the mouth.

"Hey, Miriya!" Suzy called out.

"Huh?"

"The phone's for you."

Miriya quickly composed herself, taking the phone and returning to her dulled present reality.

Lorena half-heartedly ate dinner the next evening while

watching the latest episode of *Sofia de Amor*. Isabel tinkered around the kitchen in solemn silence, moving around her children and mother, Julia, as if they were fleshy obstacles in some domestic boot camp. Francisco, sporting a new fade haircut and trim goatee, seemed oblivious to the awkward silence. He only glanced at the TV every so often, shoveling in the food, as he had a date that he needed to get ready for.

"Where are you and Lizette going?" Lorena asked. They almost always spoke English to each other. Julia glanced at them, cocking an ear toward their conversation. Although their *abuelita* didn't speak English, ever, she understood a lot more than she let on to.

"We're going to *Lucha Va Voom*, at the Mayan," he replied in his deep, soft voice.

"*Punk*! I wanted to go to that!"

"You still can," he said, shrugging his shoulders.

He wiped his mouth and stood, giving Isabel his dirty plate.

"Aw, hell no, I ain't gonna be no third wheel," Lorena said. "Who else is going?"

"Mike. His girlfriend...Chuy, and a couple of his buddies. I think this other girl might be coming, too, but you don't know her."

"Is Louis going?" Lorena turned to Francisco.

"I think so."

Lorena made a face, wrinkling her nose.

"Nah. Louis is always trying to get with me. He bugs."

"Suit yourself."

Dramatic music revealed Carmen, sitting alone at a dark, candlelit table in a discreet bar. She checked her watch and her cleavage. Her big, brown eyes eagerly sought out her lover among the patrons that entered.

Arturo de Amor would not leave his lover waiting. He blew into the bar, his long dark hair trailing his tall, muscled form like a hero's cape. His cheekbones sat high atop a square-jawed, chiseled face. His mouth was strong and sensuous.

Lorena raised an eyebrow at the handsome lothario.

"What the...," she mumbled absently.

Julia glanced sideways at her granddaughter.

"All right, I'll see you guys," Francisco said, stepping into the kitchen. He leaned down and kissed Lorena on the cheek. She turned to him.

"*Damn*, you look good! If you weren't my brother, *I'd* go out with you!"

"Yeah, whatever," Francisco mumbled. He leaned over and kissed Julia, telling her good-bye in Spanish. She made the sign of the cross in his direction, as she always did when family left the house.

"*Santa Julia* just blessed you," Lorena said, grinning.

"I saw that," Francisco replied.

Lorena turned back to the TV.

"Arturo, mi amor," Carmen stood, *lustily embracing Sofia's husband.*

"Carmen! Carmen, baby, I missed you so much!"

"I was afraid you wouldn't come," Carmen said.

"I could never be away from you, mi amor! Mi vida!"

"What will become of us, my Arturo?"

Arturo held her tightly and lightly blew aside a strand of dark hair that covered her hungry, longing eyes. His breath smelled of alcohol and cigarettes.

"Soon, we will be together forever. I've come up with a plan to get rid of Sofia. She will never prevent us from being together. I want a new life! A life with you, my love."

"Ai, mi amor, can it be true?" Carmen kissed him passionately.

"Maldito!" Lorena spat, shaking her head.

Julia chuckled at this.

"What's he gonna do?" Lorena turned to her *abuelita*, wide-eyed.

"Watch!"

"Is he gonna kill Sofia?"

Private Investigator Abel Solorzano sat at the bar, watching the lovers through the reflection in the large mirror behind the bartender, while sipping a cerveza. The bartender, a tall, blonde chilanga with wide brown eyes and a big mane of curly hair to match her big chest, wiped the counter in front of Abel.

"Hello, Miss. I was wondering if you could help me," Abel said.

"Yes?"

"There's a gentleman back there that looks like an old school chum of mine, but I can't be sure. I don't want to disturb his evening with his lady friend. Do you know his name by any chance?"

"Arturo de Amor, I think," she replied.

Abel frowned.

"Hmmm. That's not the last name I remember my friend having. Oh, well, perhaps it's not him."

Abel quickly glanced in Arturo and Carmen's direction.

"Still, it sure looks like him. Does he come here often?"

"Those two are here the same time every week, same table."

"Thank you."

The next day, Miriya's friend, Nathalie Faresi, sat at a small table in a busy corner of Il Fornaio restaurant after having a late lunch with Arturo Suarez. He had excused himself to go to the restroom to call Miriya. While waiting, Nathalie checked her teeth and reapplied her lipstick. She sat up straight, fixed her blouse and glanced quickly at her chest.

Nathalie was struck by the number of couples who appeared to be dining at the moment; old and retired, some young and busy. There were business types meeting for a brief, romantic lunch with their wives or girlfriends. Nathalie wondered how many were mistresses. She thought about her future husband. Would he be Persian? Would he cheat on her someday, after she had borne him children and gotten older?

"Hey, gotta go," Arturo said, coming up behind her and half-startling her. He took his seat and signed his credit card receipt.

"Oh, did you get hold of her?"

"Nah, I left a message for her to meet me at, uh, your guys' favorite place."

"Starbucks or Equator? Mine's *Starbucks*."

"Oh, Equator."

Arturo sat restlessly across from Nathalie, considering her for a moment before taking a last sip from his glass of water. He got a piece of ice in his mouth and chewed it, making a crunchy noise as he spoke:

"It was good seeing you," he said.

"Yeah, same here," Nathalie replied, averting her gaze. She smiled warmly as she stood. They quickly hugged and both went their separate ways.

Lorena fought the urge to visit Blick's again, fearing it would tip Steven off that she was interested. Instead, she sought quiet refuge in Equator, slunk down in one of their soft sofa chairs, drinking *sangria* and wondering if she would see the Argentinean girl today. She also caught herself thinking about *Sofia de Amor* and couldn't believe that she was getting hooked on a stupid *novela*.

Just as Lorena was getting ready to stand up and return to work, Miriya walked in, oblivious to anybody else's presence in the coffee shop. She plopped down on a couch near the entrance, crossed her legs, and had a cell phone up to her ear in no time. Miriya's eyes were transfixed on the empty wood table in front of her, and her foot bounced forcefully, as if she hoped to shake it off her leg.

Arturo appeared in the entrance of Equator. Lorena did a double take as she caught a glimpse of the handsome Argentinean.

"Oooh, who's this?" Lorena said under her breath.

She watched Miriya slam shut her cell phone and stand, arms folded across her chest, as Arturo approached her, arms open.

"Where the hell have you been?" Miriya demanded, eyes shimmering.

"Babe, I got here as fast as I could. I told you I had a meeting."

"My father's dying in the hospital, Arturo! My mother calls me in tears, telling me that today could be the day, and they need me down there—*I* need you down there, and I call you and leave you three fuckin' messages, and you just now get hold of me and leave a message telling me to meet you *here*? You should've met me at Huntington!"

"Babe!" Arturo reached out for her arm, but she jerked away from him.

"Don't fuckin' touch me!" She shook her head and stormed out of Equator.

Lorena quickly stood, hoping to stay on Arturo's tail as he followed his girlfriend? Fiancé? Wife? Who knew? Lorena had to play it cool in Mills Place, as she didn't want Miriya to notice her interest in their lover's quarrel.

"Miriya, where you going?" Arturo stood in the middle of the alley with his arms outstretched.

She turned with fire in her eyes.

"To the hospital, idiot!"

"Will you just hold on a minute?" Arturo trotted after her.

Lorena had her cell phone up to her ear, as if she were talking on it.

"Are you coming or not?" Miriya asked, only half-caring about his answer.

Arturo ran his fingers through his hair.

"Babe, you know I want to. I feel terrible about your dad. You know I have this deal I got going right now that I'm working on. I gotta meet with investors."

He lamely checked his watch.

"In fact, I gotta be in West L.A. in forty minutes."

"That's great, Arturo," Miriya said calmly. "When, and if, we ever get married, you know, and I'm, uh, in the hospital giving birth or-or, heaven forbid, getting chemo for some cancer, I'll be thinking about you while you're out at one of your damn business meetings!"

She pointed at him.

"You are a fuckin' piece of work, man!"

She turned and stormed off. Arturo shook his head and pulled out his cell phone. Lorena, who had put her own phone away and was now "window shopping," turned in time to see him punching in a phone number. Arturo kept glancing over his shoulder to make sure that Miriya was out of view.

Lorena frowned.

Jerk.

"Hey, baby, it's me," Arturo said in hushed tones.

Lorena's eyes widened as she put her hand to her mouth. She quickly turned away from him so that he would not see her instinctive reaction. As he walked by her, Lorena cocked an ear in hopes of catching some of his phone conversation.

"...She's bent, but it's okay. She'll be out of my hair for a while. You want to get together?...*You* know!...Okay, where do you want to meet?"

Lorena's eyes narrowed at him, but he was soon out of earshot. Lorena had heard enough, though. She recognized this man and had seen him before recently, but her mind had not made the connection at first. Lorena quickly racked her brain, then it hit her like a runaway train: He was *Arturo* from *Sofia de Amor*! Not the actual actor who played the character, but the type! And to think that his name was even Arturo!

Poor Argentinean girl, Lorena thought. Daddy's dying and Arturo's fucking around on her.

Eva stood, red-eyed and tired, with her husband Jim Fuller, a bushy-haired, bespectacled college professor with soft features and kind blue eyes, who was as tall as she was. Eva's hair was dyed a dark auburn and fell in clumps around her wide face, no longer than her shoulders. She had battled with her weight most of her adult life, struggling between 150 and 180 pounds. She carried it well, though, and always dressed smartly and modestly.

Eva and Jim were outside the critical care unit of Huntington Memorial Hospital, along with Anna Fronzini. Anna's hair was pulled back in a ponytail, and she wore no make-up. She had on a gray college-logo hooded sweatshirt, tight blue jeans, and flip-flops. She wiped at her teary eyes and runny nose.

When Miriya turned the corner of the hallway and saw her sisters, her adrenaline went into high gear. She hoped she wasn't too late. She embraced her little sister.

"*Hola, que tal, Anna?*"

"Where've you been? Where's Arturo?" Anna asked.

"Don't get me started." Miriya turned and hugged Eva and her husband. "How's dad?"

"Barely holding on." It was all Eva could do to compose

herself. "He wants to see you. Mom's in there, too."

"Veronica's here," Anna mumbled. "She went to the bathroom."

"Oh." Miriya frowned. "Who called her?"

"Mom."

Miriya entered Fabio's room cautiously, almost afraid that just disturbing the quiet could push her father into the afterlife. A nurse attended to one of the many beeping monitors and IV wires that led to her father's taped and tubed body. Miriya, Sr., sat by the bed, holding Fabio's hand.

"He'll be gone soon," Miriya, Sr. said in Spanish. "He wanted to see you."

She stepped aside so her daughter could sit by the edge of the bed. Miriya took her father's gnarled, arthritic fingers into her hand and held him gently. Fabio was nearly bald, the only hair on his face being a salt and pepper goatee that had grown out over his shrunken double chin. A tracheal tube was attached to a white wrap around his neck. Miriya saw his bare, bony shoulders, the loose yellowish-gray skin dotted here and there with liver spots and lesions. Her face wrinkled as she reached over and rubbed his forehead.

"*Papa*," she said, softly. "*Papa*, it's me."

A gurgling sound welled from inside his throat, and he seemed to stir slightly. Miriya squeezed his hand, hoping to will her father back to health. Fabio opened his eyes, which were more gray now than blue. He blinked at the ceiling before turning slowly toward his favorite daughter. Miriya stood so that he could see her better.

Fabio gazed at his 30-year-old daughter, recognizing the honey-brown, narrow face with straight, fine hair and sparkling brown eyes; Miriya, the beautiful one, unmarried with no kids. How he had longed to hold one of her children one day! He closed his eyes and could still feel her frail body, tiny rib cage as she tucked her little legs in to cuddle next to him, under the stars. He remembered what it was like to hold her close. Amazingly, he recalled a statement he made to her at that time, that it saddened him that she would not remain that size forever; that some day she would grow to be a woman, too big for him to hold and carry. He also remembered her reply:

"Daddy, don't ever forget that I was little."

Fabio slowly opened his eyes.

"Hi, Junior," he said, in a gravelly whisper.

"Hi, Daddy." Miriya wiped her nose as the tears rolled down her face.

"You...wanna see the stars?"

Miriya nodded, unable to speak.

He squeezed her hand back while staring at the ceiling. It was a struggle to focus his eyes anywhere, let alone back at her.

"Anybody...you want me to...say 'hi' to?"

Miriya looked confused.

"In heaven?" he clarified. "Remember?…Anybody you wanna meet…"

"All secrets revealed." Miriya remembered now.

"*Eva Perón*?…Anyone?" He tried to smile, but the gurgling returned. He closed his eyes and tried to clear his throat. Miriya felt helpless. Veronica had been watching by the door and turned to get Eva, Jim, and Anna.

The rest of the family shuffled in as Fabio turned to Miriya.

"I…love…you, *mono*."

"I love you, Daddy," Miriya replied. She leaned over and kissed his dry lips. Eva stood behind her and rubbed her back. As Miriya pulled away, she saw that his eyes were half-open, lifeless. The beeping machines had changed their tune as hospital staff checked monitors and examined Fabio.

Miriya stood and wiped her eyes.

"Is that it?" she asked, frowning. She put her hand to her mouth. "Is he gone? *Daddy*! I can't believe this. My dad's not supposed to die."

While a doctor came in and confirmed to Miriya, Sr. that her husband had indeed finally succumbed to lung cancer, Junior stumbled backward in a daze. Veronica put her arm around her friend. They walked out of Fabio's room while the rest of the family sobbed quietly near his bed.

In the hallway, they found a bench. Miriya buried her face in Veronica's bosom and collapsed in grief, crying like

Veronica had never seen her cry before. Veronica held Miriya's trembling body tightly. Fabio had been the outgoing, affectionate father Veronica never had. She had never realized this until now.

"I don't know what I'm going to do," Miriya whispered. "My daddy's always been there for me. I'll never find a man like him. Never. Never. Never."

Nathalie Faresi stared at her ceiling while Arturo snored lightly next to her. She lay naked, half-wrapped in an ivory satin sheet, a bare leg sticking out and practically hanging off the edge of the bed. In these quiet moments, after having sex with Arturo and after he had passed out in blissful slumber, she reflected upon their relationship with sweet leisure. Nathalie thought about the way his sensuous lips felt when hers pressed against them: "heart kisses," she called them. She dwelled on how her body fluttered in his strong, muscled arms, how he literally drained her when she was on top of him.

"*What?*" Taylor Jorgensen had asked recently, while gossiping about Arturo with Nathalie. Taylor was the only one privy to Nathalie's secret.

"Squirts, gushes—call it what you want—but my cum shoots out like a guy!" Nathalie said in hushed tones, afraid someone would hear.

"My God." Taylor couldn't believe it. "How? Why?"

"I don't know! It only happens when I'm on top. He

must hit the spot—some gland inside me, or something—because, it's like, after some good foreplay, the moment I get him inside me, I can feel it build quickly, and then...*whoosh*! My whole body shakes and I can feel myself squirt! And I just keep coming and coming. I swear I can have like, twenty orgasms one after another."

Taylor's shoulders drooped further. "I can't even have one," she said.

"It's addicting! No matter how many I have, I just want more. The only reason I stop is because it literally takes everything out of me. It's like I almost pass out! Totally spent!"

"I've never even heard of that," Taylor mumbled, shaking her head.

Nathalie's eyes widened.

"Imagine how I felt. That never happened to me before. I mean, I've never had a problem having an orgasm, but it was usually through oral sex. Sometimes I had one on top, but it was never like this. It freaked us out when it first happened. His sheets were soaked to the mattress. It was like his ass was sitting in a puddle of my cum on the bed."

Taylor grimaced.

"That's disgusting!" she said.

"We tried putting a couple of towels under us, but they soaked through. We then had to go out and buy one of those pads, you know, that you put under the babies so they don't wet the bed, and then put a towel on top of that! It's amazing! I can't get enough of it."

"Do you think he makes Miriya come like that?"

"I don't know. You know Miriya never talks about Arturo that way. What if it's just me? Can you imagine? I can't give that up. What if nobody ever makes me come the way Arturo does?"

"What if?"

"Then I'm stuck."

Stuck, Nathalie thought to herself, in more ways than one.

She sighed and looked over at Arturo, who was as peaceful and vulnerable as a napping baby. Nathalie reached over and dragged a finger gently across his tan, freckled back, wondering why someone like him would need a woman like her. Arturo was already practically engaged to one of the most beautiful, charming women that Nathalie had ever known, not that she doubted the allure of her own beauty. Nathalie would be a catch for any man, but Miriya was *Miriya*—Argentinean like Arturo, and with smarts and personality for both of them.

And big fake boobs! She begrudgingly thought.

Nathalie shook her head. Men were all the same to her, immature, selfish little boys who never knew a good thing when they had it. They were never satisfied with anything they had, always wanting more. Miriya Fronzini could have been the richest, most beautiful woman in the world, and Arturo would still have cheated on her with someone less attractive. It made no sense to Nathalie.

No wonder I'm still single, she thought.

Nathalie scratched her left nipple and elbowed Arturo, causing him to stir with an irritated grunt.

"Get up, loverboy," she said in a flat voice.

He slowly pushed himself up on his elbows, one eye closed.

"Huh?" He licked his lips.

"Miriya's dad is probably dead by now. Why don't you be a good boyfriend and go see her, or something. I've got shit to do."

Arturo shook his head and chuckled.

"Cold-blooded," he mumbled.

"That's right," she said, standing and walking to her bathroom to urinate.

Arturo dashed home and took a quick shower before calling Miriya. It was getting close to 6 PM, and he had not heard anything from her. He was surprised when Veronica answered the phone.

"Hold on," she said. Arturo thought he heard sniffling in the background.

He prepared himself for bad news.

"Hey." Miriya sounded like she had been crying or was still crying.

"*Hola, amor,*" Arturo said, softly. He checked his hair in the mirror and sprayed on some cologne. "How is he?"

"He's gone."

Arturo closed his eyes.

"I am *so* sorry, baby. Where are you right now? Can I see you?"

Silence.

"Yeah, I'd like to see you. Hold on."

There were jagged, muffled sounds on Miriya's end, as if she had covered the mouthpiece and was having a conference with Veronica. Arturo rolled his eyes while imagining what Veronica was saying to his girlfriend.

"Meet me at my place," she said finally.

"I'll get there as soon as I can."

Arturo breathed a sigh of relief.

Miriya walked through the front door of her dark, still, one-bedroom apartment on South Oakland Avenue, in Pasadena's Madison Heights neighborhood. She paused before flicking on the light switch, as there was ambient light from outside casting an eerie blue glow upon her living room furniture. The place looked different. It felt like something was missing, as if her apartment had been broken into and burglarized by an unseen force, snatching from her the only man who had ever truly loved her. That Fabio Fronzini no longer existed in the world made the air feel thinner, as if the molecules that had been pushed closer together by his animate body, now spread out in a futile effort to fill the void made by his being gone.

Miriya closed her eyes and took a deep breath, hoping to catch a faint whiff of her father ever having been inside her apartment. Nothing. She could not remember the last time Fabio had been there. She put her hands to her face, pressing numb fingers into her eyes in the frail hope of smothering the tears.

When she turned on the lights, she realized how empty her life was. Her sparsely decorated apartment reflected this: a white couch nondescript against a white wall; a large, looming flat screen TV beside a small, bare coffee table; undecorated walls except for a framed poster in her living room; a squat, two-shelved bookcase filled with ten or so odd DVDs and a few books. No warmth, no color, no joy was visible in her apartment, as in her life, Miriya thought sadly. She had a job, not a career. She had a pretty boy, good-for-nothing boyfriend who was no closer to giving her a ring than he was when they first met four years prior. She had hoped to marry Arturo and buy a house with him, so she hardly had anything inside her own apartment.

Miriya threw her keys on the pale Formica kitchen countertop, where they slid and came to a stop next to a plastic pencil holder. She slipped out of her black leather loafers and took off her socks, needing to feel some softness at the moment, even if only the soft give of the white carpet on her tired bare feet.

Her cell phone rang. She checked the caller ID screen and glanced at her watch.

"Hey, you." She mustered up a dose of loving warmth for her friend and sat on the couch. "Yeah...yeah, thank you, sweetie...It was bound to happen...Listen, babe, it means *so* much to me that you called, and I wish I could talk to you more, but the BF's gonna be here any minute, so can I call you later? I'm sorry..."

Miriya closed her eyes and brought a hand to her forehead.

"...Me, too, sweetie. I'll see you later...Bye."

She closed her cell phone and smiled. A knock at the door chased it away, and she stood rigidly, preparing herself for Arturo. She opened her front door and took a deep breath. Then she lost it. Arturo was upon her as she collapsed into his protective arms. He held her tightly. Miriya felt suddenly safe in his embrace, the strength of his arms engulfing her within his very being. He said nothing and just soothed her as her tears fell onto his dark wool pea coat.

He led her to the couch, where he continued to hold her. Miriya could smell the fresh scent of soap on him and knew that he had showered before coming over, washing away God only knew what, or whom. She said nothing. What could she say? she wondered, as she remembered her last phone conversation and thought about *him*.

An hour later, Miriya dug her nails into Arturo's shoulders for leverage while grinding her glistening hips faster upon his slippery loins. Her breathing grew heavier, and her heart raced so fast that she thought she would faint. Arturo watched her intently, her hair stuck to the skin of her face, neck, and shoulders in darkened, wet strips as sweat beaded and dripped across her golden skin. He thoughtfully removed a hand from the soft flesh of her thrusting hips and wiped her forehead, cheek, and chest, dragging his hand across the path of wet skin between still, firm breasts.

"Oh, *amor,* I love making you *sweat,*" he said in a grunt.

Miriya, eyes closed, ignored him and focused on the pressure building between her legs. She decided it was time. She arched farther back and placed both hands on Arturo's muscled thighs.

"Okay, now," she said, almost in a whisper.

Arturo reached up and gently rubbed and twisted her swollen nipples between his thumb and forefinger. This was all she needed to push her over the edge. Her face wrinkled and contorted in a sudden wave of intense pleasure. Tightlipped, she finally let out a faint squeal. Her body shook, convulsing toward Arturo's chest.

Miriya slid suddenly from on top of Arturo—one of her bare feet almost knocking him in the face—and landed on her side among the musky sheets. She turned her back toward him, moaning as she settled her body. She wanted to fall asleep right then and there.

Arturo frowned and slapped her rear.

"Hey, it's my turn," he said, perplexed.

"Mmm…Go ahead," she mumbled.

"Huh?"

"Do your thing. I'm just gonna lie here. I'm wiped out." She shifted her tired hips and moved her left leg forward in case he wanted to slip inside of her from behind. Arturo shook his head.

"Thanks," he smirked. "Don't strain yourself."

Miriya was already asleep.

PART FIVE:
EL OTRO

Miriya stood before the neat glass shelves of bath and body, aromatherapy, and other spa products displayed in the lobby of Burke Williams and admired their orderly arrangement. Erin, the young receptionist at the front counter, looked sharp and answered the phones with professional courtesy. The marble floor was polished and there was a tranquil, organic scent in the air.

Miriya closed her eyes and breathed deeply through her nose. Her jet lag was minimal and she felt on her game today.

"Hi, thank you for calling Burke Williams Spa. This is Erin…"

Miriya's cell phone text message alert went off. She walked behind the counter and discreetly checked her message.

Hey, you. Missed you this weekend. Call me when you get a chance. Muah.

147

Miriya smiled. "Muah" was their code word for a kiss, as it roughly resembled the sound of an affectionate "muah" on the lips. She looked toward the door as two burly Caucasian men walked in—aging frat boy types, Miriya thought to herself.

"Hi, welcome to Burke Williams Spa," Erin said politely. Miriya hung around behind Erin and pretended to be inventorying something, while one ear was cocked toward the girl's conversation with the walk-ins.

"Hi, uh, what kind of services do you have here?" asked the one wearing a USC sweatshirt. He wore loafers without socks and had a large belly.

"Are you guys interested in massages, facials…"

"Massages," replied the one with the baseball cap turned backwards. He had bad, unkempt toenails hanging over the front end of dirty flip-flops.

"Well, we have deep-tissue massage," Erin said, pulling out a brochure and price guide. "That's a harder massage where they work on specific parts of your body. We have the lighter, more relaxing Swedish massage…"

Tommy Trojan raised his eyebrows at flip-flop boy as Miriya folded her arms across her chest.

"That, uh, Swedish massage, is it full body?"

"Do we gotta be naked?"

"Can we have a woman masseuse or does it have to be a man?"

"You can request a female masseuse if you'd prefer

one," Miriya said, stepping in for the flustered Erin. "We don't take walk-ins, though. You should make an appointment."

She quickly glanced at the appointment book.

"We appear to be booked today; perhaps another day? Here is a brochure with a list of our services and prices."

She handed the USC fan the brochure.

"What about Saturday?" he asked.

"We don't take men until after six on Saturdays," Miriya said, sighing.

"How much extra for 'happy ending'?" He said the last part with a faux Asian accent, as he and his buddy snickered and elbowed each other. Miriya frowned while striking a more defiant pose.

"Perhaps this facility is a little too high-brow for what you gentlemen are looking for. Why don't you try the back of the *LA Weekly*. I think there're plenty of happy endings there. Have a nice day."

They mumbled something about snooty bitches as they turned and sullenly shuffled out of the spa. Miriya shook her head and turned to Erin.

"Can you believe those two?"

"I'm so glad you were here," Erin said, shaking her head slowly. "I wouldn't have known what to say to them. How do you keep your cool?"

"Trust me, sometimes it's hard to, but I've dealt with my share of idiots before."

Lorena had not seen the Argentinean girl in Equator in over two weeks and had no idea where she could have gone. Remembering the argument Miriya had with her man, Arturo, Lorena figured that something might have happened with the girl's sick father. Maybe he had died already, and she was on bereavement leave. This made Lorena wonder what Miriya did for a living, and if her job would even grant her bereavement leave. Lorena thought about her own father and could not imagine something happening to him.

How sad, Lorena thought. I wonder if Ramin would give me bereavement leave.

"Good morning. Fayed Law Corporation," Lorena said, cradling the receiver on her shoulder as she typed a brief for Ramin.

"Fayed Law Corporation? This Ramin's outfit?"

Uh-oh. Lorena recognized the voice.

"Yes, it is."

"This is Chet Rasmussen down the hall. Say, is this Ramin's cute little secretary? What are you, uh, Armenian? Mexican? Hard to tell with your light skin. You ain't *A*-rab are you?"

Lorena rolled her eyes.

"Hello, Mr. Rasmussen. This is Mr. Fayed's Office Manager. How can we assist you today?"

"Oh, the ol' formal routine, eh? Well, listen here, I'm going over the company phone bill, and there're a bunch o' calls placed from my office to yours. Now, I know none o' my partners and I are calling Ramin, so what gives?"

"Your secretary, *Lupe Mercado*," Lorena said, in as thick a Spanish accent as she could, "and I are friends, Mr. Rasmussen. We often call each other to make plans for lunch, get help or advice with a work-related matter, and the like."

"She ain't giving away company secrets, is she?"

"Not likely, Mr. Rasmussen."

The nerve of this guy!

"Okay, uh…Lorena. You let me know if you ever want a job with a *real* law firm. Hate to see you get wrapped up in some…*homeland security* investigation."

Chet chuckled as he said this.

"Thank you for the offer, Mr. Rasmussen. You have a good day now."

Lorena hung up before Chet could say anything else. Within a minute, her phone rang again.

What now?

"Good morning. Fayed Law Corporation."

"Girl, did Chet just call you?"

Lorena laughed.

"That guy's such an idiot!" she said.

"He jammed me up for calling you too much, so I thought I'd call you."

"What's goin' on, *carnala*?"

"Did you watch *Sofia de Amor* last night?"

Lorena brought her hand to her mouth.

"*Ai, sí, guey*! Can you believe that shit?"

"That *pinche cabrón* Arturo!" Lupe spat.

"Can you believe he confronted Abel, like he knew he was being followed?"

"Yeah! Abel's a *dick*! I can't believe he would turn on Sofia for $10,000."

"Now Abel's gonna try to *kill* poor Sofia!" Lorena said. "I'm like glued to that shit now."

Lorena shook her head as she thought about the real Arturo and the Argentinean girl. She checked her watch and decided that she would go to Equator.

Steven ducked into the stretched canvases aisle and brought his cell phone up to his ear. The caller got the butterflies going in Steven's stomach and stirred the ire Steven had felt growing over the last week and a half.

"Hey, sweetie, what's up?…Just working. What about you? How's your day going?…I'm fine…No, no, seriously, I'm fine. You know, uh, I knew what I was getting myself into when we started this…Well, since you bring it up, did you?…I wanna know! I'd rather know when you guys do have sex, than not know. At least I can, like…lie to myself that you're being totally honest with me, and tellin' me everything…"

He nodded while making a face.

"Well…good. That's great…As long as *I'm* still your favorite…Yeah, *right*!"

Steven saw Lorena approaching the entrance to his store.

"Hey, baby, listen. I gotta get going. We got a long line of customers…Okay…I adore you, sweetie. Take care… Bye."

Steven hung up and quickly re-opened his cell phone, using the mirror-like face of the interior screen to check his appearance and make sure he had nothing stuck in his teeth. He then tried to remember the girl's name.

Laura? Lauren…Lorena!

"Hi, mister." Lorena saw him and waved.

"Hey, Lorena, how're you doing?"

"Fine, how are you?"

Steven noticed that Lorena wore a powder-blue blouse under an ivory-colored sweater, tight jeans, and powder-blue tennis shoes. Her hair was pulled back in a tight pony-tail and her non-prescription, cat-eye glasses hung low on the bridge of her nose. She pushed her glasses back with a delicate finger while considering Steven.

"I'm good—better now, actually, that you're here." He cleared his throat. "I wondered when you were going to come back in."

Lorena chuckled.

"You're cute," she said. "Smooth talker, I see."

"Wha—*hey*! I'm not a smooth talker," he protested mildly. "I just wanted to see your face one more time. It's too pretty just to see once."

"Yeah?" Lorena beamed, eating it up. "What's so pretty about it?"

"Your eyes, of course." Steven nervously looked around to make sure customers or co-workers weren't eavesdropping. Luckily, the store was fairly empty. Jorge was ringing someone up at the cash registers. "They're big and, uh…are a very…pretty …brown color."

He frowned. Quit while you're ahead!

"What gives with the casual clothes today? Your day off?"

"No. I'm at work," she replied. "There's not a lot of people coming in today, and I'm filing, and moving stuff around. Copying tons of documents."

Steven nodded.

"You're still not going to tell me where you work, huh?"

"Mmmm…Nah, not yet."

"Maybe over dinner?"

Lorena smiled.

"You asking me out on a date, mister?"

"Yeah."

"How do you know I don't already have a boyfriend?"

"I don't, but I doubt you would've come back here if you had."

"Maybe I cheat." She raised an eyebrow at him.

"Maybe you do," Steven said, distantly. He thought of *her*.

"Would you still go out with me if I said yes but you knew I had a boyfriend?"

Steven considered this while looking toward the floor. Lorena noted the shift in his demeanor.

"No," he replied, meeting her eyes with a newfound confidence. "I wouldn't. That's not for me."

Lorena gave him an approving smile.

"Good answer, mister."

"Thank you, miss."

"When?"

"When what?"

"When would you like to take me out?"

Lorena had a noticeable pep in her step as she walked into Equator after making a date with Steven. Miriya, who sat by herself on one of the soft couches near the front, recognized Lorena and watched her with rising curiosity as she got in line for a drink. Miriya wondered who the girl was, why she was always at Equator, and what she did in the Old Pasadena area. Miriya was intrigued by the girl's un-self-conscious beauty and quiet confidence: her head held high, back straight, and arms by her sides like a dignified Barbie doll. Lorena, it appeared to Miriya, strolled into a room as if there weren't anywhere she didn't belong, yet she didn't draw attention to herself. The calm, reserved expression on the girl's face was that of a thoughtful woman who probably had few close friends. When Lorena got her drink and turned around, Miriya caught her breath as she saw Lorena approach her table.

"Hello." Lorena smiled warmly at Miriya. "Mind if I sit?"

"Hi—no, not at all. There's plenty of room on the couch."

Miriya instinctively slid away from Lorena, as close to the opposite arm as possible. Lorena appeared not to notice and sat a respectable distance from Miriya, placing her drink on the low table in front of them and her purse between them.

"I haven't seen you here for a while," Lorena said. Miriya felt flattered that the girl had noticed. "My name's Lorena Sandoval, by the way."

Lorena shook Miriya's hand.

"Miriya Fronzini. No, I, uh…I just got back from Argentina. My father passed away recently, and we flew back to Rosario to bury him."

"I'm sorry to hear that," Lorena said.

"He had cancer, so we knew it was coming."

Lorena nodded her head, tight-lipped.

"It's still sad," she finally said.

There was an awkward silence between the women for a moment.

"So, you're from Argentina?"

"Wha—no. I mean, my parents are. I was born here, in Glendale, so I'm American. And you?"

Lorena stifled a chuckle.

"Well, *I'm* Mexican, but I was born at Huntington. In fact, my birthday just passed recently. On Halloween."

Miriya had a funny look on her face.

"My little sister was born at Huntington on Halloween," she said, wrinkling her nose. "What year?"

"1985."

Miriya laughed.

"Oh, my *God*! So was Anna! You guys could have been born down the hall from each other."

"Small world," Lorena said. She took a sip of her drink.

"Don't take this the wrong way, but you don't look like any Mexican girl I've ever seen. You're as white as a white girl, and you've got red hair and freckles. What gives?"

Lorena thought she detected a slight sneer when Miriya said "Mexican" but gave the Argentinean the benefit of the doubt.

"Oh, c'mon. There're light-skinned Mexicans just as I'm sure there're light- skinned Argentineans. I get the hair and freckles from my dad's side, though."

"Well, I'm the darkest one of three kids—all girls," Miriya said, holding up a golden brown arm. "The other two have skin like yours. You have siblings?"

"My sister's the oldest, and we have a brother in the middle."

"Do you work in Old Town?" Miriya had to know.

"Yeah. I'm a legal secretary-slash-office manager at the Fayed Law Corporation over on Raymond. It's in the Braley Building. You work near here?"

"I'm a manager at Burke Williams Spa."

Lorena's eyes widened slightly.

"Oooh, girl, I'm glad I metchoo!"

They both chuckled.

"I could use a trip to the spa," Lorena added.

"Couldn't we all! I can't believe I don't go more often."

"You got the hook-up?" Lorena had a mischievous look on her face.

"I wish!"

"I'm just kidding."

Lorena took another sip of her drink and checked her watch.

"*Donde está tu novio?*" Lorena asked.

"Who knows?" Miriya replied in English. "Arturo's always got some business scheme he's trying to cook up." Miriya suddenly remembered that she thought she had seen Lorena there when she and Arturo had fought in the alley. "Oh, man, were you here when I had it out with him in the alley recently?"

Ooops! Lorena thought. Busted.

"I caught a glimpse," Lorena admitted.

"Talk about drama." Miriya rolled her eyes.

"How long have you guys been together?"

"Four years."

"Are you guys gonna get married?"

"We're not even engaged."

"Wuuuuuut?" Lorena said in her dull hum.

"Tell me about it."

"What's holding him up?" Lorena told herself that *she* would not have put up with that.

"Who knows?" Miriya shook her head. "He says he wants to be 'secure in his career' before we get married, but what career is that? The guy sells phones for Verizon and works as a bouncer at a club in Hollywood."

Uh-oh, Lorena thought.

"He just got his real estate license and is trying to get his own real estate investment company going, but who knows when that's going to happen. Meanwhile, he's getting hit on by hot blondes with big hair and boob jobs—*I* have a boob job, by the way. Just wanted to get that out there. I'm not hating or anything."

"Okay." Lorena chuckled, amused by Miriya's conversational style.

"And he's getting who knows how many honeys' digits at the Verizon store."

"Is he all that and a bag of chips?" Lorena thought that Arturo was good-looking, from what she remembered, but she would not have gone out with him. He wasn't her type.

"Well, you saw him—he's *gorgeous*! Who wouldn't want to marry him? And if he ever does get his real estate gig underway, I'm sure he'll be loaded, too. He's a hard worker. Very driven."

"You don't strike me as a materialistic type," Lorena mumbled.

"Not really." Miriya looked guilty. "But, we're all materialistic to some degree. A woman wants a man to be able to provide for her and her future family. We all want a good life."

Lorena nodded.

"Fair enough," she agreed.

"And just between you and I," Miriya said, leaning over and whispering. "The sex is awesome!"

Lorena raised an eyebrow and smiled mischievously.

"Oh, well, you go then," she said.

"Are you married?" Miriya asked.

"Nope."

"Engaged?"

"Uh-uh. Don't even have a boyfriend."

Miriya was incredulous.

"You've got to be kidding me. You must have just got out of a relationship then?"

"I've been single for a little over a year."

Miriya frowned.

"Are you talking to anybody?"

"Well," Lorena said, hesitantly. "I just met a guy recently, and he asked me out for a first date, so we'll see."

Miriya seemed relieved by this.

"Hey, listen, Miriya," Lorena said, glancing at her watch. "I've lost track of time, and I've got to get back to work. It was good to finally meet my Equator buddy."

Miriya smiled warmly as Lorena stood.

"Yes, it was nice meeting you, too."

"I guess I'll see you around," Lorena said, waving at her.

"Yeah, I hope so!" Miriya was all smiles.

Lorena set off for work. Miriya sat back down on the couch and felt curiously cheered. What a genuine person, she thought to herself, smiling. Miriya suddenly wished that she knew Lorena better and had a brief daydream of what it might be like if she were friends with the girl. She pictured the two of them meeting for lunch, gossiping about friends and lovers, shopping together and doing girl things. Miriya had a vague feeling that Lorena was vastly different from her own friends. Miriya suddenly felt amazingly renewed. It was as if she had turned a page in her life to a fresh chapter. She had not felt this way since she'd met *him* a year ago.

Before Miriya decided to give up on Suzy, she appeared at the doorway on her cell phone. Suzy looked irritated and Miriya could tell she was on the phone with one of her Armenian male friends, maybe even her ex-boyfriend Arten.

"Why are you even talking to me this way?" Suzy asked, shaking her head. She shot Miriya an apologetic glance. "You say you're my friend, and you talk to me disrespectfully! I don't need this! You're *not* my friend! I'm dumping all the negative people in my life and you're one of them. Friends don't talk to friends like this!...Oh, really?...You are a fuckin' piece of shit, you know that?...*Fuck you*, too!"

She slammed her cell phone shut.

"Fuckin' bastard!" she added. "Sorry 'bout that, Miriya."

They hugged each other quickly.

"What was that all about?" Miriya looked considerately horrified.

"You remember that guy I told you about a few months ago? We met at my Armenian girlfriend's wedding. We went out on a couple of dates, and all he did was talk about his friends, like 'Oh, so-and-so's the man. He's so cool. Blah-blah-blah'."

Suzy and Miriya sat back down on the couch.

"Well, he was like, trying to kiss me the whole time we were at the movies, and I'm like, 'Dude! Get a fuckin' clue, I'm tryin' to watch the movie. I'm not going to kiss you here!'...I just wasn't feeling it with him, you know? He had the car, and the bling-bling, and his family had money, but you know? There's more to it than that! He's getting' on my fuckin' nerves."

"I remember him." Miriya lied, absently. She thought that if she ever bumped into Lorena again, she would try to get her cell phone number.

Suzy considered getting a coffee. "Now all he does is

claim that he's my friend and he's just looking out for me, but all he does is call me and tell me about all the Armo women he has, and how they all think he's a catch and want to marry him, and how I don't hold a candle to any of them."

"What?"

"Fuck him, *asshole!*"

"What a dick," Miriya agreed. "Where do you find these creeps? I swear it's like…you must dream them up in your nightmares and then they get created out of shit, or something, and crawl out of a hole to meet you."

Suzy laughed.

"Huh? I probably do that! It wouldn't surprise me. *Uugh!*" Suzy grunted, holding out her hands like claws. "Why can't I just meet a good, loyal, well-to-do Armenian man?"

"These guys treat you like shit because they know you're a virgin. They have nothing to lose!" Miriya argued. "They figure if they treat you bad, you might give in to them. They just want the challenge of getting in your pants. They're horrible."

"Do you think that's it?" Suzy frowned.

"I *know* it's it!"

Miriya smiled.

"I met somebody," she added, tiring of Suzy's man stories.

Suzy frowned.

"What? What are you talking about?"

"Today. Right here, just before you got here, I met someone." Miriya felt liberated playing as though she were revealing a dalliance to Suzy.

"Are you shitting me? What about Arturo?"

"Not a guy, silly!" Miriya laughed. "I met a girl."

"Okay, now you've lost me." Suzy was getting impatient.

"No, recently I've noticed this girl here at Equator. We've never said anything to each other—I think we've kinda waved 'hi' a couple of times—but today she approached me and struck up a conversation."

"Is she a lesbian?" Suzy scowled.

"No, nothing like that!" Miriya felt herself suddenly getting irritated. "You know, I told her my dad had died and she was sad for me. Oh, and she was born the exact same day as my sister Anna, same hospital, everything! Weird, huh?"

"Whatever."

Miriya quietly added: "I can't remember the last time I met somebody new. It's kinda nice to make a new friend."

The following Friday night, Steven arrived in front of Lorena's house right on schedule. Steven hated being late to anything, especially a date, and he always made sure to be at least 5-10 minutes early. He checked his appearance in his rear view mirror and placed a Listerine fresh breath strip on his tongue. He was ready, and pleased that he had that nervous feeling in the pit of his stomach—the "butterflies." That was always a good sign in reference to dating somebody new. He wondered if Lorena felt the same way as he got out of his car.

Steven took in the almost stereotypical exterior of Lorena's house as he approached the front door. A low, beige brick wall with short columns connected by wrought iron fencing surrounded the modest front yard. There was a matching wrought iron gate, which opened to a short, concrete walkway, lined on both sides by a well-kept lawn, and rose bushes. Steven was amazed by the numerous and varied types of chili plants growing along the well-trimmed edges of the front yard, just on the other side of the wall. There were fruit-bearing trees that included an avocado, a lemon, and a lime tree. The covered front porch was also surrounded by wrought iron fencing, complete with exterior locking gate, with matching bars on the house windows. There were cactus plants with other succulents on the front porch, as well as an old stuffed armadillo.

Interesting décor, Steven thought.

Within a minute, Isabel answered the door with a polite smile and cautious eyes. It was not common for men to come calling on her youngest daughter.

"Hi, I'm Steven." He shook her hand.

"Hi, Steven, I'm Lorena's mother, Isabel. Come in. She'll be ready in a few minutes."

Steven stepped into the dimly lit living room and glanced around at the interior. There was a mirror on the wall to his right, which he figured was used to check one's appearance before leaving the house. Its wood frame was decorated in hand-carved and painted sunflowers with a matching table below it. He recognized an adjacent bedroom as probably being Lorena's brother's room, as there was a single twin bed with a duffel bag stuffed with athletic gear on it, as well as a drum set in the corner. Steven smiled to himself upon seeing the large replica of the *Virgen de Guadalupe* on the living room wall.

"*Habla español?*" Isabel asked Steven, as he sat on their couch, back straight and hands folded politely in his lap.

"No. I'm sorry," he replied, suddenly feeling ashamed. "I'm Hispanic, but my parents didn't speak Spanish in our home." Ironically, Isabel seemed more embarrassed at this than he did. He cleared his throat and tried to think of a topic change.

"You have a pretty house, *Señora Sandoval*."

"Thank you. Please call me *Isabel*."

He heard a *click-click-clack* coming from the area of the kitchen and looked up in time to see Lorena emerge from her bathroom. The sound made by her high heels upon their tile kitchen floor announced her presence in a subtle, earthy manner. Steven stood, his eyes widening at the sight of her tall, slim figure standing erect, her slinky, black cocktail dress clinging to her like an afterthought. The neck of her dress was so low, that it dipped to just above her navel, leaving exposed the creamy skin between her breasts, which hung freely just inside the fabric.

"Hi, mister." Lorena smiled in her full, toothy way.

"Hi, miss," he replied. She approached him slowly and gently leaned in, giving him a fleeting hug with an air kiss just away from his cheek.

"You ready?"

"Yup." He was still checking her out.

"*No vengas tarde,*" Isabel said to Lorena. Isabel looked at Steven and reiterated for him, "Please don't keep her out late."

"I won't," Steven said, hoping he was lying.

They had a pleasant dinner at Bar Celona in Old Pasadena, opting for drinks at Bodega wine bar. Bodega was a low-lit, trendy hipster bar, tucked away in the Paseo Colorado—an upscale, mixed-use outdoor residential-shopping-dining mall in downtown Pasadena. Steven liked to bring dates to this casual lounge bar, which played music like Air's "Moon Safari" while couples huddled closely on comfy love seats.

Since this was a first date, Lorena and Steven sat in less comfortable metal chairs and tables in Bodega's outside dining area, the crisp November air being tempered by tall, standing heaters.

"You come here a lot?" she asked.

"Eh, maybe…once every two months or so. You?"

"Once in a while. It's cool."

Lorena was surprised at how nervous she was. Steven, too, struggled to think of something to say.

"They got a lot of beautiful people here."

"Us included?" Lorena raised an eyebrow, smiling.

Steven chuckled.

"Of course."

"So why did you ask me out?" Lorena wondered aloud.

"To get in your pants," he said, straight-faced.

"I knew it!" Lorena feigned shock and disgust.

"No-no," Steven said, shyly. "I asked you out 'cause I was attracted to you. You're pretty and you're charming. Why else does a guy ask a girl out? You act like you don't get asked out a lot."

Lorena said nothing, which made Steven curious.

"Do you?"

"Do I what?" Lorena replied, sipping from her glass of merlot.

"Get asked out a lot."

"I get asked out. I'm just not very interested in many of the guys who notice me. Where I grew up isn't exactly known for its abundance of quality men."

"Where'd you grow up?"

"The 'hood," Lorena replied, vaguely proud.

"You don't look like a girl from the 'hood."

"I was sheltered effectively—no going to friends' houses, no hanging out in the street, and no dating until I had a serious boyfriend, late in high school. I had to come home every day and do my homework, and go to church every Sunday. I grew up in a traditional Mexican household. Don't get me wrong. I was sheltered but I'm not square. I just don't say 'yes' to boys very often because I'm kind of picky."

Steven nodded.

"What are you looking for?"

"A man," Lorena replied.

"Huh?"

"Most of the boys I meet are just that—*boys*. I'm looking for a *man*, with a j-o-b and a degree, who wants to settle down and get married."

"I got a job," Steven said.

"I'm here, aren't I?"

Steven smiled.

"Are you in college?" Lorena asked.

"Yeah, I'm a junior at UCLA."

Lorena was impressed.

"What's your major?"

"English."

I guess we'll be poor, she thought.

"What do you want to do?" she asked.

"I dunno yet really. I've thought about teaching, but I might just try my hand at writing. And you? What do you wanna do?"

Lorena stared at him with a blank expression on her face, then:

"I already do what I want to do."

"Oh, yeah! I'm sorry," he said, shaking his head. "What an idiot. Legal secretary, right?"

She nodded and reached for her glass of wine. She took a slow sip and considered him across the top of her glass.

"Did you ever want to be a, uh, paralegal, or a lawyer, or anything?"

"My boss offered to send me to paralegal school—even *law school* actually—but, uh, no, I'm fine where I am, for now. Again, you know, I'd like to get married and start a family. That's usually how it goes where I come from."

Steven nodded.

"Interesting," he mumbled.

"Do you want to get married some day?" she asked him, taking another sip of her wine.

"Wha—*yeah*. Yeah! Sure, someday."

Lorena chuckled.

"How old are you?" she asked.

"Twenty-six."

Lorena nodded.

"Good age. That's about, um, twenty-one, twenty-two in guy years."

"Guy years? What's that?"

"Whenever a guy tells you his age, just subtract five

years. That's about how mature he is."

"I'm mature!"

"You don't still play video games, do you?"

"No way!"

"What's your last name anyway?"

"Meztaz."

"*Mez*-taz?" Lorena clarified in her Spanish accent. "*Tú eres Latino? Mexicano?*"

"Huh? Oh, yeah, uh, but I don't speak Spanish."

Lorena looked at him sideways. A sly grin was forming at the corners of her mouth.

"Wuuuuut?" she hummed. "What's up with that? What kind of *Latino* are you?"

"What?" Steven shifted uncomfortably in his chair.

"*Americano!*" Lorena said this with feigned indignation. "Relax, I'm just messing with you. Your parents speak Spanish?"

"Yeah, my dad better than my mom."

"And they never spoke Spanish to you guys at home?"

"Nah."

Lorena sucked her teeth three times while shaking her head.

"Mmm-mmm-mmm. They did you wrong. I need a man who'll speak Spanish to my kids." She laughed as she said this.

"Hey, I can speak English to them while you speak Spanish!" he protested.

"*Oooh*! Who said it's gonna be you?" She was smiling flirtatiously.

"Well…hopefully," he said softly.

Lorena chuckled.

"You're cute," she said. "Maybe I'll teach you Spanish."

"I'd like that."

"How do you feel about pre-marital sex?" Lorena raised an eyebrow.

"Ummm," Steven had to think fast. Was this a trick question? He had never even considered this.

"I don't know, to be honest. I can't say I've ever given it a thought one way or the other."

He quickly gulped some wine as Lorena nodded without expression.

"Are you a virgin?" Lorena asked suddenly. Steven almost spit out his wine.

"Umm, no. Are you?"

Lorena thought about James.

"No."

Whew! Steven relaxed some.

"But I'm seriously thinking about saving myself for marriage now," she said. "It's what God would have wanted for me."

Steven wondered if Lorena was a Jesus freak.

"Are you like, uh…"

"I'm not a nun, Steven," Lorena said, smiling. "I'm

human. I like to party like the next young person. I like to dance. I get ripped sometimes—although I don't drink and drive. I get horny. I don't think everything's a sin, if that's what you were worried about."

"Oh, okay."

"I do go to church every Sunday. And I pray a lot. Are you Catholic?"

Steven took a deep breath.

"I was baptized Catholic. We don't really go to church, though."

Lorena nodded.

"Interesting," she mumbled, sizing up the young man before her.

On Monday, Miriya caught herself watching the clock. Equator was less than a hundred yards away, but it seemed like forever until she could get there. Suzy noticed her friend's distraction.

"Hey, you," Suzy said with a tired tone.

"Oh, hey," Miriya replied.

"What are you doing for lunch?"

"I dunno. I was thinking about just getting a salad at Equator. What are you doing?"

"I'm meeting Nathalie and Taylor at Saladang. They felt like Thai food."

"Oh?" Miriya asked, absently. "Why not City Thai? It's just around the corner."

Suzy shrugged.

"Beats me. It was Taylor's idea."

"Is Veronica going?"

"I don't think so—*I* didn't call her."

Miriya nodded.

"You're welcome to join us," Suzy said.

"No thanks. I'm not feeling Thai right now."

"You okay?"

"Yeah. Why?" Miriya frowned.

"Just wondering."

Lorena glanced at her watch as lunchtime neared. She had made sure to bring her own lunch and eat it while at her desk. She didn't want to waste any of her lunch hour standing in a line for food somewhere. She wanted to sit at Equator with a coffee.

Perhaps she would see Miriya.

Lorena was startled by her phone and picked it up, momentarily forgetting where she was.

"Hello?"

"*Hello?*" It was Lupe. "Girl, where do you think you are?"

"Oh, shit!" Lorena said. "I'm sorry!—Good morning. Fayed Law Cor..."

"Yeah-yeah-yeah! Shut-up, *cabrona*, it's me!"

Lorena laughed.

"I can't believe I did that," she said. "That shit was

funny! What's going on?"

"*You* tell me!"

"*Qué*?" Lorena played dumb.

"Look at you! '*Qué*?' With *papi chulo, carnala*!"

"Oh! Well, we went out Friday night. And Saturday night. And he took me to Third Street Promenade in Santa Monica last night."

"*No chingas, guey*! Did he give you a ring an' shit? Look at you guys! Any kissy-kissy?"

Lorena chuckled.

"There was a little kissy-kissy, if you must know. Out on the Santa Monica pier."

"Romantic," Lupe said. "Any sucky-sucky?"

"Oh, no, you did not just say 'sucky-sucky'!"

"You guys didn't do nuttin' else?"

Lorena shook her head.

"There was a little feeling up going on," she finally admitted.

"*Damn*! That was the most action you've gotten in a while, huh?"

"Shut up!"

As Miriya approached Equator, she was surprised to feel a tense euphoria—she had butterflies in her stomach. Upon entering the coffeehouse, she felt both relief and disappointment when she did not see Lorena. What am I doing, she asked herself? She wondered if she even had the time or energy for a new friend. Miriya hardly had time for her present group of friends, not to mention her family, work, and Arturo!

Ugh! Arturo!

She shook her head as she remembered how they had fought all weekend. She hated the feeling that everything in her life was right on track except in the area of romance. Arturo should have been helping to make her dreams come true, joining forces with her—as a team—to build a life together. Instead, he was bringing her grief.

And now Lorena! What did Miriya hope to achieve by pursuing a friendship, if it were possible, with this girl? What if she and Lorena were so vastly different that they would never "click"? Would any relationship with Lorena just degenerate into a forced acquaintanceship they would regret so much that they'd end up both avoiding a cherished gathering spot, out of fear of running into one another?

Miriya ordered her drink and plopped down in her favorite couch, staring at the empty table before her. She thought she needed to get her life in order.

"Is this seat taken?"

Miriya looked up and saw Lorena standing next to her as if she had magically appeared there—*poof*! The redhead wore a bun like a pastry on the top of her head and flashed a wide grin, her lipstick matching a red flower decoratively placed above her right ear.

"Hey, you!" Miriya said, the butterflies returning.

Lorena sat close to her new friend.

"I was hoping I'd run into you here," Lorena said, not missing a beat. She set her purse down by her sandaled feet.

Miriya squinted her eyes in pleased curiosity toward Lorena.

"Yeah? I have to admit I hoped I'd see you, too."

Lorena's back was as straight as a board. Miriya noticed this and sat up straighter. "Not that you wouldn't have," Lorena said. "I mean, we're here all the time."

"I used to see you walk in here," Miriya started, "always by yourself, tall and elegant—you have great posture, by the way."

"Thanks. Modeling classes."

"Huh?"

"You know, the ol' book-on-the-head routine?"

"Oh," Miriya smiled.

"I used to watch you, too," Lorena confessed. "You always sat in that chair there, your friends sat here; very handsome group. I can tell you're quite the social butterfly. I even got a little envious sometimes."

"Why?" Miriya frowned.

"Mmm…Because I don't have friends the way you do. I don't have like, a group of girls that I get together with."

"That's unusual. How come?"

"I dunno. I just never did. It was always my family. I'm real close to my cousin—my brother and his friends. I hang out with them, but that gets old because he has this buddy who has the hots for me and I'm not interested."

"Hey, speaking of! Did you ever go out with that guy?"

"Oh, yeah! He and I had the best time on Friday night! We had dinner at Bar Celona."

"Nice!"

"But the *best* part," Lorena continued, "is that he asked me out again the next night, *and* the next night!"

"Wow! You sure you guys weren't seeing *too* much of each other so quickly? You don't wanna move too fast if he's someone you care about."

Lorena considered this.

"I know what you mean," she said. "But he asked me out, you know? He's really sweet. Nice. You don't meet too many guys like him."

"Don't I know!" Miriya said, smiling.

"So, I'm taking a chance on him. I got a good feeling about it. Besides, he's a really good kisser!"

Miriya smiled.

"Well, good! Good for you. I'm happy for you."

"How are things with Arturo?" Lorena asked, averting her gaze as she asked this.

"Oh, sucky as usual," Miriya replied. "We fought all weekend."

"Over what?"

"Stupid shit. Same stuff we always fight over. 'Why is your cell phone on vibrate now?' 'Who's calling you?'

'Why don't you answer your phone?' 'Where were you yesterday afternoon? Last night?'...Take your pick."

Lorena made a face.

"Is he cheating on you?" she asked.

There, I said it, she thought.

"Hmm, I don't know," Miriya said in an unusually calm manner. "Maybe. Probably. You never know with guys. Most guys cheat."

Lorena nodded.

"What are we to do?" Miriya asked, rhetorically.

"Find one who doesn't." Lorena paused. "Don't you know a guy anywhere who would never cheat on you?"

Lorena frowned, curious as to the answer. Miriya considered this and smiled to herself.

"I do know one," she said.

"Oh?" Lorena had a mischievous smile on her face. "And is this 'the one that got away'—an old flame perhaps? Or maybe someone you're thinking of leaving Arturo for?"

Miriya shook her head with a wistful smile on her face.

"No, he doesn't belong to me. I mean, I'm kinda seeing him on the side."

Lorena arched an eyebrow.

"No shit?" Was all Lorena could say to that bombshell.

"Yeah, so I guess that's why I can't really get too bent out of shape over the possibility of Arturo seeing someone else."

Lorena chuckled, as did Miriya.

"But I've made my choice and I have to live with it—make it work. That's what you do in a serious relationship. You make it work, even when it sucks. One of these days, Arturo will get his shit together and he'll ask me to marry him, and then things will be different. We'll have a good life."

Lorena nodded slowly.

"I hope so. I'm curious, Miriya, do you go to church?"

"On holidays an' stuff, why?"

"Just wondering. I find that it often helps sort things out for me."

Lorena left it at that as Miriya smiled uneasily. She checked her watch.

"Oh, *shit*! I have to go back to work," Miriya blurted.

"Oh, me, too," Lorena said.

They both stood and looked as though neither wanted to leave yet.

"I—" Lorena started.

"Would you—oh, I'm sorry, go ahead."

"No-no, you go ahead."

"Um…Hey!" Miriya took out her cell phone. "Would you want to exchange phone numbers? Maybe if we're ever in the area, which I guess we almost always are, we could meet for lunch or coffee, like today, you know? Talk girl talk."

"That'd be nice." Lorena smiled and took out her cell

phone. They exchanged numbers.

Sofia de Amor opened her front door wearing nothing but a lime green bathrobe. Thunder and lightning exploded and flashed nearby, revealing the wet form of the private eye, Abel Solorzano. Water poured from the brim of a black hat held low, half-covering his nervous eyes.

"Mr. Solorzano," Sofia said. "What are you doing here? What is it?"

"Mrs. de Amor, may I come in, please?"

Sofia clutched at her chest, pulling her bathrobe tightly around her.

"It's late, Mr. Solorzano."

"Please, I won't be long. I have some startling news to tell you. It's about your husband."

"Arturo? Is he okay? Please come in."

Sofia closed the door securely behind Abel, who took slow, methodical steps into the elegant foyer of the de Amor home. He kept his hands in his pockets and quickly scanned the room he entered.

"Have you heard from him?"

"Yes, I have. I'm afraid I have bad news."

Sofia got wide-eyed.

"What? What is it?"

"Your husband is not coming home, Mrs. de Amor. He has run off for good with Carmen, your housekeeper."

Sofia brought her hand to her mouth, gasping with mild shock.

"So it's true," she mumbled, tears welling up in her eyes.

"I'm afraid there's more."

She turned her back to Abel.

"I don't know if I can take any more, Mr. Solorzano," she said, shaking her head. "My life feels over. My heart has been crushed. I feel like dying."

Abel removed his hands from his pockets. They were covered in black leather gloves. A length of short nylon rope was curled in his right hand as he approached Sofia from behind.

"NO! Look out!" Lorena yelled at the TV.

That same evening, across town, Miriya's white breath left her mouth in quick staccato puffs as she trotted through the crisp late evening air in high black leather boots. *Click-clack-click-clack* they echoed across the rain-dampened concrete patio of the Starbucks at Hill Avenue and Walnut Street. A green and navy blue striped scarf warmed her neck. She wore a gray turtleneck sweater and a knee-length darker gray wool skirt over her restless legs.

Once inside the warm coffeehouse, Miriya bypassed the line and breathlessly took a secluded table where she could talk in private. She brought her cell phone up to her ear while checking out her surroundings.

"Hey, sweetie," she said, grinning from ear to ear. "How are you…I missed you last night. Wha—*no*, I just didn't hear from you…No! The BF was…Who knows where he was? But *I*, on the other hand, was home all by my lonesome…*Yes*!…I miss you. I haven't seen you for a while…I know-I know, I'm sorry…You know how hard it is for me to get away sometimes…Oh, c'mon! Look, I'll make it up to you, I promise…Okay…Okay, baby doll, I'll talk to you later…Bye."

Hmmm.

He didn't even ask if he could see me. He seemed in a hurry to get off the phone, and wasn't his usual cheerful self. Miriya wondered if he was seeing someone new. She conceded to herself that he would have been within his right if he were. Still, the thought made her melancholy.

Miriya checked her watch. Within minutes, Veronica pushed open the front door and stood hovering near the line like a strikebreaker. Miriya waved to attract her attention. Finally, Veronica noticed her friend and gave a head nod with a half smile. The two of them had not seen each other in over a week. While Veronica secretly blamed Arturo for this, Miriya felt that it was because Karen was back in town.

Veronica leaned over as Miriya stood, the two of them catching each other in an awkward hug, and exchanged greetings.

"How are things with Karen?"

"Fine. She's getting along well," Veronica said woodenly.

Miriya frowned.

"Are you guys doing well?"

"You mean are we still together?"

"Yeah."

"Uh, I don't feel like talking about it."

Miriya was mildly taken aback. This was not like Veronica.

"Okay," Miriya said, suddenly at a loss for words.

"Suzy told me you met someone new—a new friend. Some lawyer, or something?"

"Oh, no, she's a legal secretary. But, yeah, she's a new friend."

Veronica nodded without emotion.

"What's her name?"

"Lorena Sandoval."

Veronica raised an eyebrow.

"On a last name basis, huh?"

"You know I don't associate with people whose last names I don't know." Miriya felt her smile fading.

"Where does she work?"

"At a law office in Old Town."

"Do you guys talk a lot?"

"We've talked on the phone a couple of times, and got together for lunch yesterday. My gosh, you seem pretty interested in this."

Veronica shrugged her shoulders and looked away.

"I just care about you, you know? I'm interested in what goes on in your life, like any good friend would be."

Miriya nodded.

"What's up with Arturo?"

"What about him?"

"How are things going with him?"

"I don't want to talk about it," Miriya said, as if rehearsed.

Veronica smiled.

"Touché, I guess."

"Yeah, you guessed right," Miriya said, leaning in closer to the girl. "I'm your friend, and I care about you and am interested in what's going on in *your* life. So don't pull that 'I-don't-wanna-talk-about-it' shit with me."

Miriya said this without a trace of anger or sarcasm, but in the warm manner her friends had grown accustomed to and thankful for. Veronica finally smiled at Miriya.

"I know-I know. Things are just tough right now with Karen. She's like, in love with me. She thinks that we can just go back to how things were before. So much has happened to both of us since then."

"Have you discussed these feelings with her?"

"Yeah, sort of. She's already kind of down about her arm, but she just gets more depressed when I try to tell her that things just aren't the same."

"Well, can't things between the two of you be different good? Kind of like a new beginning, or something?"

"I don't know. I don't know if that's what I want right now."

Miriya considered this.

"You mean, you don't know if you want to be with Karen anymore?"

Veronica nodded. "Yeah, probably. I'm just not feeling it with her like that."

"You need to tell her, Veronica. You should be honest with her. She's in a vulnerable state right now. You don't want to lead her on."

Veronica slunk down in her chair with a low moan, as both her hands went up to her face.

"Ugh! I don't know what to do with her!"

"Yeah, you do. You just don't want to do it."

Veronica thrust out her arms.

"Look at you! You're so lucky. Why can't we have found the partner of our dreams like you! Despite any problems, I know that you and Arturo will get married, you'll have a big rock on your finger and you'll be set!"

Miriya looked unemotionally at Veronica, as if she were going over in her head the wild claim her friend had just made. Veronica frowned when she realized that Miriya wasn't looking at her, in her eyes, but was staring at a point somewhere near her nose or mouth, her mind far, far away.

"You can't be sure of that," Miriya finally said, almost mumbling.

"Huh?"

Miriya looked into Veronica's eyes now.

"You can't be sure of anything like that. Who's to say if

Arturo, or anyone, is the man of my dreams—*please*! The man of *my* dreams doesn't even exist. Not anymore."

Her voice trailed off. She stared at the floor for a moment, her eyes getting shiny. She then composed herself and forced a smile for Veronica.

"He lives only in my imagination: in heaven, looking down at me from the stars. Whom are we kidding? There's no perfect person 'of our dreams.' True love is elusive, just a myth, that we spend our lives yearning for—chasing—even when we have someone good right by our side, who treats us well, and is kind to us. Nobody's ever satisfied with what they have because they never believe they're worthy of it. Then we settle for things we can see: good looks, money, a fancy car, a big cock, and we tell ourselves we deserve those things. And we fool ourselves into believing we're happy."

Miriya shook her head.

"Arturo's hardly the man of my dreams. He's the man of my dream of getting married someday, as I'm slowly realizing."

Miriya grew quiet as she thought about Lorena. What would she think about this pitiful clinging to Arturo? Lorena would never settle for a man like Arturo.

"You wanna know what I think about all the time?" Miriya looked at Veronica.

"That I've spent all this time with Arturo; invested all this energy, only because Arturo was the one I thought was in the best position to marry me. Is that what I want? Is that what any of us wants—just someone who'll marry us? A dear friend of mine once told me that a woman gets married to fulfill a childhood dream, but a man gets married only to keep the girl, so that she won't sleep with anybody else. Who wants that shit?"

That weekend, Steven had a family event to attend on Saturday night, so he told Lorena that they couldn't go out. Lorena hinted that she was interested in meeting his parents. He told her that the event was not an appropriate setting to introduce her to his folks. Lorena had been slightly hurt by this, but when Steven explained that he wanted it to be more of a private affair, like a dinner with just him, Lorena, and his mom and dad, she understood. The fact that Steven was planning a formal introduction to his family pleased her conservative sensibilities.

So instead, Lorena called Miriya, who was home alone thanks to a "business meeting" that Arturo and his partners had to take, and suggested they get together. Miriya was all for it, saying they should dress up for the occasion.

When Lorena picked Miriya up, she asked the Argentinean for a special favor.

"Would you mind," Lorena started, hesitantly, "accompanying me to St. Andrews so I can light a candle and pray for a friend of mine? He was killed in Iraq a year ago today."

Miriya was immediately empathetic.

"Oh. I'm sorry about that. S-sure, of course." Miriya thought about Karen. "Were you two very close?"

"Yeah. He was my brother's best friend. He kinda had a crush on me but nothing ever came of it." Lorena cleared her throat.

Miriya nodded while Lorena drove in silence. Miriya had never seen her new friend this solemn before and thought it best to leave Lorena to her thoughts. Lorena's outfit made more sense, now, as Miriya had wondered about the nondescript black dress, long, black wool overcoat, and black woolen scarf. Lorena looked like she was going to church.

Lorena parked across the street from the large, venerable Catholic Church—one of Pasadena's most famous religious edifices. Miriya couldn't remember the last time she had set foot in a church—last Easter? She was raised Catholic and had attended a parochial school or two, received her First Communion, and, if asked, would say she believed in God. Still, Miriya couldn't help feeling out of place as the two women walked up to the south side entrance in their heels, and wondered if she was dressed inappropriately with tight blue jeans and a turquoise halter-top, and a light, white wool sweater.

Lorena made the sign of the cross, kissing her thumb as they passed a gray stone statue of the Virgin Mary just outside the large wood doors. Once inside, Lorena dipped her fingers in a pool of holy water and crossed herself again.

Miriya followed her example and was soon taken in by the quiet grandeur of the interior. She craned her neck as her eyes followed the giant polished marble columns leading to the high ceiling. There was a smattering of devout worshippers seated here and there in the pews, some kneeling with hands clasped and heads down in prayer.

Lorena led Miriya to a side alcove where several rows of lit and unlit candles glowed on a rack before the iconic statue of a crowned baby Jesus, tucked inside an elaborate marble shrine, atop which sat a larger marble statue of a seated Christ. Lorena lit one of the candles and knelt before the altar, apparently unconcerned with whether Miriya felt like joining her or not.

Miriya knelt next to Lorena and slowly brought her hands together as if to pray. She felt a haunting peace envelop her and could not take her eyes off those of the baby Jesus.

Why are you here?

Miriya felt the question pop into her head suddenly, as if someone behind her had tapped her shoulder. She glanced at Lorena, whose head was bowed, eyes shut tight. Tears rolled down Lorena's cheeks as she cried in muffled sobs. Miriya reached out and placed a soothing hand on Lorena's back, rubbing her gently, as a sudden sadness enveloped her, too. Why was she here, she wondered? How did she get to this place in her life?

Miriya thought about Fabio and what he would have

said to her. She looked out toward the baby Jesus. Daddy, where are you? Can you hear me now?

Miriya closed her eyes.

What am I doing with my life? I'm so sorry I've wasted so much time, Daddy. I'm sorry I never gave you grand-children. Please forgive me. I'm going to get serious, I promise. I'm going to get my life together. I'm going to make things work with Arturo. I'm going to cut out those things that are keeping me from giving myself fully to him.

Miriya took a deep breath and could almost hear her heart beating in her chest.

You will do the right thing, *mono.* Miriya opened her teary eyes as the thought flashed through her mind.

"Daddy?" she called out in a whisper. Lorena wiped her face and turned to Miriya. Lorena saw that Miriya, too, was overcome by some hidden emotion, and felt suddenly closer to her. Epiphanies came in all forms and perhaps Miriya had just had one, or was praying for her dreams to come true. Either way, Lorena was happy to see that her friend was moved by the experience.

Lorena put her arm around Miriya's shoulder. Miriya leaned her head close to Lorena's and the two of them held each other, sniffling and wiping away the last tears. They composed themselves and finally stood, smiling at each other awkwardly as if they had just shared a sacred rite of sisterhood.

The two women were more talkative on the drive to the

Chalet nightclub in nearby Eagle Rock. They didn't talk about their experience at St. Andrews much, as Lorena was more interested in learning about Miriya and Arturo's relationship. Miriya went into detail about their four-year history, and about Arturo's big plans for their future, and how he was getting busier with business meetings.

"On a *Saturday* night?" Lorena asked Miriya.

"Yeah, right! *Exactly*! Business meeting, my ass." Miriya shook her head. "More like a guys' night out, I'm sure. They're probably going to a strip club or something."

"Does Arturo go to strip clubs?"

"C'mon, all guys do," Miriya said with authority. "It's like watching sports to them."

"That doesn't bother you?" Lorena frowned.

"I've been to one with him before. Spearmint Rhino in Hollywood."

Lorena was surprised.

"They're not hookers or anything, just strippers. So I'm not too worried. Still, you never know when Arturo and his buddies get together. Who knows what they're up to?"

If Arturo's even with his buddies, Lorena thought.

"What about you? Have you ever been to a strip club?" Miriya was curious about straight and narrow Lorena.

"Yeah, just recently, in fact. For my twenty-first birthday my sister and her husband, and my brother and his girlfriend took me to Vegas, where we went to Olympic Gardens."

"Oh, yeah, I've been there." Miriya smiled to herself. "What'd you think?"

"It was fun. I was drunk off my ass and my brother tried to buy me a lap dance with one of the female strippers." Lorena smiled mischievously. "I declined but I watched him get one. Later, one of the male strippers pulled open my top and said I had nice *chi-chi*s."

They laughed.

Miriya was on her third Cosmopolitan at the Chalet, a hipster bar in northeastern Los Angeles. Lorena was slowly sipping her second apple martini, and they had both settled into an interesting evening of people watching.

"Oh-oh, look over there," Miriya said, making a motion with her head. "It's the, uh, five nerdy guys with the one kinda cute nerdy girl."

"Huh?" Lorena strained to see where, among the thick crowd, Miriya was pointing. "Oh, yeah, I see 'em."

"You know she's either seeing one of the guys, or they all have a crush on her and she only likes one of them, though."

"Oh, right." Lorena knew the situation. "And he's probably too shy to do anything about it."

"The one I like is the two guy buddies who go out together, and one of them has a girlfriend, so he brings her along, too."

Lorena chuckled.

"I think I saw them here," she said, sipping from her martini.

"Why would I want my boyfriend's buddies to go out on a date with us?" Miriya frowned, holding out her hands. "You know the buddy always has a crush on the girl anyway! Guys are so lame!"

Lorena nodded and took another sip of her drink. She caught Miriya's gaze and the two women broke into laughter.

"You know." Lorena took a serious tone. "Like I mentioned before, uh, aside from my family, and this girl at work, who I really only talk to on the phone, I don't have any close friends like this." Lorena made a sweeping gesture between the two of them.

"Really?" Miriya still found this hard to believe.

"Yeah. It's refreshing."

"I know I definitely don't have any friends like you."

"How so?" Lorena was curious.

"I don't know. It's hard for me to put my finger on it sometimes. With you it's like there's no hidden agenda. You're not trying to compete with me. I feel like I can tell you anything."

Miriya sighed while looking in her glass.

"When I was a kid," she continued, "and started school here in the States, I hated being Argentinean. Kids in school were so mean, and no kid wants to be different. I was called all kinds of nasty things. Told to go back to Argentina, that I was a 'foreigner'—God, I *hate* that word! They even thought I was Mexican!"

"God forbid," Lorena mumbled.

"I'm sorry," Miriya said, touching Lorena's thigh. "Nothing against Mexicans—it's just…Nobody wants to be confused as anything else! I mean, I was as American as they were!"

Lorena nodded.

"And I became as American as I could be," Miriya added, "even to the point of responding in English when-ever my parents spoke to me in Spanish."

"I remember doing that," Lorena said, smiling.

"Really? See—"

"We all did that at one point."

"—I would have thought that you were always so con-tent and sure about your heritage: the way you talk about your family and how fun all the cultural things are, how you look forward to going back to Mexico all the time."

"*Girl*! I'd much rather go to Argentina, trust me!" Lo-rena chuckled.

"I know. I'm fine with it now, but it's so…*different* for someone with my experience to meet someone with your experience."

"Miriya, we were never allowed to do anything grow-ing up that wasn't family-related. I could never go to friends' houses, or-or play in the street. All I knew was Mexican! You're nine years older than me. You came from a different era and probably went to high school with a lot of *blanquitos*. By the time I was in school, it was all brown and black. Everyone looked like me and spoke Spanish. I never felt all that different."

Miriya's voice was subdued: "I never thought about that."

"Girl, I need to get you back in touch with your *Latina* roots!" Lorena downed the last of her drink. "And I know just the trick."

"This I gotta hear!" Miriya looked skeptical.

"We need to go on a good ol' fashioned road trip."

"Huh?" Miriya wrinkled her nose. "Where?"

"My family's going to Tecate soon. Whenever we go for a long weekend, we usually drive down to San Felipe. You'd love it! The beach, the food, everything! It's not Argentina, but it might give you a new outlook. Kind of a way to, uh, recharge the batteries, as they say."

Miriya considered this. She had only been to Tijuana and Rosarito—the usual tourist traps south of the border.

"Deal!" Miriya blurted. "I'd love that. How exciting!"

PART SIX:
TELENOVELA

Karen sat barelegged, wearing only gray sweat shorts and a white tank top, her back propped up against her bed's pillow-cushioned headboard. Her left arm was tucked awkwardly behind and around the small of Veronica's back. Veronica was sure that this position was uncomfortable for the girl, and kept squirming and shifting her butt to give Karen's arm more breathing room. Veronica was fine with this small display of affection, but would not cuddle any closer to Karen or lay her head on the veteran's shoulder, as the two of them watched TV.

Karen's hair, which hadn't been washed in two days, slipped off her shoulders like black spaghetti. She wore no make-up and was breaking out near the corners of her mouth. Veronica had heard that Karen had lost a lot of weight in Iraq. Looking at her now, Veronica saw that Karen had gained most of it back, and then some, while recovering at the various hospitals along the way. Karen wore a white, sock-like covering around her stump.

"You ever watch this show?" Karen asked, raising her stump toward the TV.

"Nah, it's one of those, uh, *telenovelas*, huh?"

"How do you know what a *telenovela* is?" Karen chuckled at the thought.

"Miriya. Her mom watches these."

"Oh." But of course.

"Is it any good?"

"Yeah, this one's pretty good—*Sofia de Amor*. It's about this rich married woman named Sofia de Amor, whose husband is having an affair with the hot house-keeper, Carmen. Sofia starts to suspect her unfaithful husband, Arturo, is up to no good, so she hires a private detective to follow him around."

"Oh yeah? Does the private dick catch him?"

"Yeah, not only that. Sofia's gonna probably take her jerk husband to the cleaners in a nasty divorce. So Arturo actually hires the private dick to *kill* Sofia for $10,000. The bastard has over a million bucks in life insurance policies out on his wife, so the private-eye-turned-killer has to make it look like an accident."

"But guess what?" Lupe Mercado said to her boss Chet the next morning. "While homeboy tries to kill Sofia, she fights him off and he actually ends up getting it!"

"The private dick gets killed," Chet replied, frowning in

mild disgust, "by this, uh, Sofia character?"

"Well, actually, it's an accident, but everyone *thinks* she did it, including the police, and the Mafia, whom the private dick owed money to, so now she has all these dudes after her, and she has to prove that Arturo is the one who tried to kill her."

"Bet he's still trying to kill her, too," Chet added, amazingly following along.

"You got it, boss man."

"And you Mexicans like this stuff?"

"'*You Mexicans*'? You try watchin' it! You'd be hooked, too!"

Chet considered this.

"Hot Mexican women? Like them wacky variety shows?"

Lupe frowned.

"How do you know about those?"

Chet shrugged.

"Flippin' through the channels," he blurted. "These Mexican chicks in bikinis are always dancing around on stage—boobs bouncing around."

Lupe shook her head.

"Them no-vellas like that?" Chet raised an eyebrow.

"Yeah, Chet. Hot Mexican women with big boobs bouncing around."

"Hmmm," he grunted.

Steven cuddled up next to Lorena on her living room couch later that night. She had invited him over to watch *Sofia de Amor*. While holding his hand, she felt a slight vibration and realized that a call was coming in on his cell phone. Steven got rigid and seemed reluctant to check the caller ID screen. Lorena looked up into his eyes.

"You can answer it," she said.

He sighed and reached for his phone. Sure enough; it was *her*.

What do I do, he asked himself? Do I lie or tell the truth? Lying has never got me anything in the past but in trouble. Maybe I'll be honest this time. I really like Lorena.

"Sweetie," he began somberly.

"What is it?"

"This person who's calling me." He held up his phone but Lorena couldn't see the screen. "She's a girl I was seeing before I met you."

"Oh." Lorena didn't know what else to say but was pleasantly surprised that he was being honest. She held her breath and waited for more.

"But I've kind of been trying to phase her out. I really haven't talked to her lately. I haven't even seen her since we've been going out. I think she's wondering what happened to me."

"Maybe she's hurt," Lorena said diplomatically. "Why don't you just tell her how you feel?"

"Huh?"

Lorena sat up straight, carefully choosing her words.

"If you haven't talked to her because you've been see-ing me, it must mean that you are more interested in me than her—I hope."

Steven smiled.

"And if so, being that I, too, am interested in you, I would want you to not see anybody else. I wouldn't want girls that you were seeing before me calling you. To me, that means that you would have to make it clear to her or anyone else, that you are seeing someone new and that you would like them to stop calling you, out of respect for your new relationship—that is, *if* this is how you feel."

Steven considered this.

"Does this mean you want us to be exclusive?" he asked.

Now this took Lorena by surprise. She hadn't thought of it quite that way.

"Well, yes," she responded slowly. "I guess…Yes, I do want that."

She paused.

"Don't you?" she added.

Steven nodded.

His cell phone rang, indicating he had a message.

"Are you, uh, gonna let her know?" Lorena raised an eyebrow.

"Yup. And it shouldn't be a big deal, since she has a boyfriend she's practically engaged to anyway."

Lorena was taken aback.

"Wuuuuuut," she hummed. "And she was seeing you, too? *Maldita!*"

Steven smiled nervously.

"Mal-dita? What does that mean?"

"It means 'bad girl'—evil!"

"Well," he said, feeling slightly defensive. "She was okay. She was just unhappy. Her boyfriend's a jerk."

"I don't like her," Lorena said, turning back to the TV.

Arturo de Amor and Carmen ran from his red Ferrari into the lobby of the secluded resort hotel. It rained hard but Carmen could see the name of the place on a wet, low, stone wall—Hotel Las Tres Mujeres. Arturo's hair, now dyed black, was pulled back in a ponytail, and he wore a black leather jacket. Carmen wore a tan raincoat and tall black leather boots.

"Why this place, Arturo?" she asked as they stood under the canopy near the main entrance. Arturo scanned the area to make sure they weren't followed.

"I've traced Sofia to this hotel. We can finish her off once and for all!"

"What about the gangsters, Arturo? Let them take care of her! I want to run away with you!"

"In time, my love. This is something I have to do."

Carmen bit her lip, unsure of where this was going or what trouble lay ahead.

"Carmen's *hot*!" Steven said.

Lorena playfully hit him.

"Arturo's *hot*!" she countered.

"Yeah, but he's a mal-dita."

"*Maldito, gringo!*—dee-*toh*! Not *dita*."

"Oh."

Lorena leaned over and kissed him.

Sofia pulled her hair back and put it in a ponytail. She wore a tight gray sweater, blue jeans, and brown boots. She was on the run and ready for action. When she looked out of the window of her second story hotel room, she saw two men dressed in black get out of a sinister-looking sedan with tinted windows. Her big, brown eyes widened with fear and she turned away, putting her hand to her mouth.

"It's them!" she said aloud.

"Who're those guys?" Steven asked, pointing to the TV.

"Those are the gangsters. Remember I told you about them? That detective, Abel Solorzano, owed them money and now they're gonna try to get the dough out of Sofia or kill her."

"*Oooh*! The plot thickens!"

"So, uh, when are you going to talk to this girl you were seeing?"

Steven turned to her. Lorena was looking at the TV, playing it cool.

"I'll tell her tomorrow."

"Over the phone or in person?"

Steven considered this.

"These things are best handled in person."

"Where are you going, Arturo?" Carmen asked, as they settled into their hotel room.

"I've got to find out what room Sofia is in. I've got to play it cool. You wait here and I'll be back for you."

Carmen frowned.

"No, don't, Arturo! I'm afraid. Don't kill Sofia. We've caused her enough pain. She was kind to me. Let's just run away together and forget about this place."

Arturo grabbed her arms forcefully and shook her.

"You listen to me, Carmen! Don't get cold feet on me now! You don't know what kind of pressure I'm under, what I stand to lose! I must do this. Now, stay here and do what I tell you!"

Arturo stepped into the hallway and closed the door behind him. He tiptoed past the quiet, closed doors of the hotel's many rooms. He saw the cleaning woman's supply cart standing alone outside an open door. This was his chance.

Arturo knocked gently on the open door before stepping into the room. There was a bathroom on his left. When he looked inside, he was surprised to see a young, tan girl of about eighteen or nineteen, barefoot and on her knees, scrubbing the tub. She wore a tight-fitting housekeeping uniform with short skirt. Her blouse was unzipped down to her mid-chest, exposing ample cleavage glistening with sweat.

The girl stood and looked at Arturo with big, blue eyes. Her sensuous mouth, lips slightly parted, moved in a quiet loss for words. She had curly, black hair that clung to her thin face, wet with rain, sweat, or both.

"Hello," Arturo said, himself at a loss for words.

"Hola, Señor."

"What's your name?"

"Maribel."

"How old are you, Maribel? You look so young."

"I'm eighteen."

"My name is Arturo. I'm a guest here—new to this place."

"Are you alone?"

"Yes. Yes, I am."

Maribel smiled to herself while giving him the once-over.

"Oh, *snap!*" Lorena yelled while covering her mouth. She broke out into laughter as Steven pointed at the screen.

"Arturo's gonna fuck the housekeeper, watch!" he yelled.

"*Ssssh!*" Lorena put her finger to her lips. "My *abuelita!*"

"Ooops! Sorry."

Victor Cass

Steven was suddenly aghast as *Sofia de Amor* ended for the night.

"What the…!"

"What?" Lorena was still chuckling.

"It's over?"

"Yeah. Come back tomorrow. Same bat time, same bat channel."

"Hey! How do you know about that?"

Suzy Hovsepian was on a roll as Nathalie and Taylor sat in front of her in various stages of apprehension and boredom. The three friends filled the dull air in a quiet corner of the near-empty Mecca Room at Louise's Trattoria in Old Pasadena. A dazed Ethiopian waiter with a five-o-clock shadow and a bulging forehead cleaned off the remnants of their lunch as Taylor tore off pieces of a remaining roll and gently placed them in her mouth.

"Can you believe this fucking guy?" Suzy said with her hands outstretched.

The waiter looked dismayed.

"Not you," Nathalie said blankly. The waiter looked relieved.

"He's been telling me for three weeks since we've been hanging out, how much he cares about me, how he's never met any girl like me before, and then this bitch calls him, who he's been ga-ga over for years, and tells him that she and her husband got a divorce, and now he's all happy because he thinks he has a chance with her.

Telenovela

"He tells me—while we're on a *date*—that he has to leave to go be with her! I looked at him like, 'You're fuckin' kidding me, right?' And then he says: 'Suzy, look, I gotta be honest with you. I've been fucking two other girls since we've been hanging out and I still like this one girl and now I gotta see if she and I can make this work.'"

Nathalie frowned and gave Taylor a look. Taylor shook her head.

"Is this normal?" Suzy asked them. "Is something wrong with me? This fuckin' asshole tells me to my face that he's fucking some other bitch."

Why don't you hurry up and fuckin' get laid, Nathalie thought. I'm tired of you being a virgin.

"He's a shithead loser, just like I told you," Nathalie mumbled. "Why do you still hang out with him?"

"I don't! I told him to fuck off to his face! Go fuck your little whores, I told him. I'm glad I didn't give it up to that piece of shit. I deserve better than that. Who says that to a girl they're dating?"

Taylor kicked Nathalie under the table. Nathalie frowned at her.

"What?" Suzy caught them.

"All right, are you gonna talk about this loser all day? I'm bored with this conversation," Taylor said, almost yawning.

"I'm sorry." Suzy frowned and slunk down in her chair. "I just had to vent."

An awkward silence hung over them.

"Are you gonna tell her?" Taylor got wide-eyed at Nathalie.

"Shut up." Nathalie avoided Suzy's perplexed stare.

"What are you guys up to?" Suzy folded her arms across her chest.

Nathalie took a deep breath.

"Look, we're all friends, right?" she began.

Suzy was tight-lipped.

"I just can't keep this in anymore, especially since Taylor already knows about it. I feel awkward you not knowing." She was looking at Suzy.

"Not knowing what?"

"Oh, Jesus Christ!" Taylor sat up straight for once. "Nathalie's fucking Arturo!"

Suzy recoiled in shock.

"*Arturo? Miriya's* Arturo?"

"Yup." Nathalie looked away.

"Are you guys shitting me?"

Nathalie shook her head and then looked up into the horrified eyes of her old friend.

"What the fuck, Nathalie? How long has this been going on?"

"For about a year-and-a-half."

Suzy shook her head with her eyes shut tight.

"*What?* A *year-and-a-half!* Does Miriya know?"

"Of course not," Taylor said, looking at Suzy as if she

were an idiot.

"I can't believe this shit. Miriya's our friend!"

"You better not say shit to her." Nathalie flared up. "Or to Veronica. She has no idea either."

"Veronica'd probably be glad, she's so in love with Miriya," Taylor muttered.

"Shut up!" Suzy snapped. "Why are you doing this to her, Nathalie? You're gonna fuck up all our friendships."

"This is between Miriya and Arturo. It's not my fault that he cheats on her. They're the ones with the problems."

"This is fuckin' great! How can I look Miriya in the eye now?"

"You better find a way." Nathalie pointed at her. "Don't fuck my shit up. I'm trusting you."

"I gotta go," Suzy said, taking a last sip from her glass of water. She stood and left in a huff.

Nathalie looked restless.

"Let her go," Taylor said, rolling her eyes. "She talks too much anyway. You know why guys treat her like shit? Because she never sleeps with any of them! Who's the Virgin Mary holding out for anyway, Prince Charming? With her list of qualities she's looking for—in an *Armenian man*—c'mon! She's gonna be single forever!"

Look who's talking, Nathalie thought.

"I just hope she doesn't blab to Miriya." Nathalie shook her head.

"Don't worry," Taylor said. "Suzy's dumb but she's

not stupid. She knows Miriya wouldn't believe her, and would end up hating her. The messenger always gets shot, right?"

"Well, don't you have it all figured out." Nathalie crossed her arms.

"Miriya!" Taylor grimaced. "Everyone always talks about her like she's a fuckin' princess—like she has it all! She doesn't have shit. She has a loser boyfriend who cheats on her."

"Yeah, with *me*! Thanks! I happen to like him."

"Oh, get real! Arturo's not for you."

"Yeah? Who is, Dr. Ruth?"

"It ain't him, trust me. He's no Mr. Right, just like Miriya isn't the perfect woman. Miss Happy-go-Lucky! I'm sick of her chipper, perky self. She's living proof that you never know what goes on behind closed doors."

Nathalie frowned at Taylor.

"You know what, Taylor?" Nathalie started in on her. "You need to develop your personality, too. Bring it up to speed with your pretty looks."

"*Excuse me?*"

"Jealousy is unbecoming on you, so check it at the door."

Nathalie stood and gathered her things.

Later that afternoon, Steven stood nervously in front of the door. When Miriya opened it, he felt queasy as the butterflies started again in the pit of his stomach. She smiled warmly at him, her sparkling brown eyes squinting at the corners.

"Hey, baby." Miriya reached for him and hugged him tightly.

"Hey, sweetie," Steven replied, with a somber but loving tone.

Miriya held his face and brought her soft lips to his. She kissed him gently, at first, like they used to, slow and fleeting. Instinctively their tongues met, and passion filled their hungry mouths. Miriya pulled him into her apartment and shut the door behind her. She led him to her couch and pulled him down on top of her.

For a moment, Steven couldn't remember why he was there. All he knew was that he was holding *her*—Miriya Fronzini—a woman he had fallen hard for over a year ago. Now, he was on top of her on her couch, where they had made love countless times before. Miriya tugged at his hips as she brought her bare foot up behind him, pulling him closer to her body.

"I missed you so much," she whispered into his ear. "Where've you gone?"

"Oh, baby, baby…"

Lorena.

Steven frowned as a wave of guilt washed over him. He pulled back and almost struggled to compose himself, sitting up straighter on the couch. Miriya leaned up on her elbows and stared at him.

"Hey, what's the matter, babe?"

"Miriya, I…"

Steven looked at his hands. Miriya licked her lips and pulled her leg out from behind him as she, too, sat up on the couch.

"What's going on?" she asked, calmly. "Talk to me."

Steven considered his words carefully.

"I, uh, I can't do this anymore."

Miriya stiffened.

"What do you mean?" Her tone was serious, harder. Steven had never heard her voice sound like this.

"This isn't me, babe—the other guy? It's just not for me anymore. I have very strong feelings for you. I always have. You know, I used to think, just stick it out. She'll leave Arturo eventually. Who was I kidding? You even made it perfectly clear to me that despite your feelings for me, you were never going to leave him. Despite all of our 'I adore yous' and our 'Madly In Love With U' texts, I knew that you'd never leave him. How do you expect me to feel?"

Miriya said nothing and crossed her arms.

"Recently I met someone—someone who didn't have a boyfriend. She's a good woman, and we're getting feelings for each other."

Miriya nodded her head slowly and glared at him.

"So that's why I hadn't heard from you."

"I'm sorry I didn't tell you sooner. I just…I guess a little part of me held out some hope for you and me. But I've realized that I want to pursue something meaningful with this other woman."

Although Miriya's eyes were shimmering, she forced a tight-lipped smile.

"So that's it, huh?" She reached out for his arm but thought the better of it. Miriya brought her hands up to her face and rubbed her eyes slowly. "I don't know what to say."

Steven, too, seemed drained of words.

"I don't think I'm even in a position to say anything," she added. "After all, I'm the one with the boyfriend."

Steven nodded slowly, feeling a burning in his eyes.

"Yup."

Miriya leaned forward and touched his face. He turned toward her as she looked into his eyes.

"I wish it was you I met years ago instead of him," she said. "I mean that. I love Arturo, but I know I would have loved you more."

Steven looked away, his face wrinkling.

"I don't need to hear this."

"Sorry."

She stood up. Steven knew this was his cue to leave. He wiped his eyes and put on his best face. As he stood, he tried to find the words.

"I'm glad I know you."

Miriya nodded.

"I wish you the best," she said.

As Miriya walked him to the door she took a deep breath. Her heart felt like it would jump out of her chest and grab Steven before he walked out of her life. As he glanced back at her, all she could think to do was to say:

"You're lucky I'm not a psycho!" She laughed uneasily.

The door closed behind him, and he was no more. Miriya leaned into the stark white door and placed her outstretched arms against it. She touched her face to the cold wood and pressed her chest into its hardness. She recognized again the emptiness of her life and burst into tears. Slowly she slid to the floor and cried herself into the fetal position.

Nathalie drove to Arturo's apartment and parked several houses away. She sat in her car, remembering what Arturo had told her about showing up at his place unannounced. Her leg bounced and she shifted uneasily in her seat. She finally decided against knocking on his door but thought it best to call him and let him know what happened.

"Hello?" Arturo's voice was businesslike.

"It's me." Nathalie looked down at her fingernails.

"Hey, baby, what's up? Where are you?"

"Just driving around—running some errands."

"Cool. Listen, I can't really talk right now."

Nathalie frowned.

"I think I fucked up," she said with a sigh. She felt a

stomachache coming on.

"Why? What happened?" There was a new, panicky edge to his voice.

"I told Suzy about you and me."

"*What*? What the fuck! Why?"

"Relax!" Nathalie was irritated now. "It's no big deal..."

"No big deal? They're like best friends! That fuckin' bitch can't keep her big mouth shut."

"Veronica's her best friend! Besides, she won't say anything to Miriya. She knows better than that. Miriya would never believe her and would end up hating Suzy for even suggesting it—even if it were true."

"It *is* true! Jesus! I can't believe this shit!"

"God, settle down. It's not the end of the world."

"What's with you Middle Eastern women? You can't ever keep your big gossiping mouths shut!"

"Fuck you!" Nathalie yelled now. "What's with you sorry-ass South American men? You can't keep your *dicks* in your pants!"

"I don't have time for this bullshit. You're fuckin' my shit up!"

He hung up on her.

"Lame ass!" Nathalie snapped her cell phone shut.

She felt like crying.

"Boy, you wanted to get off the phone fast," Nathalie said aloud. She looked down the street and decided to sit there for a little while. Soon a silver Mercedes SLK230 sped up from behind Nathalie and stopped in front of a tight parking space directly in front of Arturo's apartment. Whoever was driving thought the better of trying to fit in it and double-parked.

Nathalie watched as the driver's side door opened and a tall, leggy blonde with an obscenely large boob job emerged, honking her horn.

"Oh, great," Nathalie mumbled. "Who the fuck is this?"

Sure enough, Arturo emerged from his bachelor pad sporting new highlights in his hair and a light gray Armani suit over a black T-shirt. He was all smiles and seemed to know the mystery woman very well as they hugged affectionately. Arturo got into the passenger side of the sporty coupe as the blonde disappeared inside. She slammed her door shut so hard that Nathalie felt it like a slap in the face. Ms. Thing revved the engine and drove off into the sunset.

Nathalie sat in her car for a moment looking out toward the empty street. She glanced up toward Arturo's apartment while processing what just happened. Sighing, Nathalie saw her reflection in her rear-view mirror and shook her head.

It was 8:00 PM when Miriya, Veronica, and Karen arrived at Jones Bar on Santa Monica Boulevard in Hollywood. Veronica had invited Miriya to join her and Karen for dinner and drinks. Miriya, not wanting to be alone tonight, had agreed to come. She hadn't felt like seeing

Arturo, who was supposed to be out with a client anyway. In fact, while Miriya was looking forward to seeing Veronica, the one who she really felt could lift her spirits was Lorena. Miriya had therefore asked Veronica if it would be okay if her new friend could come along. Veronica, interested in seeing who this Lorena person was, had readily approved. Lorena had been equally thrilled to hear from Miriya. Lorena asked Miriya if it would be okay if she brought along her new boyfriend. Miriya was pleased that it was shaping up to be a night out with a group of friends that did not include Suzy, Nathalie, and Taylor, and told Lorena what a wonderful idea that was, and how she couldn't wait to meet her new man.

Veronica smiled at Karen and stroked her thigh as the three of them squeezed into a dinner booth inside the boisterous watering hole. Jones was a low-lit, cozy hipster joint that doubled as an Italian restaurant, complete with red and white checkered tablecloths on top of small, cramped tables surrounding a central, angular bar, packed elbow to elbow with bed-headed Hollywood types, rockers, first-daters, and both tourist and ex-patriate Euro-trash. Jones was a favorite nightspot of Miriya and Veronica. Karen had never been there before. Lorena told Miriya that she had only been there twice.

"Where's your friend?" Veronica asked Miriya.

Miriya checked her watch.

"She should be here any minute. She called me and told

me they were just getting off the freeway."

A waitress with dyed blonde hair and bright red lipstick approached them and asked what they wanted to drink.

"I'll have a Stella." Veronica admired the server's Betty Page hairdo.

"Jack and Coke, please," Karen said. Her hair was down, her face made up, and she wore a black-beaded sweater over a cream camisole. The sleeve covering her stump was pinned up underneath her armpit, as she never wore her prosthesis out. Veronica thought that Karen looked beautiful tonight and had told her so.

"And for you?"

"Oh, uh, I'll have an apple martini." Miriya placed her gum inside a napkin and absently picked up her menu. She kept looking toward the door and scanning the bustling interior of the bar. Miriya saw Lorena walk past a burly doorman, and waved at her. Lorena saw her friend and acknowledged her with a big smile. Miriya thought that Lorena's black cocktail dress was slinky and elegant. She had never seen Lorena in date attire before.

"Hey, sweetie." Miriya stood from the edge of the booth and gave her friend a tight hug. Lorena kissed her cheek.

"Hi," she said. Lorena stood while waving delicately at Miriya's friends. "I'm Lorena." They all greeted her in turn.

"Here," Miriya said, making room. "Sit next to me.

Where's your boyfriend?"

"He's parking the car. He dropped me off because he thought we were late."

"Oh, well, I'm glad you came."

"Thanks for inviting me."

Lorena smiled at Veronica and Karen.

"I remember you two. I saw you guys once at Equator. You were in your uniform. Army, right?"

Karen nodded. "Yeah, Army Reserves."

"Still in?"

"Nah, I'm out. I wanted to stay in, but…"

She lifted her stump as Lorena nodded, unsure of what to say. At that moment, Miriya saw Steven approaching their table and her heart caught in her throat. What's he doing here? Steven had an equally shocked look on his face as he saw that Miriya sat next to Lorena.

"Hey, babe," Lorena said, reaching for him.

"Hey." Steven gave Miriya a confused look as she turned away in stunned silence. Her adrenaline made her heart feel like it was going to explode. He absently kissed Lorena and quietly sat next to her.

"This is my boyfriend, Steven." Lorena held his hand in hers, smiling proudly. "This is my friend, Miriya."

"Hey." Steven hardly looked at her.

"Hey." Miriya licked her lips and took a deep breath.

"These are her friends, Veronica and Karen."

"Hi, pleased to meet you guys." Steven limply shook

their hands. "Did you guys order already? I need a drink."

The waitress showed up with the first group's order. Miriya could not gulp her martini fast enough, while Lorena frowned at the strange air that had suddenly settled over them all. Veronica, too, had noticed a mood shift and glanced at Miriya, hoping to catch a clue as to what was going on. Steven, meanwhile, ordered a Tom Collins while Lorena got a Cosmopolitan.

"So, what's been going on?" Lorena touched Miriya's arm. Miriya turned to Lorena, her eyes watering, and took hold of her hand. Miriya squeezed gently and smiled the warmest smile she could muster.

"Nothing," Miriya said, softly, holding Lorena's gaze in hers. "I'm really happy for you."

"Are you okay?" Lorena asked.

"Yeah. I'll be fine." Miriya said. She quickly turned to Veronica and whispered: "Let's go to the little girl's room."

"Okay. Whatever. Excuse me." Veronica slid across the booth as Karen stood to let her out. Lorena also made way for Miriya's exit while noticing that she appeared to purposely avoid looking at Steven.

Miriya could not get to the restroom fast enough.

"Hey! Slow down. What's with you?" Veronica reached for Miriya's arm. Miriya turned toward her friend in the darkened hallway in front of the restroom entrance, and started crying.

"Miriya, what's going on?" Veronica stood in front of

her, arms akimbo.

"I'm sorry, Veronica," Miriya stammered, wiping her eyes.

"Sorry for what?"

"I'm sorry I never told you this. You're my oldest friend."

Veronica touched Miriya's shoulder, rubbing it gently.

"You can tell me anything, babe," Veronica added.

"For over a year now, I've been seeing someone else besides Arturo."

Veronica's eyes widened.

"*What?*"

"I can't believe I'm missing *Sofia de Amor* tonight," Karen said, chewing on some bread. They had ordered pizza.

"You watch that show, too?" Lorena almost laughed.

"It's the bomb!"

"I got Steven hooked on that shit," Lorena said, rubbing his shoulder. "Ain't that right, babe?"

He had a blank look on his face.

"Sweetie, uh."

Lorena turned to him.

"You okay? You've been acting weird ever since we got here."

"Can I talk to you outside?" he said, curiously looking away.

Chet plopped down on his sofa holding a beer and a TV dinner. He wore faded "Wonder Woman" boxer shorts, a stained white T-shirt, and grayish-white socks with a hole in the left big toe. He fumbled with his TV remote, but eventually found what he was looking for.

Arturo de Amor licked his lips while caressing Maribel with his eyes. The young housekeeper stood before him in the bedroom of the empty hotel room. Arturo watched her intently as he stepped back and closed the door behind him.

"Maribel, you are the most beautiful sight these eyes have ever seen."

"Arturo, I have never met a man like you—so strong and handsome."

Maribel unzipped her uniform some more while sitting down on the bed. She brought her bronzed, lithe legs up, pointing her toes out toward Arturo.

Chet frowned while taking a swig of his beer.

"Jesus," he mumbled. "Whatever she's saying, it sure sounds good."

He picked up a Spanish-English dictionary he had purchased earlier in the day.

"What the hell did she just say?" He clumsily flipped through the pages.

Carmen sat with her arms folded on the bed. She looked

at the nightstand clock and shook her head. She stood and walked briskly out of the room.

"Where are you, Arturo? I know you're up to some-thing!"

Lorena stood hugging herself and shivering in the night air. She frowned while watching Steven's face. He fought the urge to avoid her big soulful eyes.

"What's going on?" she asked, feeling that churning in the pit of her stomach that always signaled bad news.

"How do you know her—Miriya?"

"She's my friend—how do *you* know her?"

Steven sighed.

"She's—that girl. The one I was seeing." He scanned her face for any flash of horror or indignation. Instead she laughed.

"Yeah, right—you're shittin' me, huh?"

Steven shook his head.

"I wish I was."

Lorena's face grew cold.

"You're not shitting me?"

Steven stared at her as she looked down Santa Monica Boulevard toward West Hollywood. She blew on her hands while thinking and then turned toward him.

"Miriya's the one who called you the other night?" she asked, still in shock. "The one with the boyfriend whom you've been seeing for a year or so?"

"Yeah."

"The one you cut off for me?"

"Yeah."

Lorena spaced out, eyes wide and eyebrows arched.

"There's always something," she mumbled absently.

"What?"

"I don't believe this shit. Just take me home, dude."

"What? C'mon. Lorena."

"I'm serious. Take me home."

Veronica couldn't believe what Miriya had just told her. This evening was turning into a disaster for everyone.

"How come you never confided in me about this?"

"I don't know. I didn't know how you'd take it. I didn't want to be judged."

"Oh, who's gonna judge you?"

"You. Suzy. Everyone."

"Miriya, I'm your best friend. You shoulda said somethin'." Veronica shook her head. "Look, we better get back out there. Karen's probably sitting by herself."

"You think they left? I can't face them!"

"Trust me. I'm sure they left."

"Go check."

"Oh, Jesus!" Veronica ducked out into the restaurant and was back in an instant. "They're gone. I'm surprised Karen's still there."

Steven and Lorena drove in silence all the way back to Pasadena. He pulled into the short alley adjacent to her rear driveway gate and turned his engine off. The mood inside his car matched the dark quiet of their surroundings. Lorena looked sick as she tightened her lips over her teeth before licking them.

"Thank you for driving," she said flatly. She stared straight ahead as she slowly opened the passenger side door.

"Lorena, please!" he pleaded. "I had no idea. What can I do about it now?"

She turned to him.

"I know." She considered him and smiled politely. "I just need some time to think, that's all."

Steven sighed in dejected resignation.

"Do you mind? This is a lot to take in," she added. "We'll talk later."

"Fine. Sure. Okay."

He started the engine.

"Good night," Lorena said softly.

Steven leaned over slightly, unsure of what to do. Almost obligatorily, Lorena leaned across the center console and gave him a quick peck on the cheek. She then bolted out of his car.

Miriya, Veronica, and Karen walked the half block down Formosa Avenue toward Miriya's Volkswagen Jetta.

Karen had given Veronica an inquiring look, which she answered with an "I'll-tell-you-later" roll of her eyes. A silver Mercedes sped past them and parked near Miriya's car. The three women watched with mild curiosity as a tall blonde stepped out of the driver's seat. Veronica's eyes widened as Arturo got out of the passenger side. He obviously hadn't seen them, since he casually met the blonde on the sidewalk and put his arm around her waist. She threw her head back laughing at something he said.

Miriya stopped in her tracks and folded her arms across her chest.

"I can't believe this shit!" she said in a huff.

"What's going on?" Karen asked, looking between Miriya and Veronica.

"It's Arturo—Miriya's boyfriend," Veronica replied, matching Miriya's aggressive stance.

"Hey, Romeo!" Miriya yelled.

Arturo stopped and realized that his girlfriend was standing in front of him. He quickly disengaged from the blonde who stood with a cool confidence that annoyed Miriya.

"Hey, baby," he said, coming toward her.

"Don't touch me!" Miriya crossed her arms. "Who the fuck is she? Lemme guess—one of your clients?"

"C'mon, Miriya," Arturo said, holding out his arms. "She's an old friend of the family. Miriya, meet Annelise. Annelise, this is Miriya…"

Annelise barely acknowledged Miriya while throwing back her head and shifting her weight to one hip. Miriya noticed Annelise fold her arms under her large breasts.

"She's practically a cousin," Arturo said haltingly.

"Kissing cousins, I'm sure," Miriya huffed. "I can't fuckin' believe you! I can't fuckin' believe you're doing this shit to me. We need to talk, Arturo! I'm serious. *To-night*! At my place!"

She shook her head as she and her friends walked away.

Chet's mouth hung open as he watched Maribel and Arturo going at it on the tossed sheets of the hotel bed. He was on his second beer and had long since abandoned the dictionary. He felt like he could almost understand the Spanish.

"Oh, Maribel, Maribel."

"Oh, Arturo."

Suddenly the door flung open as Carmen stormed into the room. Arturo practically fell off the bed, shirtless, with his muscled torso glistening with sweat.

"You bastard, Arturo! I knew it! How could you do this to me?"

Maribel was horrified and scrambled to get decent.

"Arturo, who is this? I thought you said you were here at the hotel by yourself."

Carmen's eyes widened.

"By yourself, huh? Well, you're by yourself now, you cheap, disgusting bastard!"

Carmen slapped Arturo and turned toward Maribel.

"Cheap whore!" she spat at her.

"Carmen, my love! Wait!"

Arturo struggled to get dressed and go after Carmen.

"Arturo, wait!" Maribel pleaded in her black lace bra and panties. "I'll wait for you!"

"Oh, yeah!" Chet yelled. "The three-way! The three-way! Go for the three-way! You are the *man*, Arturo!"

Miriya waited for Arturo in her impatient manner, arms folded across her chest, bare foot bouncing nervously over her knee. She sat on her white couch, glaring at the time displayed on the DVD player on top of her TV. It was past 1:30 in the morning. Every so often, she stood and paced the living room floor, going over in her mind the things she needed to say to her wayward boyfriend. Miriya was determined to maintain calm in the face of his predicted denials, lies, and sugary talk. She needed to keep her wits about her; develop an airtight argument and stick to it, no matter what he said. And most importantly, she would not let him touch her.

Just before Miriya sat for the third time, Arturo knocked at her door. She let him in, holding out her right arm in a gesture meant to shepherd him to her couch where he would wait in judgment. They didn't kiss or exchange affectionate pleasantries. She said nothing and Arturo avoided eye contact. Head down, Arturo plopped down in the center of the couch, his shoulders hunched forward. He looked toward his shoes as Miriya struck a defiant pose in the middle of the floor, her right leg stuck out at an angle.

"What the fuck!" she started in on him, holding out her hands. "What is wrong with you, Arturo?"

What's wrong with me? She asked herself.

"What?" he finally looked up at her, wrapping his arms around himself. "I told you, she's practically family."

"I swear if you say that one more time!"

Like I'm one to talk, Miriya thought. What if Steven was here?

"Baby," Arturo started.

"Oh, shut-up! You need to get your shit together, man!"

As do I, she confessed to herself.

"I can't believe you," Miriya continued. "You think I'm just gonna sit around and wait for you to start getting serious about us? You'd better wake up, mister!"

She was on a roll.

"By the time you realize I was the best thing you had in your miserable little life, I'm gonna be out the door—long gone, in the arms of someone who's going to treat me the way I deserve. Look at me!" Miriya commanded, standing in all her glory. "Don't think that I can't have any man I want!"

I'm probably getting what I deserve, Miriya painfully

admitted to herself.

"I know you can!" Arturo countered, coming to life. "Just like I can have any woman *I* want—big deal! Is that the game we're going to play?"

"No, Arturo, I don't wanna play games! This relationship isn't a game to me, as you sometimes make it out to be."

"Wha—" he started.

"Shut up and listen to me!" Miriya pointed at him as she started to pace again. Arturo was wide-eyed in stunned silence. "I'm deadly serious about us, Arturo. I've been with you too long, have invested too much of my time and energy to throw this all away! You think a woman like me is in this for *fun*? You think I *like* sucking your cock all the time?"

Miriya grimaced as she said this.

"Cum is disgusting! 'Worship the cock,'" she imitated him. "You try swallowing a load or two, see how *you* like it!"

Her words hit him like paintballs.

"I'm thirty years old, Arturo. I'm looking to get married."

And even though you're a cheating bastard and I'm a hypocrite, you are fucking hot! Nobody's ever made me feel the way you do in bed. Passion is a powerful thing.

Miriya closed her eyes, almost sickened by her lust for him.

"I'd like to be married to you, Arturo."

You're Argentinean, after all.

"But I'm getting tired of your shit. If you're just gonna drag your feet and string me along, I'm outta here, as in 'Peace out, see ya later.'"

Yeah, right. I'm sprung on you, jerk.

She waved at him for added emphasis. Arturo said nothing and glanced up at his woman, as she stood arms akimbo, waiting for his reply.

"*Well?*" Miriya raised her eyebrows.

"Well, what?" Arturo grumbled. "I guess I know where we stand now."

He got up as if to leave.

"Where are you going?" she asked him, feeling the shameful twinge of panic welling up within her being.

I blew it!

"I guess I'm going nowhere, at least with you. Now that I know how you feel. I'd hate for you to have to swallow any more of my disgusting cum."

"Oh, lighten up, Arturo! I was just trying to make a point."

Don't panic.

"You made it," he said, opening her door. It was taking every ounce of Miriya's strength, as she bounced gently on her toes, to keep her from throwing her body in front of him, closing the door and effectively blocking his escape. But then he would know that he could walk all over her.

Bluff him!

"You know what?" Miriya raised her right arm and flicked a limp hand in his direction. "Get out! Go be with one of your blonde bimbo *whores*!"

"There's an idea," he mumbled, disappearing from sight as the door slammed behind him.

"Bastard," Miriya mumbled, her face wrinkling.

Oh, shit.

PART SEVEN:
DRAMA

Ramin strolled into work the following Monday whistling *Sleigh Ride* and carrying a small Christmas wreath. He had a happy air about him. He removed his coat and hung it on an old wooden hat rack.

"Thanksgiving is Thursday," Lorena mumbled, barely looking at him. Her hair was pulled back in a tight bun, and she looked glum behind her glasses. "And you're already whistling Christmas tunes."

"Let's just say that Christmas came early for Tahra and me," Ramin said, smiling broadly, as he stood before Lorena's desk. He smelled nice, Lorena noticed, as she sat up straight and folded her arms across her chest.

"Oh?"

"I'm gonna be a daddy." Ramin held out his arms. Lorena's happiness for her boss overpowered her funk, and she cracked a pure smile.

"Congratulations, mister," she chuckled. "Wow!

Ramin the daddy! I can't wait to see you pushing a baby stroller. I'll be *laughin'*!"

"I hope it's a boy."

"It'll be a girl, watch. When did you guys find out?"

"Friday. Thank goodness, too! Sex was beginning to be a chore."

"Oooh! TMI." Lorena shook her head.

"On that note." Ramin looked embarrassed.

"Yes," Lorena said, pointing to his office. He continued whistling as he disappeared behind his door.

Lorena turned to her computer screen and stared at it for a few minutes until her cell phone rang. Her recently updated ring tone was Chakira and Alejandro Sanz' *La Tortura*.

"Hello?"

It was Miriya.

"Oh, hey, what's up?" Lorena sighed. "Working."

Her work line rang.

"H-hold on a second."

Lorena picked up the receiver.

"Good morning. Fayed Law Corporation. Can you please hold? Thank you."

She hung up and brought her cell phone back to her ear.

"So, uh…Nah, it's cool…When?"

Lorena glanced at a clock on the wall.

"Twelve, twelve-thirty usually…Okay…See ya."

Lupe Mercado wrinkled her nose when she heard Chet enter the office. She sat painfully at her desk with a growing stack of case file folders in front of her. As he approached, she held up a stack of pink "While You Were Gone" message pad sheets without saying a word. She hardly looked at him.

"*Gracias, Señora Mercado*," Chet blurted with a passing accent. "*Cómo está usted?*"

Lupe's jaw dropped as her glasses slipped down her nose.

"*Qué, guey?*"

"Been catchin' the hot *señoritas* on that *novela*, 'Sofia de Amor' you turned me on to. Even picked up a few phrases here and there, *mamacita*."

"*Ándale, cabrón!*" Lupe laughed. "Well, lookitchoo!"

"*Anda*-lay, *ca*-brone," Chet imitated. He uttered this phrase under his breath several times as if trying to learn it by rote, then stepped into his office.

"Oh, *heeeell* no!" Lupe picked up her phone to call Lorena.

Miriya walked into Equator unsure of what to say when she saw Lorena. Of all people, Miriya couldn't believe her new friend was caught up in this. In just a few weeks Miriya and Lorena had bonded fast. Lorena was happy, supportive, and this resonated with Miriya. Miriya could have handled this crisis fine if it had involved Taylor or even Nathalie, but Lorena wasn't like those girls. Miriya thought there wasn't a catty, mean-spirited bone in Lorena's body. Miriya wished more people in her life were like Lorena.

Now Miriya prayed that the damage wasn't irreparable. Steven Meztaz! Why him? Miriya saw Lorena sitting in the far corner and smiled at her.

Lorena kept her mohair coat on and clutched at her sides with gloved hands. She stood awkwardly and gave Miriya a quick hug.

Miriya spoke first: "I feel kind of yucky about what happened the other night." She felt her eyes start to water and told herself she wouldn't get emotional about this—after all, it wasn't anybody's fault.

Lorena's big brown cat eyes were open wider than normal as she considered her friend's sincerity. Miriya couldn't read the expression on Lorena's face and thought it blank, which worried her.

"It was a little unexpected," Lorena said with a smile.

This lightened the air a little for Miriya.

"I'll say! I had no clue, Lorena." Miriya shook her head. "I can't believe that in our conversations about him, we never mentioned Steven's name. Not that we would have necessarily put two and two together…"

"Who knows?"

"I feel so bad." Miriya sighed. "I know how excited you were about meeting somebody new, and now, I just…I can't imagine what's gonna happen."

Lorena stared off, past Miriya to another point in time.

"I was there when Steven decided to cut things off with—well, with you," Lorena mumbled. "I remember thinking that 'you'—although I didn't know it was you—probably wouldn't take it so hard anyway since I knew you already had a boyfriend, whom Steven was convinced you would never leave. I didn't feel bad for you, because of what I knew Steven had gone through emotionally by getting caught up with you."

Miriya took a deep breath and felt her face burn.

"But it's weird now," Lorena continued, frowning. "Because I know what a good guy Steven is, I can understand a little of why you fell for him, despite having Arturo. I can't pretend to know how you felt about Steven, or what went through your mind when he called it off between the two of you—whether you were sad, relieved, glad—but, uh…now that I know it's *you*, Miriya Fronzini…*Junior*."

Miriya smiled through welling tears.

"*My* Miriya," Lorena added, quietly. "I feel bad for you."

Miriya wiped her eyes.

"He broke my heart," she confessed.

Lorena's breath caught in her throat and she frowned.

"Why? Why didn't you dump Arturo and snatch Steven up then?"

Miriya shook her head and covered her face with her hands.

"I don't know! I don't know! I'm stupid." She wiped her eyes. "I was with Arturo for four years. Look at him! He's stunning, gorgeous! Any woman would want him. I remember I used to feel like a million bucks on his arm."

Lorena frowned at this but kept quiet.

"And I hate to say this, but Arturo's fucking awesome in bed! Oh, God, does that make me shallow?"

Lorena considered this.

"No, I guess not," she said. "Chemistry is a powerful thing. I know that when I get married, someday, I hope that my husband and I share a passion that makes the hard work of marriage worthwhile."

Miriya absorbed this.

"Hard work," she muttered. "Boy, has it been work! Lorena, I feel like I'm getting what I deserve. I know I cheated, too, and that makes me a big hypocrite, but I always justified it by telling myself that Arturo didn't make me happy; that he was probably cheating on me, too, with God only knows how many of the bimbos he likes to surround himself with—what did I expect, right?…I dunno, Steven seemed like just a casual fling to give me the strength to handle Arturo's infidelities. I thought Arturo would grow out of it later and come to realize that he wanted me more than anyone else."

"And he still might." Lorena gently touched Miriya's

face and turned it toward hers. "What will you do then?"

Miriya shrugged.

"I want to get married, Lorena. I'm thirty years old. I want to have children. And sadly, as terrible as this sounds, I'm willing to settle. At least I'll have a hot husband, who probably will make a load of cash someday, and we'll have an awesome sex life. Plenty of women settle for this all the time."

"You will have children, Miriya," Lorena said. "When it's meant to be. *We* don't choose when it's time to have kids, *He* does," Lorena said, pointing toward the ceiling.

Miriya stared at her feet.

"What about us?" Miriya finally asked.

"What do you mean?" Lorena bit her lip.

"Are we still friends?"

Lorena's mouth broadened in a toothy grin.

"I don't know. Are we?" she playfully asked.

"Yes!" Miriya said firmly.

"Then we are."

"What about Steven?"

"What about him?"

"Are you still going to see him? You can. I don't mind. He's a good guy. He'd be perfect for you."

Lorena considered Miriya's words.

"I don't know. We'll see. It's too weird right now. I didn't sleep with him. I'm not invested emotionally, you know?"

Miriya clutched at her chest.

"I have a lot of praying to do about Steven and every-thing," Lorena added, smiling. "Jesus will show me the way."

Lorena thought she knew the answer already.

Karen sat next to Veronica at a table in the outside patio area of Starbucks. Karen sat slouched in her chair, more dolled up than usual in a flower-print dress, bare legs and flip-flops. She used the hooks on her prosthesis to take a cigarette out of a worn pack.

"Didn't know I could light one of these bad boys with my hooks, did you?" Karen said, cigarette dangling from her lips. Her hair was pulled back in a ponytail, and she wore glasses.

Veronica watched with mild amusement as Karen's hooks manipulated a match from a matchbook held in her left hand. Veronica shielded her eyes from the sun as sev-eral Marines from a nearby recruiting office approached.

"What's up with these guys?" she asked.

Karen took a long drag of her cigarette.

"Marines," she replied. "Who're we meeting here any-way?"

"Suzy. She said she had something important to tell me."

"This I gotta hear."

One of the Marines stood outside, talking on his cell

phone. He noticed Karen and lifted his head toward her. Karen responded with a tight-lipped smile, straining to see the ribbons on his chest.

Veronica saw Suzy's car pull into the parking lot.

"She's here."

When the Marine's buddies walked out with their tray of coffees, the one who was on his cell phone, a dark, well-built Latino staff sergeant, said something to them. They stopped and considered Karen. The staff sergeant approached her.

"*Cómo está, mi 'ija? Eres una veterana?*"

"Army," Karen replied.

He motioned toward her prosthesis.

"Where?"

"Iraq. Near Baghdad."

"Got my purple heart in Fallouja. It's good seeing a Latina who served. You go, girl!" He held his fist out to her, which she tapped obligatorily with her left fist.

"Hoo-ah," she added for effect.

The Marines seemed pleased by this and walked off as Suzy approached.

"Bonding moment?" Suzy asked.

"They're hooked on me, what can I say?" Karen raised her prosthesis.

Suzy frowned as Veronica chuckled.

"So, what's going on? What's this big news you had?" Veronica checked her fingernails.

"Okay, I don't know how to break something like this to you guys, so I'm just gonna say it. I can't keep it to myself any longer. There's way too much lies and bullshit going on among all of us."

Karen gave Veronica a look.

"Nathalie and Taylor hit me up the other day and told me that Nathalie's been fucking around with Arturo."

"What?" Veronica sat up straighter as Karen's jaw dropped. "What do you mean, like…they *slept* together?"

"No, like they've been having a fucking affair for over a year—behind Miriya's back. Miriya doesn't know shit."

"Ooooh!" Karen snickered.

"Shut up! That's not funny." Veronica put her hands to her forehead. "I can't fuckin' believe Nathalie! Miriya's not stupid. She doesn't exactly trust Arturo."

Veronica did not want to tell Suzy about Miriya and Steven.

"Fine, but I doubt she suspects he's cheating with one of her friends," Suzy said, throwing up her hands.

Karen looked at her girlfriend.

"Well, we have to tell Miriya." Veronica looked from Suzy to Karen. "That's fuckin' bullshit! Arturo's a piece of shit."

"I'm not telling her shit. She won't believe me and will just hate me," Suzy said.

"Don't look at *me*," Karen blurted.

Veronica sighed.

"This is just fuckin' great." Veronica shook her head. "I'll tell her—I don't care. I hope she kicks his ass to the curb!"

On the TV that night:

Mexican police cars drove up the front of the Hotel Las Tres Mujeres. A swarthy lieutenant with slicked-back hair and a thin mustache got out of a black sedan with a radio held to his lips.

"Surround the hotel. Block the exits. We have the murderess Sofia de Amor cornered."

He motioned to a uniformed sergeant.

"Sergeant Robles, take your men inside and secure the lobby area. No one gets in or out. And find her husband!"

"Yes, Lieutenant Madero!"

Chet stuck a slice of pizza in his mouth while holding a beer in his other hand.

"This shit's better than *Law and Order*," he said with his mouth full. He put down his pizza slice and grabbed his remote. He turned up the volume.

"Hah! Lookit them Fed-er-*ah*-lees!" Chet yelled, pointing at the screen. "You can run, but you can't hide, Sofia *dee* Amor!"

Carmen stormed down the hall muttering under her breath:

"That bastard Arturo was only using me! Who knows who else he's been seeing behind Sofia's back—and my back! Poor Mrs. de Amor! I must get to her and help clear her name!"

The two gangsters, dressed in black suits and ties, quickly climbed a flight of stairs. The tall one with the thin face, acne scars, and a short ponytail wore black leather gloves. The shorter, fat one had thinning hair and wore dark green sunglasses. Both hoods had their guns drawn and were closing in on their prey.

Miriya opened her front door to find Nathalie standing by herself, uninvited. Miriya was surprised that Nathalie remembered how to get to her apartment, as the girl had only been there once before, at a party thrown two years prior. Miriya wondered if Nathalie was truly alone and poked her head out to check the hallway.

"Nathalie, what are you doing here?"

"Can we talk?" Nathalie's voice cracked.

Miriya frowned.

"Sure. Come in."

Miriya closed the door behind her friend.

"Please," Miriya said, pointing to her couch. "Have a seat. What's up?"

Miriya sat rigidly next to her. Nathalie fidgeted with her fingers as if they were tied in a knot.

"I, uh…I don't know how to start, or how to say what I'm about to say…I'm a terrible friend, and you *never* deserved any of this, but, uh…I've been having an affair with Arturo for the last year."

Miriya almost chuckled.

"That's not funny, Nathalie."

"Do you see me laughing?" Nathalie's eyes watered and a single tear rolled down her cheek. Miriya sat in stunned silence as Nathalie wiped her face.

"What?—*Wait*! You've been having an affair— *sleeping* with Arturo? My boyfriend?"

Nathalie nodded, unable to look Miriya in the eyes. Miriya stood suddenly and pointed toward the door.

"Get the fuck out of my apartment, you whore!"

Nathalie winced, eyes shut tight and hands clasped on her knees as if praying for a way out.

"Miriya, please."

"I don't fuckin' believe you, Nathalie! How could you do this to me?"

Miriya paced the room with her hands to her forehead.

"So all those times Arturo said he was working a deal."

"He was with me."

Nathalie finally looked up at her as Miriya cringed.

"When my father died in the hospital, and he was supposed to be meeting a client?"

"He was with me," Nathalie repeated softly, her eyes closed.

Miriya brought her hands to her mouth.

"*Ugh,* I think I'm gonna be sick."

Nathalie stood and reached out to her.

"Miriya, please, I'm so sor—"

"Don't fuckin' touch me!" Miriya yelled, stepping back from Nathalie. "I've been nothing but a friend to you. Always supportive, always listening to your guys' *bullshit* all the time! How could you *do* this to me, Nathalie? You were my friend!"

"I feel terrible, Miriya."

"Why even tell me? Why not just keep fucking him behind my back?"

"Because he's fucking someone else, too, and who knows how many other women," Nathalie's voice took on an edgy tone that made Miriya want to slap her. "He's a lying bastard. You deserve better."

"I deserve *better*? Do I deserve one of my friends fucking my boyfriend, Nathalie? You haven't invested four years of your life with this man like I have. It's easy for you to say, 'fuck him' and walk away. This is the man I wanted to *marry*, Nathalie. Of all the fuckin' guys out there, you couldn't find one of your own? You had to have *my man*?"

Miriya sighed and plopped down on her couch. Suddenly she was calm, at peace.

"Who else, Nathalie? Who else knew about this? Did Suzy or Veronica?"

"Wha—*no*! No…only Taylor. I only told Taylor."

Miriya shook her head.

"You guys are a real piece of work, man, you know that?"

"I'm sorry, Miriya. I don't know what else to say."

"There's nothing else to say, Nathalie. I'm sorry that our friendship had to come to this—that it had to end this way. I can never be friends with you, Nathalie. Not now, not ever...I don't care if you change, become a better person, or-or join a convent. You're out of my life forever."

Nathalie nodded.

"I know. I mean, I knew it—I knew that's what you'd say."

"Yeah? What'd you expect?"

Miriya got up and walked to her front door. She calmly opened it and stood by, holding the knob, without saying anything. Nathalie walked toward the door and paused next to Miriya. Nathalie stuck her hand out.

"It was good knowing you, Miriya."

Miriya raised her eyebrows and refused to look at her. She closed the door behind Nathalie and picked up her phone.

Veronica was surprised to see Miriya at that late hour and wondered what Arturo was doing. Miriya walked into Veronica's apartment with barely a peep.

"Uh-oh," Veronica mumbled. "I knew when you called something was up."

"Guess what I just found out tonight?" Miriya stood,

arms akimbo in the middle of Veronica's living room.

"That 'god' is 'dog' spelled backwards? I don't know."

"That Arturo is *Nathalie* spelled backwards!"

Veronica got wide-eyed.

"Oh, my God, Miriya! I was going to tell you, I swear!"

"You *knew*?" Miriya blurted.

"I just found out! I was gonna say something to you first chance I got. Suzy told us. She was gonna break it to you herself but was afraid you wouldn't believe her and that you'd end up hating her. I told her I'd tell you because I couldn't stand to see you with that lying cheater."

Veronica took a deep breath.

"It's a good thing you haven't been captured by *Al Qaeda*!" Miriya said in a huff. "You'd tell 'em *everything*!"

Miriya crossed her arms and sat on Veronica's futon sofa.

"Oh, Veronica, I don't know what to do."

"About what?"

"About everything! I feel like such a fool. I always knew Arturo had trouble staying on the straight and narrow when it came to other women, but—*Nathalie*! Of all people, how could she? How could he?"

Veronica thought it best not to bring up Steven Meztaz.

"I mean…I had Steven," Miriya said. "So, what can I say?"

"Yeah, but…Steven wasn't Arturo's buddy."

"I should fuck Carlo and Jorge just to get back at him!"

Veronica tried to get that image out of her head.

"Veronica, I may be dumb, but I'm not stupid! I know what's going on a lot of the time."

Miriya sized her up.

"I know, for instance, that you've always had a thing for me. Call it a crush, or whatever, but I've known since we were in junior high school!"

Veronica shifted uncomfortably on the futon but said nothing.

"And it's okay!" Miriya said. "You've been a great friend. You never tried to get with me, and I always appreciated you for that. But look what it's done to your relationship with Karen! In high school and college…All the times you let her down to be around me. Those weekends in the reserves were a way for her to get away from the pain you caused her. She finally volunteered to join a unit that was shipped to Iraq and she almost *died* there."

Miriya shook her head.

"Most people never know a good thing when they got it. They only realize it after the person they loved has been driven away—too little too late. You got a chance with Karen like Arturo had with me—don't blow it! Run to her and embrace her! Tell her how much you love and appreciate her, because no day is guaranteed. We might not be here tomorrow."

Miriya's face wrinkled.

"I thank God…everyday…"

She wiped the tears from her face.

"…that I told my dad how much I loved him. He died knowing I loved him."

Veronica wiped tears from her face as Miriya spoke. All she could think about now was Karen.

On the other side of town Lorena had a meeting of her own. She had agreed to speak with Steven at her place. Steven was dressed nicely in a sweater and dark wool pea coat, as the two of them sat chastely on Lorena's living room couch, the eyes of the *Virgen* looking down upon them.

"So, what'd you want to talk about, dude?" Lorena talked as if she were speaking to her brother.

"About us."

"You mean 'us'—you and me—or 'us' as a couple?"

Steven knew that Lorena could be annoyingly coy.

"Us, as a couple."

Lorena raised her eyebrows and stared at her dark TV set. She thought of the alien's reflection in the movie *Signs* and shuddered. She then turned to Steven.

"I don't know."

Steven frowned.

"You don't know what?"

"I don't know if there is an 'us.' I don't know how I feel about 'us' anymore."

"*C'mon*, Lorena!" Steven blurted.

"*Sssh*! My *abuelita's* trying to sleep." Lorena glanced toward Julia's bedroom.

"Oh! I'm sorry." Steven lowered his voice. "Lorena, I explained to you what happened. I didn't know. She didn't know. How could we help it?"

"I know what you said. I understand every-thing...Miriya's my friend, Steven. She's my best friend. I couldn't be with you knowing that you were with her...I mean, uh...I'm glad we never did anything because I really care about her."

Steven shook his head and sighed. He knew Lorena well enough to know that her mind was made up. If there was one thing Lorena knew, it was her own mind. She had a wisdom that she trusted and would never stray from.

"So that's it, huh? We don't have a chance?"

"It's nobody's fault, mister," Lorena said with a girlish voice. "It just happens like that sometimes. I'm sad, too. I really liked you."

"Great." Steven tapped his shoes on her floor. "What if, like...five years from now we were to bump into each other again and find that we were still single?"

Lorena looked at the floor with a wide-eyed blank stare. She turned to him and her full lips parted in her trademark toothy grin.

"I don't know," she said, shrugging her shoulders.

Well, that's something, I guess, he thought.

Steven stood up and thrust his hands in the pockets of

his pea coat. Lorena quietly walked him to the door. As she opened it, he turned to her and gave her an awkward hug.

"Good-bye, mister."

"So long, miss."

And he was gone. Lorena took a deep breath and smiled to herself. She wondered if her dad was home and went out to their rear yard to check under some hoods.

Midnight found Arturo in bed with the blonde, Annelise, who owned a boutique on Rodeo Drive. She was half-Norwegian and half-Venezuelan, and the combination was almost too hot for Arturo to handle. The room was candlelit and Carlos Santana played on the stereo.

"Oh, baby, baby, baby," Arturo moaned as Annelise kissed his neck and chest.

Her flowing mane of blonde hair poured from Arturo's hands like silky sand.

"Baby, you get me so hot," Annelise purred while running her clawed fingers gently over his muscular chest and abs.

She wore a hot pink tank top that barely contained her enhanced 36 DD chest, and a matching G-string. Arturo had guessed her cup size because she had said there was a "double D-lite" waiting for him. Arturo was only wearing boxer briefs divided into the colors of the Argentinean flag, with a smiley sun over the growing bulge in the front.

Arturo looked toward the ceiling as Annelise raised

herself up while straddling his waist. He thought that Annelise was the most beautiful woman he had ever laid eyes
on and asked himself what he had done to deserve her.
Other questions raced through his mind. He wondered if
she was on the pill; did she do anal? Were there skid marks
on his underwear?

Annelise appeared to hug herself as she lifted her tank
top slowly over her head. Arturo's eyes bulged at the vision
of her perfect, gravity-defying, tanned breasts jutting out
toward him, her nipples erect like accusatory fingers boring
into his conscience.

That's when it hit him! Arturo's hands stopped just
short of grabbing at Annelise's hungry chest and he
propped himself up, nearly knocking the blonde backward.
Annelise struggled to get her balance while Arturo looked
dazed.

"Baby?" Annelise frowned. "What is it? What's
wrong?"

"Your tits," Arturo said, almost stuttering.

"What about them?"

"They're...*perfect*."

"And? I already know that! Let's get it on, baby!"

"And Miriya's tits are perfect."

"So? Who's *she*?" Annelise was losing her patience.

"So! So, what? *Exactly*! Tits are tits are *tits*."

Arturo ran his hands through his hair.

"My, God, it's all the same." Arturo was on a roll as he

struggled to get untangled from her sheets. He sat at the edge of Annelise's bed, as she propped herself up on her knees, arms akimbo. "Pussy is *pussy!*"

Annelise shook her head.

"All right, *genius*, what the fuck are you talking about? I warned you not to start thinking!"

Arturo stood and paced her bedroom, talking to himself.

"You've had one piece of ass, you've had 'em all! I can't even remember all the pussy I've gotten over the last few years. They're all starting to blend into one another. All I can remember is Miriya! She's always been there for me."

Arturo frowned as he turned to look at Annelise.

"You! You'll grow old and wrinkly!"

"So will *you*, limp dick!"

"I know! We all will…So will Miriya…She'll get old, and maybe fat, but she will have known me—the real me! Warts and all! And she will have been by my side. And when I'm an old fart, fat and balding, and can't even get it up with viagra, and sexy hot blondes like you are laughing at me and calling me limp dick!"

"That's 'cause you are a limp dick! Get out!"

"Miriya will still be by my side! And you, where will *you* be!"

"Fucking some boy toy who knows a good thing when he has one!" Annelise said this while squeezing her tits together. She licked one of her own nipples.

"I've got a good thing!" Arturo yelled while putting on his clothes. "I've had a good thing going for four years and just didn't know it. Miriya's the best thing that ever happened to me! I just hope I haven't blown it."

"Go blow yourself, queer!"

Arturo had called his buddy Carlo the moment he left Annelise's. Arturo was in a jam and he needed his help. Where was he? Carlo said that he and Jorge were sweet-talking two hot Brazilian women at Firefly's in the Valley. Arturo wasted no time in getting there before last call.

"What the fuck!" Carlo yelled. "You left Annelise there naked and wanting it?"

"Will you two shut up and listen to me!"

Jorge shook his head while downing the last of his drink.

"What am I gonna do? What if I've pushed her away for good this time?"

"So, marry her!" Carlo said.

"What?"

"*Boludo*! What's the one thing Miriya's always wanted?"

"A ring!" Jorge added.

"You give her a ring and she's yours! Forever! Then she's happy and she can't have sex with anyone else. And you? You keep doing what you're doing! It's a win-win situation."

Arturo let this sink in. Carlo was right. Miriya just wanted to get married. That's what she always wanted. He was too stupid to realize that he couldn't put it off forever and expect her to stick around. She was thirty after all, and wasn't getting any younger. To think that if he had just gotten her a ring, he could continue getting as much tail as he wanted—It was a win-win situation!

"That's it! I'll marry her! I'll go out and get a ring, first thing in the morning! I'll propose to her tomorrow evening at that restaurant on Green Street. You guys'll be there, right?"

"Oh, I wouldn't miss it for the world," Carlo said, chuckling.

The next morning, Arturo went out and bought a diamond engagement ring of a style that Miriya had once pointed out to him as being the kind that she would want on her finger one day. He also made reservations at Madeleine's for a party of eight that evening.

PART EIGHT:
I DO...OR DO I?

Lupe noticed that there was something different about Chet when he came in to work that morning. She couldn't put her finger on it. It wasn't that he was lingering around her desk after getting his messages—he'd been doing that more lately, ever since he had gotten hooked on *Sofia de Amor*. Lupe knew that tonight was the final episode. She couldn't wait till the whistle blew so that she could head home and hunker down in front of the TV with her *novio*.

Lupe looked up over her computer monitor and watched Chet, as he stood, almost posing before her, turning his head from one side to the other.

What is this *cabrón* doing now?

"Well? What do you think?" Chet asked.

"*Qué, guey?*"

Then she saw it. Lupe threw her head back and covered her mouth, laughing.

"Oh, *NO* you didn't!"

Chet had styled his hair like the popular Mexican soap opera star Sebastian Rulli.

"Huh? *Huh*? Am I a *Papi* Choo-low?"

"*Papi Chulo!*" Lupe shook her head. "It looks like you've been watching more than just *Sofia de Amor*."

"Even taking a Spanish class at night," Chet said proudly. "I just gotta know what Derbez is saying on his show. It looks hilarious!"

"I can't believe you're watching *Derbez* now!" Lupe looked at Chet in a whole new light. Maybe the *gringo* wasn't so bad after all. "Aren't you a little old for the Rulli look, though?"

"Latin honeys love older men." Chet said this with dubious authority. "All ready for the final episode tonight?"

"Of course! I can't wait. I was thinking you might even let me go home early tonight."

"Fat chance, *Mami* Choo-la! What do you think's gonna happen tonight? Do the gangsters get it, or do they get Sofia? Do the cops get her? Or does she kill Arturo? Or do the cops kill Arturo? The possibilities are endless!"

"Maybe they all die in the end."

"You think?" Chet was wide-eyed.

"*Vámonos, cabrón*! I'm on the phone. Go run your law firm." Lupe dismissed him with a wave of her hand while dialing Lorena's office line.

"Good morning. Fayed Law Corporation."

"Hey, *cabrona!*"

"What's up?" Lorena sounded preoccupied.

"*Girl*, you should check out Chet. We're gonna have to start calling him *Chuy*, *guey*!"

"Why?"

"He's hooked on Spanish TV, he's taking Spanish classes, and he even styled his hair like *Sebastian Rulli*."

"Wuuuuuut?"

"*Sí, carnala*! He's gone plum loco," Lupe said, with an American accent. "It's a trip! Hey, are you watchin' *Sofia de Amor* tonight? It's the last episode."

"You know I am."

"Who you gonna watch it with?"

"Probably just my family."

"What about, uh…Aren't you gonna invite your friend, Miriya? I thought she was gonna go with you guys to San Felipe. Don't you guys leave tomorrow?"

"Eh, I don't know. I was gonna call her to see if she still wanted to, but, uh, I haven't heard from her. I don't know if she remembered. Whatever."

"Call her! She's your friend!"

"I don't know. We'll see."

Lupe could tell that Lorena didn't feel like talking about it.

Miriya asked Veronica, Karen, and Suzy to meet her for lunch at a favorite Thai restaurant. Miriya didn't want to run into Lorena at Equator while with her other friends.

After ordering their food, Miriya got down to brass tacks.

"I already talked to Veronica about what happened," Miriya began matter-of-factly. "I don't know what else has been said among the group, or whether you guys have heard from Taylor or Nathalie. Needless to say, Nathalie and I aren't friends anymore. You guys can continue your friendship with her, or Taylor, if you'd like, but it would put a strain on your friendship with me."

Suzy glanced at Veronica, who sat stone-faced.

"I think what's been going on is fucked up," Miriya said, folding her arms across her chest, trying to maintain her composure. "Fine, you guys didn't know what was up until Taylor and Nathalie came clean, but I can't shake the feeling that there was a lot of shit-talking going on behind my back. I don't even want to know whether you guys were involved or not. I'm going to believe that you weren't."

"Good, 'cause we weren't," Suzy huffed.

"Whatever. We're fuckin' friends!" Miriya said with her hands outstretched. "We all need to act like it. We need to stick up for each other and support each other. No more bullshit. I can't believe that Nathalie did that shit to me! And I can't believe that Taylor could look me in the face and pretend to be my friend when she *knew* what was going on behind my back!"

Miriya stopped to catch her breath.

"But anyway, that's all in the past," she continued.

"Forgive and forget. I've got more important things going on right now, and I just want you all to know that Arturo has asked my family and me to get together for dinner tonight at Madeleine's on East Green Street. I think he's going to ask me to marry him."

"What?" Veronica could not believe her ears. "Don't tell me you're going to say yes!"

Miriya frowned.

"And what if I decide to, huh?"

"After what he pulled?" Suzy chimed in. "C'mon, Miriya, you can do way better than him."

"Oh, yeah? Arturo's a good man. He's made mistakes but who hasn't? You even said yourself, Veronica—what was it? 'Show me a man who doesn't cheat and I'll give you a million bucks'? All men are the same. If given the chance, they'll all get a little on the side—they're not angels."

Veronica shook her head.

"You don't believe that," she said.

"*I* cheated!" Miriya blurted, throwing her hands out.

"That was different!"

"No! No different. I was unhappy. He was unhappy. Big deal. I'm not going to blow four years so I can be alone and miserable. Arturo and I can have a good marriage. Things will get better. Maybe he realizes that I'm the best thing that ever happened to him."

"Miriya, don't get married just to get married," Suzy

said. "Wait for the right person."

"I'm tired of waiting!" Miriya said. "I've got the best man I'm going to find. This is my last chance at happiness. I'm taking it!"

Lorena checked her watch.

4:45 PM. The day was almost over, and she had not heard from Miriya. Lorena wondered if all that talk about remaining friends was just talk. If Miriya was serious about being her friend, she would have at least called. Miriya knew that Lorena's family was scheduled to leave for Mexico the next day. Miriya was not only invited, but had said she would go. She should have the courtesy to call and cancel if plans had changed, Lorena thought.

Lorena picked up her office phone and dialed Miriya's number.

"Hello?"

"Hey, it's me."

"Oh, hi, Lorena. What's up?"

"Listen, we should talk. Could you meet me after work for a little minute?"

There was a pause. Lorena shifted uncomfortably in her chair.

"Um…Sure, okay. I don't have a lot of time, but I can meet you at Equator later. Say…6:00? I have to go home and get dressed after work," said Miriya.

"Cool. I'll see you there."

Nathalie sat at her desk and stared at her computer. None of the designs made sense to her. She forgot what she was looking at. She closed her eyes and sighed just as a be-spectacled colleague approached her with some idea boards.

"Nat! What do you think of the colors now?" he asked, startling her.

Nathalie squinted as if she needed glasses.

"What rooms are these?"

"The master bedroom," he replied with an exasperated tone. "It was your idea!"

"Fine. Whatever. They look good."

He turned away with a confused look on his face. Nathalie ignored him as if he had never been there and checked her cell phone. No messages. No phone calls.

No friends.

Nathalie wanted to cry but couldn't do it at the office. It was time to go. She stood and quickly packed her things, choosing not to look at any of her co-workers. Within five minutes, Nathalie was behind the wheel of her car, heading home.

While driving, Nathalie glanced toward the dark sky. The radio had reported that it would be a wet Thanksgiving weekend and the prediction was right on. Rain started to fall hard, quickly making the streets slippery and the traffic tricky.

"This is just great," she mumbled to herself.

Nathalie's cell phone rang. Although it was inside her purse on the seat next to her, it stuck out, revealing her Caller ID screen. It was Taylor. Nathalie took her eyes off the road to reach for the phone. When she looked up she saw that traffic had stopped in front of her. She jerked her steering wheel to the right and then tried to over-correct, which sent her car into a skidding spin.

Chet fumbled with his windshield wipers just as Nathalie's car spun out in front of him. He tried to avoid her but it was no use as both their front ends crunched into each other. Nathalie's car was pushed into a concrete light pole, which sheared off at the base and fell over into the street, nearly hitting two other cars as it came down.

Chet slowly came to his senses as cars honked and tires screeched around him. He felt his chest, arms, and legs, and took a slow, deep breath to make sure that he wasn't injured. The car's airbag was in his lap like a deflated beach ball and there was a strong odor inside the car. He coughed and waved the smoke out of his face while unlocking his seatbelt.

"Christ," he muttered under his breath when he saw the streetlight blocking the lanes of traffic.

Chet stumbled out of his car and looked for the silver BMW that had crashed into his gold one. He saw it resting up on the sidewalk next to the base of the broken light pole. The driver, an ethnic-looking young woman, was still inside, her face in her hands.

"Hey! Are you okay?" Chet called out to her through her rolled up window, as he rapped on it with his knuckles. Nathalie turned her tear-streaked face toward him.

"Are you okay, miss?"

Nathalie frowned and scanned the interior of her wrecked car.

I don't know. Am I?

Nathalie shook her head.

"I-I-I don't know," she stammered.

Chet pulled on her door and it opened about two feet.

"Can you get out?" he asked.

"I think so." She unlocked her seatbelt.

Chet helped Nathalie squeeze out of her car. He frowned at her appearance. Despite her smeared mascara he could tell that she was pretty. Elegant was the word that popped into his mind. Still, he couldn't tell what her ethnicity was. She looked exotic, like one of the women on the Spanish-language TV stations.

"What happened?" Chet asked.

"Something stupid! I took my eyes off the road," Nathalie said, wiping her face. "I just started spinning out or something."

She shook her head as she gazed upon her car.

"Oh, man! My car's *totaled*!"

"Yeah, mine looks pretty bad, too."

Chet saw the traffic backed up over two blocks then turned back to Nathalie.

"You okay? Need me to call anyone for you?"

"I can't even think right now," Nathalie replied. She looked up at Chet and took a deep breath. "No, uh...there's no one to call."

Chet had his cell phone out.

"C'mon, there has to be somebody. Husband? Boy-friend?"

Nathalie let out a short, sharp laugh.

"Ha! Don't get me started!"

"What?" Chet smiled.

Nathalie gave Chet the once-over. He wasn't bad look-ing for an older white guy, she thought. And he looks like he has money.

"No, I don't have a husband. No boyfriend. No one." Nathalie started to cheer up. "So, uh, what happens now? Are you gonna sue me or something? You look like a law-yer."

Chet laughed.

"You're pretty good. I am a lawyer, but I'm not gonna sue you. C'mon, this was an accident. The road was wet, you spun out. Coulda happened to anybody. You mind if I ask you something?"

"What? Do I have insurance?"

"No-no, uh, what nationality are you?"

"I'm American." Nathalie looked amused.

"Yeah? Born and raised?"

"Right here in the good ol' USA."

"'Cause you looked…"

"Did you mean nationality or *ethnicity*?" Nathalie said, crossing her arms.

"Oh, then I meant ethnicity."

"Why? What do you think I am?"

"Well, I dunno. You look, uh, Mexican, or-or A-*rab*…"

Nathalie laughed.

"'*A*-rab'! What's up with that? No, I'm not Mexican or Arab. I'm Persian."

Chet frowned. Like Ramin Fayed!

"Iranian," he said.

"Yeah, whatever. My parents were born there."

Nathalie noticed that Chet looked at his watch. They heard sirens somewhere in the distance.

"You gonna be late for dinner?" she asked. "Your wife waiting for you?"

Chet smiled.

"Don't have a wife."

"Girlfriend?"

"Nope."

Good. Nathalie smiled.

"I was just afraid I was gonna miss my favorite TV show. Tonight's the final episode."

"Oh, yeah?"

That was when the two of them noticed the burly motorcycle cop standing to the side with his arms folded across his chest.

"You two gonna exchange information," he started, "or phone numbers?"

Lorena checked her watch.

6:05 PM.

Her mind was a jumble of chaotic images and emotions. She thought about *Sofia de Amor*, San Felipe, and what she wanted to say to Miriya. When Miriya finally walked through the door, Lorena noticed that she was all dolled up.

"Hey, what's up?" Lorena said, as they exchanged a quick hug.

Miriya sat down next to Lorena and looked like she was at a loss for words.

"You look nice," Lorena commented flatly. "Special engagement?"

"Thanks," Miriya replied. "Funny that you say that."

Lorena gave her a curious look.

"I have news," Miriya said, choosing her words carefully. "I think Arturo's going to ask me to marry him tonight."

Miriya braced herself for the response she had received from her other girlfriends. Lorena stared at her for a moment, eyes wide, and took a slow, deep breath. She gave Miriya a tight-lipped smile, and reached out and held her hand.

So you're gonna settle, huh? Lorena thought. Miriya, why would you do this to yourself?

"Where?" Lorena asked.

"At Madeleine's on East Green Street. He has kind of a whirlwind weekend planned for us afterward."

So much for San Felipe, Lorena thought glumly. You're making a big mistake, Miriya.

"Congratulations," Lorena said softly.

Miriya was taken aback.

"Wow!" she started. "That's it?"

Lorena frowned slightly.

"What do you mean? What do you want me to say?"

"Uh—well…I dunno. 'Don't do it! How could you?' No words of warning?"

"Is that what you want?"

Miriya considered this.

"No."

"I'm your friend. I'm going to support you no matter what."

Miriya gripped Lorena's hand tightly and looked away.

I almost wish you would tell me not to, Miriya thought. You, I would trust.

"Thanks, Lorena."

"I wish you the best."

Miriya nodded as they stood and embraced. Lorena knew that their friendship was going to change once she became Arturo's fiancé, and later, his wife. She would be a new Miriya, and would probably not have time for her old single girlfriends, opting instead to spend time with new "couples" friends.

Gerardo frowned when he saw Lorena step out of her red Jeep Cherokee. The look on her face was not one he was used to seeing on his normally cheerful daughter. She had had tiring days at the office, but he could tell that she was not exhausted. Gerardo looked at his wristwatch and saw that Lorena was also home later than normal.

He wiped his hands on an oily rag and took a few steps in her direction as she shuffled up to their rear door.

"*Que onde, mi 'ija?*"

"Hey."

"You okay?"

"Yup."

Lorena didn't stay and chat. Isabel also noticed her daughter's sullen demeanor as she gave her a hug and a kiss. Lorena barely uttered a peep to her mother and grandmother. Julia shrugged this off as she settled in front of the TV in the kitchen. Her granddaughter was allowed to be moody.

It was every girl's right.

Lorena opted not to watch the final episode of *Sofia de Amor* in the kitchen with her family, but chose to sit alone in the darkness of her living room watching the *telenovela* on their big TV. Lorena sat, hunched over, squeezing a large pillow close to her chest.

Sofia de Amor peeked out from behind her hotel room door and saw Carmen running in her direction. Sofia got wide-eyed and tried to close the door before her former housekeeper could get at her. It was too late as Carmen threw her body against the door, preventing it from being closed.

"Sofia! Sofia, please listen to me! You're in danger!"

"Leave me alone, hussy! You've ruined my life!"

Carmen pushed her way into the room as Sofia backed up in mortal dread.

"Please, Mrs. de Amor, I'm here to help you! There are gangsters coming to kill you. Arturo is still trying to kill you, and the police have the building surrounded!"

"Why should I trust you?" Sofia demanded to know.

"What I did was wrong, Mrs. de Amor. You were always good to me. You didn't deserve all this trouble. I just wanted to be loved by Arturo. He turned out to be a lying, dirty bastard! I caught him with the hotel housekeeper! He doesn't want my love or yours. He's only interested in money!"

Carmen got down on her knees and took Sofia's hand.

"Mrs. de Amor, you must believe me! I want to help you. You don't have to like me or give me my job back, but please let me help you clear your name! Perhaps Arturo can receive the justice he deserves, too!"

Sofia considered the tear-streaked home-wrecker.

"Okay, Carmen. I'll trust you. I may never forgive you, but I'm sure that we need each other now. What do we do?"

"We get out of here!"

Shortly after leaving Lorena at Equator, Miriya drove eastbound on Green Street, hoping she wouldn't be late to Madeleine's. It was going to be a night to remember, she thought to herself. She didn't want anything to go wrong.

Miriya didn't have to wait long for that. As the monsoon-like rain pelted her car, she realized that traffic had come to a complete stop. Up ahead she saw the telltale orange overhead lights of public works trucks, as well as the blue and red lights of emergency vehicles.

"Oh, what now?" she blurted aloud.

She craned her neck and could barely make out that there must have been some kind of accident. A concrete light pole had been knocked over into the street, effectively blocking all lanes of the one-way traffic.

"You've gotta be fuckin' kidding me."

Miriya quickly scanned her surroundings as car horns blared. She looked over her shoulder.

"Unbelievable!" Miriya hit her steering wheel.

She was stuck. There were cars stopped behind her and in front of her, and she had the misfortune to be mid-block. There was nowhere to turn off. Miriya checked her watch and thought of calling Arturo to tell him of the delay. As she reached for her cell phone she reconsidered. Who knew how long this would take?

Miriya saw an empty parking spot next to where she

was stopped and decided to park her car. She grimaced as she turned the engine off and watched the rain. She looked at her dress and strappy sandals.

"Great!" She shook her head and scanned the interior of her car for something to cover her head. She found an old issue of the *LA Weekly*. "Here goes nothing!"

Miriya cringed at the shock of the cold hard rain on her bare skin. Holding the weekly over her head, she knew that her hair, make-up, and dress would not survive the four-block trip to the restaurant.

This was stupid!

Arturo Suarez shifted uncomfortably in his chair while glancing at Carlo and Jorge. The two of them checked their watches and gave Arturo a supportive smile. He knew what they were thinking: Don't worry, she'll show.

Would she? Arturo wondered. He grinned uneasily at Miriya, Sr., seated across the table from him sipping a glass of merlot. Eva, Jim, and Anna sat around the matriarch like a board of inquiry. Arturo subtly examined their faces for any hint that they knew about the other women, the cheating and the lies.

You're not worthy of my daughter's hand! Arturo pictured Miriya, Sr., blurting out to him after getting sloshed on the vino.

Arturo quickly downed his Jack and Coke. Eva leaned over and caught Anna's attention. The youngest Fronzini was checking her lipstick in a compact mirror.

"Hey! What's taking Junior?" Eva asked.

"Maybe she's finally wised up," Anna mumbled with a sly smile. Jim chuckled as Eva playfully hit him.

Miriya ran harder as the rain pelted her soaked body. She had discarded the pulpy *LA Weekly*.

Sofia and Carmen ran down the hall toward the main stairs leading to the lobby, just as a cadre of Federales, led by Sergeant Robles, suddenly appeared to block their path.

"Halt!" Sergeant Robles commanded. All guns were pointed at the two out-of-breath women.

"No, don't!" Carmen yelled. She stood between the police and Sofia, arms outstretched as if to shield her former boss. "Sofia de Amor is innocent!"

There were confused looks on the faces of the policemen. Sergeant Robles stepped forward.

"Who are you?" he demanded.

"I am Carmen Santiago! I am Mrs. de Amor's former housekeeper, who ran off with her husband!"

"Sofia de Amor is wanted in connection with the death of Abel Solorzano," Sergeant Robles said.

"He was killed in self-defense," Carmen said. "I can prove that Arturo de Amor hired him to try to murder Sofia."

Sergeant Robles was stunned at this news. Suddenly,

the two gangsters emerged from an elevator to find the po-lice holding guns on their intended prey. Sergeant Robles recognized the tall gunman, Maximillian Termite, as a no-torious killer.

"Max Termite!" Sergeant Robles yelled, wheeling to-ward him to shoot.

The police and gangsters exchanged gunfire as every-one dove for cover. Sofia and Carmen screamed while cowering in a doorway.

At that moment, Arturo de Amor climbed slowly down the stairs, only mildly concerned that he had stumbled into a gunfight. Sofia saw him and knew that Arturo was trying to escape.

"Carmen, there's Arturo! He's trying to get away!"

Sergeant Robles also noticed Arturo and radioed to Lieutenant Madero that they had located the real culprit behind the De Amor-Solorzano caper. Arturo saw Sergeant Robles low-crawling toward him. Arturo turned and ran back up the stairs just as the cornered gangsters ran out of ammunition.

"Get him!" Carmen yelled.

As the police took Max Termite and his sidekick into custody, Sofia, Carmen, Sergeant Robles, and the rest of the police chased Arturo up several flights of stairs toward the roof.

"Get him! Get the bastard!" Chet yelled, while huddled next to Nathalie on her living room couch. After Chet had helped her, Nathalie had invited him over to watch *Sofia de Amor* at her place so he wouldn't miss any of it.

Chet was an interesting character, Nathalie thought to herself. Maybe there's something there.

Miriya made it to Madeleine's just as Carlo and Jorge were going to throw in the towel and give condolences to their buddy for getting jilted at an engagement. All heads turned toward the doorway as she stepped in dripping from head to toe. Arturo was shocked to see his would-be fiancé drenched to the bone.

"*Dios*! Miriya, *mi amor*!" He quickly removed his jacket and held it out to cover her.

"Junior! *Ai quierdo*!" Miriya, Sr. said under her breath at the spectacle of her cold and shivering daughter.

"No, thank you, Arturo," Miriya said softly. She kissed him. "Sorry I'm late. My car got stuck."

She kissed her family members awkwardly, trying not to get them wet, and gave meek hellos to Carlo and Jorge. Miriya took a seat to Arturo's right, as he motioned for her wine glass to be filled. Just as the waiter finished pouring, Miriya took a quick drink, spilling some on her chin.

"Well," Arturo began, "now that we're all here—a toast!"

Everyone reached for his or her glass, as Arturo stood.

"Here's to family…" He smiled at Miriya, Sr., who avoided his gaze and took a sip of her drink before he was finished.

"Good friends..." He glanced at his buddies. Carlo gave him a "thumbs up."

"And to true love...in all of its complex, heart-wrenching, and heart-warming forms." Arturo lifted his glass to Miriya, who gave him the warmest smile he had seen in a long time.

As they toasted, Arturo's free hand fumbled with the ring in his pocket. Miriya pretended not to notice as her heart raced. She quickly searched her soul for answers.

Arturo put his glass down and opened the small, black velvet box. He stepped to the side and got down on one knee as Eva and Anna gasped aloud.

"Miriya, *mi amor*," Arturo said in Spanish. "I know that it has taken me some time to get to this point, but I know in my heart of hearts, it is what I truly desire, to make you the happiest woman in the world, to make you my wife, and to be the best husband a woman can have...Will you marry me?"

Miriya couldn't take her eyes off the diamond. There it was, just a foot away, snug in a tiny little box, burning with fire and brilliance. Her eyes welled with tears as she looked into Arturo's eyes and smiled.

"You did good," she said, almost in a whisper. "That's the one I wanted."

Her voice cracked.

"I really did."

Arturo frowned as Miriya turned to look at her mother.

Say something, Mama.

Miriya, Sr. smiled at her daughter while fingering a small crucifix pendant that hung around her neck. Fabio had given it to her.

"Miriya," Arturo said with more firmness, "will you marry me?"

Arturo de Amor made it to the roof of the Hotel Las Tres Mujeres where the rain fell hard and the escape routes were few. His face showed that he knew that this was the end of the line for him. Everything that he had done in his life until this point had now come back to haunt him. He quickly examined his options, figured the angles, and calculated the odds. Perhaps there was one more trick left, one final story he could weave, one last line of sweet talk that he could string together to help get him out of this jam.

He stood near the edge of the roof and could see the ground four stories below. There were no fire escape stairs up there, at least none that he could see.

Arturo heard a noise from behind and turned around to see Sofia and Carmen run toward him with a squad of federales in tow, led by Lieutenant Madero and Sergeant Robles.

"Arturo!" Sofia yelled, her face contorted in anguish. She stepped up to him and slapped him across the face. "How could you?"

Sofia started hitting him, pounding at his chest and shoulders.

"How could you do this to me, mi amor? I never did anything but love you! I was good to you! And all you could do is cheat on me and poison my love for you! You would have killed what was so pure and honest!"

Sofia broke down crying and fell into his arms. Carmen looked on, aghast that Sofia was weakening in her resolve.

Arturo held onto his wife. He looked up and saw that the police had their guns pointed at him. He knew that he was the wanted man now.

"Sofia, my love!" Arturo cried out to his rain-soaked wife. He stood dangerously close to the edge of the hotel roof as the guns remained leveled at him. "I'm sorry for everything I've done. Please forgive me. Can you forgive me? Take me back! We can start over!"

He looked into her hurt and angry eyes and held her tighter.

"Arturo...How could you?" Sofia started. She looked warily at the edge near her feet. She looked up at Arturo, as the music cascaded to ominous heights.

Sofia pulled herself up and withdrew from his arms. Raising a finger at him, she stepped backward into the gathering puddles of rain.

"No, Arturo! I can never forgive you for what you did. You are a cruel and heartless man! I want a divorce! I want you in jail!"

Arturo was wide-eyed with terror as these words were spoken. Lieutenant Madero motioned for his officers to close in on Arturo de Amor. As the police moved toward him, Sofia backed up into Carmen's arms. The two women comforted each other.

Lorena tossed her cell phone aside. She gave up on trying to reach Miriya and buried her face in her hands.

"Miriya, no!" she said aloud. "I can't believe it! Why? Why didn't I say something to you? I should have warned you! I should have yelled at you like I wanted to!"

Lorena felt like crying. She took a deep breath and turned her weary eyes back to the TV.

Arturo stepped back, his feet nearing the edge of the roof.

"If Sofia cannot love me, I am not worthy of anyone's love! I'm going to end it, once and for all!"

Arturo jumped off the roof as the women screamed. Lieutenant Madero shook his head as he motioned for the officers to head to the ground floor.

As Arturo fell, he smiled, thinking that he had escaped justice. These thoughts were quickly dashed when he landed in a trash dumpster filled with rotting food and used toiletries. Instead of being dead, Arturo de Amor was covered in filth and slime.

The police took him into custody, whereupon he would face trial for trying to kill Sofia de Amor—in effect, for betraying her love.

Lorena sat wide-eyed as she watched the close of her favorite *telenovela*. It was an interesting ending, Lorena thought, the Sofia character not ending up in the arms of a hero. Lorena told herself that sometimes the girl didn't get the guy. Perhaps this was a lesson, she wondered, that there were often more important things than being swept away by a knight in shining armor. There would always be time for love, and it was never too late to love again.

There's nothing like a new start, Lorena thought to herself. She switched off the TV and sat alone on her couch, thinking about her life, about Steven Meztaz, and about Miriya, and Arturo Suarez, who were probably happily engaged already, embarking on their own new start.

Lorena came to the conclusion that she was meant to cross paths with Miriya. Miriya had been good for her. Miriya had brought to Lorena a zest for life and sociability that she felt she had lacked. Miriya wasn't afraid to be out there, in the arena, laughing, loving, hurting; getting knocked around and taking her lumps with the rewards, always smiling, but never afraid to cry or get angry. Lorena knew that she could learn a thing or two from that.

Lorena sighed and stood to get ready for bed. She had a big day ahead of her. She cherished and looked forward to her family's trips to Mexico. Perhaps San Felipe would be a new beginning for Lorena Sandoval, a chance to recharge the batteries, as she once said.

As she turned off a small lamp in the living room, she

heard a knock at the front door. Lorena frowned and checked the clock. She didn't exactly live in the best neighborhood and was cautious when she cracked open her door. Although the porch light wasn't on, she recognized the thin, brown face with the squinty, sparkling eyes and warm smile. There was still a light rain out, but Lorena saw by her clothing and the bag on her shoulders, that Miriya had changed and packed for the trip.

Lorena beamed with a wide, toothy smile.

"Hey, miss," Miriya said.

"Well, hello to you, miss."

They hugged and held each other tightly. Lorena saw that Miriya did not have a ring on her finger.

ted in the United States
65LV00002B/104/P

9 781432 736903